THE
LIST

Carys Jones is a thriller writer based in Shropshire where she lives with her husband, daughter and dog. When she's not writing she can often be found indulging two of her greatest passions: either walking round the local woodland or catching up on all things Disney-related.

www.carys-jones.com

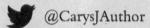 @CarysJAuthor

THE
LIST

Carys Jones

ORION

First published in Great Britain in 2020 by Orion Fiction,
an imprint of The Orion Publishing Group Ltd.,
Carmelite House, 50 Victoria Embankment
London EC4Y 0DZ

An Hachette UK Company

3 5 7 9 10 8 6 4 2

A CIP catalogue record for this book is
available from the British Library.

ISBN (Paperback) 978 1 4091 9598 6
ISBN (eBook) 978 1 4091 9599 3

Typeset by Born Group
Printed and bound in Great Britain by Clays Ltd, Elcograf S.p.A.

www.orionbooks.co.uk

For Rose

'When falsehood can look so like the truth, who can assure themselves of certain happiness?'

Mary Shelley, *Frankenstein*

Prologue

The nightmare started the same as all the others. Screaming, terrible and tormenting, pitched like an animal caught in a trap desperately squealing for its life. It rattled through Beth Belmont's bones, causing sweat to prickle on her skin. In the early hours, she awoke gasping, the screams still ringing in her ears.

'Hey, it's okay, just calm down.' Her boyfriend, Josh, rolled over and folded his arms around her, holding her close, waiting until the shaking subsided and her breathing levelled out. Beth lay wide-eyed and staring into the darkness of their bedroom at the swollen shadows in every corner. 'It was just a nightmare,' he calmly assured her as he ran his work-hardened hands in circles over her lower back.

Just a nightmare.

Drawing in ragged breaths from this latest twilight terror, Beth focused on that.

It was just a nightmare.

The Green Day T-shirt she slept in was soaked through, her long dark hair damp and matted. How long had she tossed and turned while the phantom in her mind shrieked like a banshee?

'Let's try and get back to sleep.'

Josh was always keen to return to his slumber. He had to be up at dawn, with the birds, for another day labouring on the new super school that was being built on the edge of town.

Beth wanted to sleep too, but the screams lingered. Each nightmare stayed by her side like an unwanted bedfellow. Even though she could no longer hear them, she could *feel* them, scraping down her spine like sharpened claws, picking her apart at her very core.

'What are you even dreaming about?' Josh had asked early on in their relationship, his tired blue eyes holding her in a concerned stare.

'Nothing.' Beth knew that the answer came a little too easily. 'I mean, I can't remember.'

'Your nightmares, they seem . . . intense.' He tilted his thick neck to watch her. Josh – who slept like the dead – never so much as whimpered in his sleep.

'Really, it's nothing,' her voice was strained, so she forced a smile, 'lots of people have nightmares. Like night terrors. Honestly, I can't even remember what they're about.'

'Well, okay then. As long as you're all right, babe.' He'd kissed her forehead and Beth wished that his touch had healing properties, like the kisses bestowed on her as a child when she scraped a knee or an elbow.

'Let Mummy kiss it better,' her mother would say, leaning in close, smelling of musky Dior perfume and cigarettes, scents that she shrouded herself in. A cloak for the senses.

But there was no kissing her nightmares better, no willing them away. Each night as Beth tucked herself in beside her boyfriend of three years, she knew what was coming – at some point, she'd wake in a pool of her own sweat, gulping deep, frantic breaths as though she'd been drowning. And the screams would continue to linger on the periphery of her mind, even when her eyes were bloodshot and wide open, a reminder that no one was ever truly free.

One

Neat. It has to be neat.

I remind myself of this as I lift the fountain pen in my hand and begin to guide it slowly and gracefully over the paper. I need silence. Stillness.

The bare bulb above me shakes. The tremble spreads across the ceiling like a stain.

'Fuck.'

The pen is down and my blood pressure is up. Fucking Mrs Norris in number five is hoovering. Again. And the old crone will labour over it as she usually does, thanks to her arthritic knee.

'It's bad again,' she always says through those wrinkled lips of hers each time I pass her in the stairwell. What does she expect me to do? Carry her? Cure her?

Now my whole flat is whirring along to the guttural groan of Mrs Norris's cheap hoover. I glance at the clock hanging above my electric fire, forgetting that for the past week it's been stuck at eight fifteen.

Batteries.

I grind my teeth, already knowing that I'll forget this addition to my shopping list, thanks to the noise which is now reaching down from above and scratching against my bones. My focus has weakened these last months, along with my body. But I'm not done yet. There's still a fire in the pit of my belly, one that takes all my energy to keep stoking. My hands tighten into fists. I could shout. I could grab the baseball bat by the front door and smack it

3

against the ceiling until my arms begin to ache. But Mrs Norris would just go on hoovering, because she's as deaf as she is lame.

No. I need to finish this.

The radio, or the television. I could turn one of them on, try to drown out the drone from upstairs. But I'm not quite sure if I paid the meter. And if I didn't . . .

Squeezing my eyes closed, I force the darkness to find me. One breath in, one breath out. Slow. And steady. Just as Roger taught me.

Silver-haired Roger with all his suggestions.

Something flutters in my core. It could be regret, or it could be a delayed response to the tin of baked beans I'd eaten at lunch which were four months out of date. But my mum always said up to six months was fine, especially for a tin.

It's nerves. It has to be.

I look down at the paper on the table. So neat. So crisp. The bulb above me swings back and forth. I begin to hum, growing louder so that the pressure builds in my head, in my ears. Eventually all I can hear is my own internal melody, Mrs Norris and her hoover overpowered. I close my fingers around my fountain pen, gripping tight. I write down the first name. Then the second. And then I deliberate over the third, as this is the one that matters. This is the one that needs to stick, that needs to work.

Satisfied, I lean back and admire my handiwork. I've stopped humming. And Mrs Norris has stopped hoovering. My skin prickles in the silence. Now it's working against me, needling up close and lingering on the back of my neck. When I was writing I needed it, but now . . .

I close my eyes, surrendering myself again to the darkness, and open my mouth wide. The scream I release is piercing, burning my throat. But no one will come running. No one ever does.

When I open my eyes again, I don't know how much time has passed, only that my throat is raw and my palms are clammy. I *imagine you running, sprinting through the sunlight. All of this hard work. For you. For us. For all of us.*

I've never liked the woods. But you do. So this is where it needs to be. Where I need to be. Two trains and one bus, that's what it's taken to get me here. It's late. And dark. The trees are still, not stirred even in a gentle rustling. The silence is suffocating. I should turn back. But I've come too far now.

I shake out my hands, fingers stiff. Cold – why is it so damn cold? With only moonlight to guide me, I scurry down a twisting path. Something stirs in the undergrowth. Instinctively, I crouch down low. Not that I need to. I'm surrounded only by shadows. No one else is here so late. But it's not always that way. Some nights as I've wandered these woods, I've caught laughter on the breeze, laced with the scent of weed. I've let it fill my lungs and draw me back in time. But the spell never lasted long enough. The hoot of an owl, the rustle of leaves, I'm always snapped back into the moment far too soon.

But tonight I won't let anything distract me. I feel buoyant with purpose. Tonight, finally, I get to act. If I could see myself, I know I'd be smiling. Too long have I waited, have I dwelt on how to proceed.

I make a sharp right as the path forks and glance around at the clearing I find myself in. The trees which border me are stoic guards. I study the area, squinting against the lack of light. It feels secluded. Hidden away. But still on the main path. My hand slips into my pocket, fingers the piece of paper concealed inside. Am I taking too much of a gamble? What if someone else finds it first?

A breeze strokes through my loose hair and my teeth chatter together, the cold of the evening beginning to gnaw at me. I look to the trees, trace the line of the path.

There. A log. I hurry to it, rest my hand on its back, imagining the tree it had once been. Perhaps birds would perch in its

5

branches, even nest there. Would squirrels twist their way up its trunk in a helter-skelter motion?

But now it's laid low and perfect for what I need. Taking the paper from my pocket, I admire the way it glows in the moonlight like a star. Carefully, I place it on the ground amidst the carpet of moss and twigs, jutting out just enough to be visible, to catch the eye of a passer-by.

Stepping back, I rub my hands together, stomach churning. What if I'm wrong? What if they're not the first person to find it? But if I'm right . . .

A charge of excitement shoots up my spine, causing me to tingle. I wish I could see it, wish I could be there in the dawn light as my little offering is discovered.

A knife twists in my stomach. Staying is impossible, my nerves already starting to devour me. But I'll be back.

I take one last look at the paper beneath the log. Then I leave. I just need you to find it. To see it. To remember.

Sunlight mottled the ground, filtered through the canopy of green leaves overhead. Blades of grass were still tipped with dew and many flowers had yet to unfurl their petals. It was early. Less than an hour had passed since the dawn chorus concluded their performance.

Beth was running. She slowed as she reached a turn in the path, dirt crunching beneath her neon green Skechers trainers. Back on the straight, she built up speed again, arms powering at her sides. Effortlessly, she leapt over a fallen tree which sprawled across the path, pre-empting the obstacle before it even came into view. She knew this route – this trail that snaked through the woodlands near her little terraced house.

'It'll be nice, being so close to the woods,' Josh had said when they went for their first viewing, a smile spreading across his face. Beth had seen the trees, the shadows beneath their canopy, and shivered in the sunlight.

'Nice, yeah,' she'd found the strength to mirror his smile. And now she had bested the woods. Found comfort in their darkness, in the stirring of leaves.

So, each morning, she followed Josh out of bed and as he showered, she pulled on her jogging bottoms and trainers. For an hour, she would run wild and free, like an untamed horse. Round and round she'd go, until her legs ached and her chest burned.

'You training for a marathon or something?' Josh had asked on one of the rare occasions he was still home when she burst through the front door, sweating and panting.

'What? No. I just like to run.'

At fifteen, Beth had discovered the liberating properties of running, of pushing her muscles to their limits. It was intoxicating thinking only about the route, her speed, the distance. Not a morning went by when she wasn't out in the woods powering around the trail.

Mr Woodson who lived at number thirteen in their little cul-de-sac was out that morning walking his Irish setter, Beau. He paused to raise a hand and offer a smile as Beth thundered past him. Beau's tail wagged furiously, but the bundle of ruby fur didn't try to chase after her, not this time.

'Morning,' she greeted him breathily as she sped by.

At this time, the woods were relatively quiet and undisturbed. Smoke hung on the air, an echo of teenage revelry around campfires the previous night. Beth passed by a lady with a trio of poodles and then reached the densest part of the woods. Here, the trees had grown thick and fast, causing a dip in the temperature as even the brightest rays of sunlight struggled to penetrate the overgrown mass of leaves above.

Birds were singing, chirping sweetly to one another. Beth felt her thigh muscles constrict and, with an anguished sigh, conceded that she had to slow down. Letting her arms fall lower against her sides, she drank in the crisp morning air, filling her lungs. Dark patches gathered beneath her armpits and down her back.

'Right . . . okay.' Raising her arms, Beth tightened the band holding her hair in a high ponytail and jogged idly through the maze of trees. She'd sprint again once she'd recovered some of her energy. Now that she'd slowed down she could more clearly take in her surroundings. Amidst the base of the trees sprouted little flowers, shyly concealing their purple petals. Spring was about to turn into summer, which meant that the snowdrops Beth so loved to see had long since disappeared for another year. As she pondered this, something white lying on the ground caught her eye. The brightness of it against the hues of browns and greens of the woodland carpet made it stand out starkly.

Beth came to a complete halt and peered down at the sliver of pristine whiteness. It was so utterly out of place and, as she moved closer, Beth realised that was because the object was unnatural. A piece of human debris, usually plucked up and disposed of by the group of volunteers who pruned and preened the woods on a weekly basis. Now crouching, Beth reached forward and grazed the item with the tips of her fingers. A slip of paper. It wasn't scrunched up, like a piece of discarded rubbish. Slightly bigger than a receipt, tucked just beyond the fringes of the jogging trail and wedged beneath an old upturned log, sticking out just enough to be noticed.

Seemingly begging to be noticed.

Curious, Beth plucked the piece of paper out from beneath the tree trunk. It was crisp in her hands. And surprisingly clean. It couldn't have been out in the elements for long at all. Straightening and turning back, she glanced at the trail behind her, then strained to look ahead. There was no one else around, no one within sight who could have dropped the slip of paper.

'Hmm.' It was folded over. Beth opened it up, expecting a shopping list hastily scrawled upon it or perhaps a discarded note. But, instead, she was looking not at a list of items, but of names.

The penmanship was immaculate. Each entry written in exquisite cursive text. Clearly great care had been taken.

Beth scanned the list. There were five names, each on their own line.

She gasped, as though someone had just sucker-punched her in the gut, doubling forwards. The third name on the list was all too familiar. Because it was her own.

Slowly, carefully, she read back over it, wondering if her eyes were deceiving her.

Joanne Rowles
Trevor Hoskins
Beth Belmont
Harry Jensen
Rebecca Terry

Her own name stared out at her, pretty and challenging in its neat cursive appearance.

'What the hell?' Beth anxiously glanced back over both shoulders, along the length of the jogging trail. There were so many trees, so many places for someone to hide. The shadows that gathered amongst the numerous trunks suddenly seemed pregnant with danger.

'Is anyone there?' Beth asked of the emptiness. Only the

birds chirped back in response. She was alone. 'What . . . what is this?' She swept her gaze over the note one final time before shoving it into the front pocket of her hooded jumper. None of the other four names meant anything to her. Yet there had to be some connection, didn't there?

Beth no longer felt like running. She stalked back through the woods, shoulders hunched and brow furrowed as she mentally worked through the list again and again. When she crossed the threshold to her home, she was no closer to finding a link between the names, and the weight of the list in her pocket now felt unbearably heavy.

The house was empty. Josh, reliable as the tide, had already left for work while she was on her run. After discarding the note on the kitchen table, Beth dragged her weary legs upstairs, keen to shower off the feeling of unease that coated her skin like a thick oil.

Two

'Ruby, do you know why you're here?'

She lifted her head to peer at the bespectacled woman on the nearby armchair but said nothing. The fibres of the sofa she was perched on were chafing against her bare legs. She wished she'd pulled on jeans rather than her pink shorts. But it was warm for April and today they might let her go outside, might let her feel the sun on her skin. Yet here she was again, in the office that smelt like old books and stale coffee. A large window showed the green grounds, glowing and lustrous in the early-morning light.

Tired of being taunted by the view, Ruby lowered her head again.

'I felt like we made real progress during our last session.' The woman regarded her notes and then lowered her glasses with a plump hand, letting them hang around her neck on the ornate chain she always wore. 'Maybe we could continue from where we left off?' It sounded like there was genuine hope in her voice.

Ruby grunted and leant forward to pick at a scab on her knee. 'I want to go home.' The words were mumbled, almost incoherent. Yet the woman in the armchair was attuned to her juvenile dialect.

'You know that's not an option.'

'But I want to go home.' Her words were a plea. Abandoning her scab, Ruby folded her arms against her chest, which had begun to swell. She wanted to see her friends, to feel the sun warm the back of her legs as she ran through a field. She wasn't supposed to be here. She was supposed to be in school like everyone else.

'Ruby, there is no going home. You understand that, don't you?' There was a gentleness to the woman's words which Ruby wasn't accustomed to hearing.

'I do but . . .' She squeezed tight against her chest, against the unfairness of it all. 'I still want to go home.'

'I understand that, truly.' The woman leant forward. She had kind eyes and a treble chin. Every day she wore the same uniform of a long flowing skirt and an ill-fitting blouse that strained against her ample bosom. And she always smelt of coffee and lavender. Her curves made her seem kind, like her body was built to give cuddles. Not like Ruby's mother, who was made of sticks, every slim bone in her body piercing and sharp. When she embraced her daughter, it felt like being pressed into a bag of needles. But already Ruby was starting to forget what it was like to be in her mother's arms. How much time had passed since Linda Renton had held her – really held her?

'Let's talk about that day, about what happened,' the woman prompted, a smile of hopeful eagerness pulling on her thin lips.

Ruby swallowed. Talking about that day was like turning the screw in a broken hinge: pointless. It never did anything, never improved her circumstances.

'No,' she told the woman sternly. 'I'm done talking about it.'

'Okay,' came the breezy reply. There was no resistance, no hand surging forward to strike her across the face. At home, any resistance always earned her a smarting cheek.

Perhaps this place wasn't that bad after all . . . 'Then let's talk about something else. About your family. Can we talk about that?'

A shadow passed over Ruby's young features as her hazel eyes gazed up sadly at the woman. 'I'd really rather not.'

'Well, we have to talk about something. It's important that we make the most of our time here.'

'Can we talk about something nice?'

'Sure, Ruby. Like what?'

'Like . . .' Ruby looked up and allowed her gaze to fix upon the window and the sunlit vista beyond. 'Like the weather. It's so sunny today. Perhaps later I can—'

'We can talk about the weather all you want.' The woman was writing while she talked, scribbling notes in her thick A4 leather-bound pad. 'But eventually we have to talk about things that are not so nice.'

'I know. I mean, eventually, right?'

'Right.'

'So not today.' Ruby continued to gaze wistfully out of the window, hoping that today could be a good day, that today she could at least pretend she was free.

'Okay, Ruby,' the woman conceded with a soft smile, 'not today. But another day. And know that there will be other days, lots of them.'

Three

Hair still damp, Beth trudged back downstairs, skin flushed from the heat of the shower. Stepping into the kitchen, her eyes immediately locked on to the slip of paper on the table, left there in haste as she'd headed for the shower, needing to feel the pressure of hot water against her back. It looked innocuous in the morning sunlight.

'Weird.' Tentatively, Beth approached the note, drumming the blunt ends of her nails against the table as she moved round it.

Five names. Alien to her. Strangers. Except for the third name, which was her own.

Dragging a chair out, Beth sat down heavily and grabbed the note.

'Joanne Rowles.' She read the first name aloud, hoping that it might bring forth some distant memory from the recesses of her mind. It didn't.

Carefully, she folded the paper along its crease and then opened it again, running her fingertips against its surface. Its material wasn't flimsy, it was the kind of thick, sturdy paper she used to feed into the printer back at school. And the writing on it. So ornate, so carefully executed. It chilled Beth to imagine someone bent over a different table, pen in hand, taking the time to write out her name so artistically, so elaborately. The list was not scrawled in haste.

'But why?' Beth stared at it hard and bit her lip. What was the point of the list? What connected her to the other names?

The brightness outside drew her attention, reminding her of the litany of chores she had to do that morning, of her shift at the cinema that commenced at six. She didn't have time to idle over the list. But still the names lodged themselves in her mind, prickly as a thorn.

After pinning a freshly washed load of clothes onto the rotary line in the small back garden and cleaning away what remained of last night's dinner, Beth once again found herself drifting towards the kitchen table and the folded slip of paper upon it.

'Why am I on there?' she asked aloud, knowing no answer would present itself. 'Could it be another Beth Belmont?' she wondered. In the woods? *Her* woods? Where she ran each morning? Her fingers twitched with the impulse to go into the lounge and fire up her laptop. A quick Google search might shed some more light on matters.

Beth's bare feet took her out of the kitchen, across the grey tiled floor towards the lounge at the back of the small terrace. The computer was in her sights when she heard gravel crunching beneath the weight of thick tyres. Turning, she saw through the kitchen window that Josh's van had just pulled into the driveway. Her chest constricted as her gaze flew back towards the list.

Beth was struck by a sudden urge to hide it. Should she? Like anyone in a relationship, Beth yearned for hers to be open and honest, built on a foundation of trust. But what would she say to him at this point? She at least needed more information, more context, before she presented the list to him. Lest he think she was being crazy. Josh saw the world in such certain terms. The list would either be an issue in his eyes or something to completely disregard. Beth couldn't risk being influenced by his steadfastness until she knew more. He wouldn't entertain her questions, that wasn't his style.

She gnawed on the inside of her cheek, stomach swirling with indecision. Could she just discard it? Throw it in the bin, forget all about it? Her mind was a machine gun, launching rapid-fire questions. She drew a breath and the door to the house creaked open.

Josh strode into the kitchen, looking harassed.

'Bloody typical,' he muttered to himself, shaking his head.

'Hey,' Beth straightened in the doorway and pulled her lips into a welcoming smile. 'What are you doing back home again?' Her voice pitched higher, 'Everything okay?'

'Forgot my lunch, didn't I?' Josh replied with a grunt as he thrust open the silver door of the fridge and stooped to grope inside it.

'Oh.' The list sat there. On the table. Out in the open.

'What time are you going in?' Plastic lunch box in hand, Josh straightened and looked over at her. Already his T-shirt was dirtied with dust and grime, his jeans spattered with paint.

'Umm.' Beth pushed a hand through her damp hair. He'd asked her a question. A direct one. A simple one. Yet it was taking a herculean effort to think of anything other than the list on the table. Had he seen it yet? Would he see it? 'Six.' She furrowed her brow. 'I'm on close tonight, so not in until six.'

'Right, okay.' Josh nodded. His six-foot-three frame seemed to completely fill the small kitchen. In fact, any room he stood in within their terraced home felt dwarfed by his presence.

This was the point where he should leave, get back in his van and return to work. Beth should be waving him off, smiling sweetly. But she couldn't do that. This was

Josh, her Josh. Josh who would hold her in the small hours of the night as she trembled away the last fragments of a terrible nightmare. If the list was an issue, then he needed to know about it. Beth knew that he'd just want to protect her – that was his default reaction to anything. She relented.

'Before you go.' She stepped closer to the table, smelling the musk of building materials that clung to Josh. 'I found something strange when I was out jogging this morning.'

'Strange?' His thick eyebrows pulled together. 'If it's anything rank, I've told you to just leave it where it is. The guys at work are always joking that people go dogging in the woods near here.'

'No, no, nothing like that. This . . .' Beth leant towards the table and grabbed the article in question, unfolded the piece of paper and passed it to her boyfriend. He clutched it with the tips of his fingers silently. 'It . . . it was just on the ground towards the back of the woods, tucked under a fallen tree. I mean, it's weird, right?'

'Your name is on here.' He looked quizzically between Beth and the list he was holding.

'I know. And those . . . those other names mean nothing to me.'

'And it was in the woods?'

'Uh-huh. Almost completely hidden beneath a fallen tree trunk.'

'Weird.' He handed the note back to her. 'What do you think it means?'

'I've no idea.'

There was no longer any urgency to Josh's movements, all thoughts of returning to work abandoned. 'Was anyone around when you picked it up?'

'Not that I saw.'

'And this was the only note you found?'

'Yep, that's it. Just the one.'

'Shit, Beth, that's weird.'

Beth nodded.

'Think it's one of the little pricks at the cinema messing with you?' Josh's tone became hostile.

It was a conclusion Beth hadn't considered, but it was plausible. She worked at her local cinema as a projectionist and was much older than a lot of her front-of-house colleagues, often still in college or university. They certainly enjoyed playing pranks on one another but had never included Beth before. She was the mature one in the group and they kept a respectful distance from her. Everyone except her manager, Colin. He was just a year younger than Beth, married with three kids and paying off an extortionate mortgage he loved to lament about whenever he had the chance.

'I mean, I guess it could have been someone at work.'

'I wouldn't put it past them,' Josh grumbled, nostrils flaring. 'Some of them are right brats. I wish you'd get a proper job, Beth.'

Proper job.

The flippant remark cut into her, piercing with its damning truth.

'You're so smart,' Josh would comment during those first heady days of living together, when their relationship was as new and untarnished as their little home. 'Do you really want to load film reels for the rest of your life? You could be so much more, Beth.'

She had dreams and aspirations, sure. But all the doors which led to them had been closed to her a long time ago. Besides, the cinema suited her. It was dark up in the projection rooms. Safe. She could drift along the corridors, move from theatre to theatre without being bothered. She felt like the Phantom of the Opera, always out of sight, and she liked it that way. Let her younger peers deal with the public, with the filling of popcorn buckets and tearing of ticket stubs.

'Well, don't dwell on it,' Josh advised as he tucked his lunch box under his arm. 'And if it is one of those acne-ridden little pricks, then I need you to write up a list of names of your own.'

'Josh—'

'They'd literally shit a brick if I showed up on their door-step with some of my boys. And they wouldn't try and freak you out again. Little bastards. I hate the way they're always looking down on you, just because the cinema is some pit stop on their grand tour to becoming wankers with degrees. You're the sweetest, kindest person I know, you deserve to work with people who respect you.' He stepped forward to lean down and plant the whisper of a kiss on her forehead.

'Have a good afternoon at work.'

'I'll try and be home before six.' He kissed her again. 'I love you.'

No matter how many times she heard it, its power never faded. She'd often cocoon herself in the sentiment, fold it around her like a warm towel long after Josh had left. She was smiling as she waved goodbye.

'I love you too.'

I repeat the names to myself as I stand beneath a tepid trickle of water each morning. I let them roll off my tongue, bounce off the tiles crusted with black mould and echo back to me. They are familiar to me now, woven so tightly into memory that they can never be unpicked. But, once, they had been new. Strange.

My search for names had led me to Roger's door, as I'd always suspected it would. In the lazy haze of twilight, his olive door had creaked open and he'd peered out at me. First came surprise, his pupils widening. Then his jaw began to quiver with fear.

'You know why I'm here,' I told him bluntly, hopping from foot to foot, arms tight across my chest. Even though it was midsummer, I was cold. I was always cold. The doctors told me it's Crohn's, eating me from the inside out, draining me down to just skin and bones.

'Look, I . . .' A single hand lifted pleadingly, fingertips calloused. I wondered if he still played the guitar or if I'd ruined that hobby for him completely when I'd smashed his beloved Gibson. 'You can't be here. Do you understand?'

'The names.' I glowered at him, felt the throb of my pulse within my inner ear. 'Tell me the names.'

'You know that I can't, I—'

'You know them.' I shuffled towards him, the worn soles of my trainers whispering against his concrete step. 'And you're going to tell me.'

'Really, I can't. Please, don't do anything . . . irrational. Look, just come inside and we can—' He eased back from the doorway to gesture to his hallway, to the plush carpet and floral wallpaper. To the black phone resting on top of a slim pine table.

I bit down on my tongue and moved fast. Side-stepping the porch, I lunged at the red brick of the house, forehead first. I heard my nose crunch before I felt the warmth of blood seeping down my face. With a grimace, I returned to the step, light-headed, to the sound of Roger gasping, the sound gargling in his throat like a fledgling scream.

'What are you—'

'The names.' My bones ached with exhaustion.

Roger's hand again crossed the threshold, trying to reach me. But his grip had always been weak.

'Tell me the names.'

'Please,' he begged, voice raw with desperation, 'don't, don't do this. Stop hurting yourself, stop—'

I smiled at him and he stopped, remembering the game all too well. I kept my voice low, level. But there was a pounding within my skull that was getting loud and desperate.

'Either you tell me the names,' I explained, 'or I'll pound my head against the wall of your house until my fucking brains are splattered across your front step.'

'Please, stop, just—'

'And when the police come . . .' I continued, holding him in a fixed stare whilst he squirmed beneath my gaze like a fish caught on a line, mouth gaping open with each anxious breath he drew, '. . . do you think they'll believe that I did this to myself? You tried so hard to bury our history, but I can dig it up again. Maybe I'll tell the police that's why you took my head and bashed my skull against the bricks until I went limp in your arms, just to keep me quiet, just to keep your sordid secrets safe?'

'Don't,' he pleaded pathetically, sweat glistening on his craggy forehead. 'Don't do this.'

'What would your neighbours – your colleagues – think?'

'I'm begging you.' He gripped the door frame, knuckles white.

'What would your wife think?'

'Don't.' It was a whisper. His shoulders sank as the last of his resistance ebbed away. I'd worn him down.

'The names and I walk away into the night.' I had to keep pushing, keen to claim what I came for.

Now he was silent.

'The names and I forget where you live.'

'And what will you do with them?'

I made the mistake of tilting my head to the side, causing spots to explode in my line of vision. Wincing, I swiped away the blood that had gathered beneath my nose and squared my shoulders, needing to look firm. 'Does it matter?' My question was followed by a guttural cough, my lungs stinging enough to make my eyes water, helping me forget the pain pulsing in my temple. The night was creeping in, I needed to get home.

Roger straightened up, ran a hand through his thin white hair, pale blue eyes never daring to move from my bloodied face. 'Will you hurt them?' His forehead crinkled.

'I'll make them remember.'

'Why can't you just move on?'

I wanted to laugh at him, at the hypocrisy of his comment. Instead, I rubbed my slick blood between my thumb and forefinger. 'I refuse to live a lie.'

He flinched and then withdrew to the plush comfort of his home, emerging less than a minute later with a folded piece of paper. My trophy.

Satisfied, I walked away, felt his eyes on me until I was out of sight.

And now the names are mine. A story I know the beginning, middle and end to. I whisper them as I trudge into town to wait in line at the job centre, mumble them into my pillow as I lie in bed and wait for exhaustion to take me.

I'm on the third one. I get a jolt of excitement every time I consider that. And yet . . .

My brother. Her. Their faces find me when I try to sleep. Their last words to me the lyrics to a song I'd much sooner forget. But this time is different. I know it is. While they were just surviving, she's thriving. I've seen it.

My excitement curdles with fear. I've lost so much that I'm hollow. Yet still I gamble what remains.

I twist onto my side and clutch a pillow against my stomach, folding into it. Cold. It's always so cold. It's hours until the sun will glow through my window, golden and warming. Until then I'm left staring at its substitute – the street lamp just a few feet

22

from my building. I can see the moths that circle it, foolish and committed in their pursuit of light.

Tomorrow, I will catch two trains and one bus. Tomorrow, I will find out if the gift I left in the woods has been found. My stomach clenches, the anticipation becoming unbearable. I can hear myself groaning as I hold my pillow ever tighter. I wish I could have stayed there, in the woods. I wish I could have waited for dawn to bleed across the sky, for birds to begin their chorus within the trees, for the animals of the undergrowth to stir. Those moments, when the world is first stirring, can feel so pure. So hopeful. But then every day ends the same, no matter how it begins.

I loop the names around my mind one final time before I surrender to sleep.

An hour later and Beth was sitting in the centre of the plush sofa they'd got on sale at Next. Her computer was resting on a cushion on her lap. She was idly checking her emails and social media, but she knew that really she was biding her time until she gave in to her curiosity and entered every name on the list into Google. She just wanted answers, which was normal, right? But what if she was just giving the author what they wanted, playing into the hands of a prankster?

Was Josh right? What if the younger team members at work were just trying to wind her up? It seemed like their style. Perhaps it was a reference to a film she hadn't seen. Her peers at the cinema had an encyclopaedic knowledge of movies. Often, they'd lace their conversations with relevant quotes or anecdotes, which made Beth feel even more excluded from their social clique than she already was.

When it came to films, Beth was sorely out of the loop. It was partly what had drawn her to the job at the cinema; that, and the fact that she managed to get through to the interview stage. As a projectionist, she could finally catch up on the world of the silver screen. As a child, she'd loved to watch fantasy adventure films, where magic and reality collided, films like *Labyrinth* and *Dark Crystal*. But as a teenager, cinema trips ended, films and their magic became lost to her.

'Trevor Hoskins.' Beth thought about the second name on the list, trying unsuccessfully to jolt free a memory that might help her find a missing link. Her hands hovered above the keyboard of her laptop, frozen with indecision. 'It's probably just a prank.'

The afternoon sun which bled through the patio doors warmed her bare feet. Beth turned to glance appreciatively at her little garden, which was so green, so lustrous. A tiny patch of lawn which she had ardently cared for since moving in. The washing on the line swung softly in a lazy breeze.

Josh had so easily served up an explanation for the list. Why was he so quick to come to a conclusion? Why not the level of intrigue which gnawed at Beth?

He's worried about fixation.

Her cheeks burned as she recalled the events of the previous summer when she'd become convinced that their new neighbours hated her. She'd googled them relentlessly, stalked them on Facebook, become obsessed, all because the slim blonde had ignored her call of *Good morning* one sunny July day. Beth had feared they saw something in her, that they had a reason to despise her.

'You're driving yourself crazy,' Josh had lamented as he'd snatched her laptop away from her, his tone like thunder. 'Let it go, Beth. She just didn't hear you, it's nothing.'

And it had turned out to be nothing. Josh was right. But the note . . . that was *something*. From the location to the penmanship, everything about it seemed deliberate.

Beth felt in her core that her happening upon it was no accident. Someone had intended her to find the note. But where was the prank in that?

With a sigh, Beth lowered her hands and began typing, punching each key with unnecessary force. She typed in a Google search:

Five names on a list, the third one is yours.

She hoped it would be a tag line from a film or a line from a song, something to connect it to some canon or zeitgeist that her co-workers ardently followed. But there wasn't anything. A few unrelated websites were listed beneath her search.

'Dammit.'

So the connection had to be the names themselves, there was nothing else. But Beth really didn't know them. The only recognisable name on the list was her own.

It has to mean something.

With steady hands, she started with the first name on the list, the one neatly written above all the authors, and typed Joanne Rowles into her laptop's search engine.

Four

Facebook profiles, LinkedIn pages, Beth scrolled through them all, reading about a plethora of people named Joanne Rowles, greatly diverse in age and location. Nothing shone out from the screen with any glimmer of familiarity.

'Who are you?' Beth wondered aloud as she read about a Joanne Rowles who was a doctor in Sydney, Australia. She knew this couldn't be the person she was looking for since Beth had never even left the UK. Surely she couldn't somehow be connected to someone on the other side of the world.

As the hours slid by, Beth tumbled deeper into the rabbit hole of strangers' profiles, becoming increasingly desperate and willing to spot any possible link. If she found a Joanne who was the same age, she'd linger on their information, scour all their available images, without even knowing what she was looking for.

The sun passed across the room, leaving her feet bare and cold. Still Beth didn't move, not even when her throat became parched and her hands began to ache.

There has to be something.

Increasingly, she couldn't accept that the list was merely just a prank. Why would anyone do that to her when her presence at the cinema was so unobtrusive? She dwelt in the projection rooms, the shadows of the corridors. What gossip she heard uttered by the others she quickly forgot. Beth lived with blinkers on, focused on what was in front of her. Her friends had fallen away. It was her and Josh. And yet the note, it had been there, directly in her path. It wanted to be found, read, investigated.

On the twenty-fifth page of search results for Joanne Rowles, Beth finally accepted that she should probably stop. It was exhausting to slam her head against a succession of dead ends.

With a weary sigh, Beth clicked on the next listed link. It took her to a page for a regional newspaper, *The Bridgnorth Bugle*, and a small story from several months ago about a fire. The headline read:

WOMAN, 29, DIES IN
SUSPICIOUS HOUSE FIRE

Beth's eyes widened with interest. She was herself only four months away from her thirtieth birthday. And where was Bridgnorth? Wasn't it a small market town in the next county over?

Gravel beneath tyres. A key turning in the lock. Staring at her laptop, Beth failed to hear the sounds which heralded Josh's arrival back from work. He burst into the lounge, cheeks reddened by a day spent out in the sun.

'Beth, what are you doing here?' He was annoyed. And confused.

'Huh?' Beth's gaze strayed away from the article to the lower right-hand corner of the screen and the little digital clock that was tucked away there in the toolbar. It was quarter past six. She was officially late for work. 'Shit.' Slamming the computer closed, she shoved it from her lap and hurried out of the room, squeezing her way past Josh, who loomed large in the doorway.

'Beth, what's going on?' his voice followed her up the stairs. 'Are you all right?'

'I lost track of time,' she quickly explained as she dove into their bedroom and began pulling open drawers, desperately seeking the items of her work uniform.

'That's not like you.' The floorboards creaked in protest as Josh followed her into the room.

'Like I said, I lost track of time.' Beth pulled on her polo shirt with the cinema's logo emblazoned in the top corner. Next came her plain black trousers. Then she'd need shoes. And her hair, what sort of state was that in?

'What were you even doing?'

'Just . . .' she shrugged as she fastened the zip on her trousers. 'You know, stuff.'

The washing. It was still out on the line. There was a lot Beth had neglected to do as she'd sat transfixed in front of her laptop, chasing a seemingly unanswerable riddle.

'This anything to do with that list you found?' Josh folded his arms, thick as tree trunks, across his chest. Was he concerned? Because he sounded annoyed. Beth couldn't risk getting drawn into a heated debate with him, she was running late enough as it was. Each minute she procrastinated in the house was another minute that would be deducted from her wages.

'I need to go.' Finally dressed, she barged past him. Her hair was loose and full of kinks from being left to dry naturally, but there wasn't time to care. Her footsteps thundered back down the stairs and in the hallway she grabbed her bag and slid into a pair of worn black ballet pumps.

'You need to bin the damn thing,' Josh persisted, following her. Now they were both in the hallway, the driveway beyond distorted by the mottled glass in the front door.

'Josh, I have to go. I'm late.'

'It means nothing,' he insisted. 'Don't get obsessed about it, okay? It's just names on a list. That's it.'

'Yes,' Beth agreed as she reached for the door handle, 'but one of those names is mine.'

Five

The door clicked loudly behind her as she was shut inside. Ruby glanced around woefully at her assigned room. Though calling it a room seemed overly charitable. It felt more like a prison cell. She rubbed at her arms as she shuffled towards the single bed on a wrought-iron frame that occupied the farthest wall.

To her left, there was a small writing desk, sans paper and pens. It was currently empty, like so much of the room. A cork noticeboard hung above the desk, but it didn't even contain any pins, let alone any pictures. There was a slim metal rail opposite the desk, where some of Ruby's clothes hung down lamely, each supported by thick plastic hangers, and along the ceiling ran a strip light, which hummed loudly whenever it was turned on.

'Just great,' Ruby muttered to herself, feeling surly as more goosebumps pricked along her skin. It was always so very cold in her room, probably because of the lack of natural light. A single window resided high above her bed, barely a sliver in the thick bare wall. Beyond the crappy little window. Ruby knew that the sun was shining, had seen it while she sat in the musty office for yet another interrogation. How long had she been here? No one would permit her to look at a calendar.

The sun was her sole connection to the outside world. She could tell from its glorious glow that it must still be summer.

Approaching her bed, Ruby kicked off the rubber-soled shoes they made her walk around in and climbed on top of the aged mattress. Rusty springs winced as she drew herself up onto her tiptoes and leant against the flat grey wall that covered her room.

Grey.

It had quickly become her least favourite colour, mainly because it barely felt like a colour at all. It was so uniformly bleak, reminding her only of rainy days. Why couldn't her room have been painted in something more vibrant, like yellow or blue?

Still straining on her tiptoes, the mattress sagged beneath her weight and the springs wheezed. Ruby didn't care. She needed to see the sun at least once more that day. Her fingertips scrambled up the smooth walls, reaching for the ledge of the tiny window.

'Come . . . on.' She puffed.

It was always just too far. Fully extended, on her tiptoes, arms stretched so that her shoulders ached, she'd find the ledge in her grip and then try to haul herself up higher, desperate to look out at something natural, something that wasn't grey. But, as usual, she was several inches too short. Even clutching the ledge, she couldn't haul herself up any more, all she was looking at was the bland surface of the wall, instead of the glorious glow of sunshine.

'Shit.' She slapped her hands against the brickwork and then slammed down against her bed in an avalanche of sagging springs and disappointed breathing. 'Shit, shit, shit.' Ruby gave the wall several punches for good measure. Her knuckles began to throb, whilst the matte grey paint remained mockingly pristine. 'Shit!'

With one final sigh, she dropped onto her back and peered up at the cracks in her tiled ceiling. It reminded her of the ceiling back in her maths class, where she'd sat beside Annie and they'd scribbled notes into their textbooks instead of following along with Mr Simmons as he tried to get them to understand algebraic equations.

'Keep climbing those walls and your bed will break.'

A voice crept into the space around her, distant yet close. Ruby rolled onto her side.

'I just want to see the sun.'

'A fart couldn't even escape through our fucking windows.'

Ruby snorted. 'You're right.'

'I'm always right.'

Dexter Griffin. Ruby had met him in the canteen during lunch and dinner service and they'd realised that they were dorm mates. A vent which ran between their rooms permitted them to chat freely with one another on still afternoons such as this, when the rest of the building was quiet. If an alarm was sounding, or they were on lockdown, Dexter's voice would be drowned out by the incessant wail of a siren.

'You coming to dinner tonight?' Dexter's question floated down the vent. He was seventeen and liked to boast that his eighteenth birthday was imminent, and thus so was his departure. When Ruby thought about him leaving, a hole opened up in the pit of her stomach, which she feared all her organs would fall through. He was the only friend she'd made since her arrival. He'd dropped down beside her on the bench in the canteen and extended his hand, smiling warmly. 'I'm Dexter,' he'd announced as she gently shook it, 'and you're new around here. I always spot the new faces.'

Dexter laughed like Muttley from *Wacky Races* and had an answer for everything. Five years her elder, he seemed so vastly worldly and his proximity to freedom made him exotic, alluring.

'Um,' Ruby cleared her throat, suddenly nervous. The bespectacled woman had been very clear about dinner service:

'Once you open up and talk about that day, your privileges will return. You know that my hands are tied over this, it's due process for someone in your . . . situation.' Glenda had offered Ruby a pitying smile. 'You just need to talk. It's really not so hard. Until you do, your access to the canteen and other communal areas has to be revoked. You need to understand that I'm trying to help. But until you talk about that day, about what happened, you'll eat dinner alone, Ruby, in your room. I'm sorry.'

Time had become untethered since Ruby arrived at her new home. She couldn't place how long her embargo from the canteen had been enforced. One week? Two? The pit in her stomach widened. If lack of direct sunlight didn't kill her, then surely loneliness would. The question was – which would take her first?

'So will I see you?' Dexter prodded.

'Not tonight, no.'

'Damn, Ruby. Just tell them what they want to hear, then they'll let you out more. You just have to play the game.'

There had already been too much playing, too many games. From now on, the only drumbeat Ruby would dance to was her own.

'I can't.'

'You can, we all do it.'

'Really, I can't.'

'Seriously, come on. I miss seeing you in the canteen and I'll be going soon, remember? Don't you want to see me?'

There were so many people Ruby wanted to see. Squeezing her eyes shut, she slowed her breathing – a trick she'd developed for staving off the onset of tears.

Crying just wore her out; it was pointless doing it alone in her room without anyone to make notes or observations.

'Ruby, just play nice with them,' Dexter urged. And he was right, she knew he was right. If she gave them what they wanted, she'd get to go outside into the common area, get to eat in the canteen, get to bask in human company instead of this imposed isolation she was suffering through.

'I . . . I can't.' Suppressing a sob, she pressed the heels of her hands against her eyes, sealing herself in darkness. 'I'm just not ready.'

'Well hurry up and be ready,' Dexter advised, 'else you're just going to waste away in here.'

Six

'You're late.'

Beth nodded in acknowledgement at Suzy Parker, who was propped up behind the ticket collection booth, eyes almost completely hidden by the thick layer of liner she always insisted on wearing.

'Like thirty minutes,' Suzy called after her, voice shrill with judgement. 'That's not like you, Beth.'

No. Beth agreed silently. *It isn't.*

When it came to timekeeping, Beth was always punctual. In her five years working at the cinema, she'd never taken sick leave or been absent for any reason. She was reliable, hard-working, the model employee. Because she forced herself to be.

'Maybe try being less aloof with the others,' Colin had gently suggested during Beth's last appraisal. At the time, she'd nodded eagerly and assured him she'd try, knowing full well he was asking the impossible. Beth could be on time, work extra hours, cover other people's shifts, but one thing she couldn't do was connect with others. She refused to.

'Hey!' She almost collided with Colin as she rounded a corner. He held his hands up and regarded her with mild confusion. Unlike everyone else, he wore a blue shirt and no name tag, a way to signify to outsiders that he was management, that he didn't work out on the floor in the public arena like everyone else did.

'Crap, Colin, sorry.' Beth tucked her hair behind her ears and glanced beyond him, at the door to the projection booth innocuously placed in the darkened wall that she was so desperate to slide behind. There would already be people in the theatre, waiting impatiently for their film to start. Beth knew she'd have to forsake the adverts and go straight to the feature, not that any of the cinema's patrons would complain. That would be a gripe only management would make.

'Running a bit late, Beth?' Colin had probably been slim as a younger man, but a comfortable adulthood had gifted him with a sizeable paunch which bulged against the buttons of his pale blue shirt. His features were soft, with round green eyes and a puckered chin. Though his blond hair was thinning, he could still be considered handsome. But he'd always remained unappealing to Beth. There was no edge to him. He drove a white BMW, had a wife and three children and gushed about the latest season of *Game of Thrones* the second it came out. He was predictable, safe. And whilst being with Josh made Beth feel safe, he wasn't predictable. She'd figured out early on that he had secrets of his own.

'I . . . Yeah,' she dipped her head shamefully. 'I lost track of time and—'

'Just work over, okay? Stay past closing, help with the cleaning in the theatres, just half an hour or so.' He smiled and gestured towards the door just beyond him.

'Thanks, Colin.' She hurried past him. 'Thanks so much.'

Heat swells above the tarmac, warping the air. I drift along the edge of the car park, focused on my feet. Occasionally, I chance a glance into the distance, at the glass doors pulled open by giggling teenagers and excited children. I knew I'd be best coming here on a Saturday, when it'd be busy, when the car park would be almost swollen to capacity and I could lurk amongst visitors, could blend in amongst the crowds.

The signage above the glass doors is large. Bold. I crane my neck to read it, squinting against the sun. This cinema is big, new. Compared to the tattered theatre of my childhood, it seems alien and almost grotesque with its barrage of primary-coloured walls. I remember the cinema on Lomax Street crammed into an old tiling factory. The ceilings were high and the seats were stiff, but the magic on the screen, that never changed. For less than five pounds you could look up at a different world, a greater world, and get away. I lived for those days. I'd pluck a crisp fiver from my dad's wallet, not caring if he'd notice or not. The chance to get away was worth the smack around the head I'd get later.

Is that why you're here? To escape?

Not that I've seen you. It's been almost three hours and despite the number of people pouring in and out, I don't think you've been amongst them. But I can wait longer. I'm patient. I've always been patient. And the sun is out. It's warming the hood of my jumper, keeping my hands from going numb. Some people who enter the cinema have completely embraced summer – they're in tiny shorts, tops that reveal their belly buttons and podgy centres, sunglasses giving them all a mirrored gaze. Do I stand out in my jeans and hoody?

I finger the fraying edge of a cuff and keep walking. I'm so close now, I can smell the popcorn, taste the sweetness in the air. My stomach performs a somersault. When did I last eat?

My mind doesn't present the memory willingly. I have to dig through the debris of the day, tracing my steps from my flat, to the station, to the train, to the bus. My stomach twists and, with a resigned sigh, I rummage in my jeans pocket, letting the shrapnel of change gathered there rattle together. Really, I need to eat.

37

I could walk into the cinema, part those glass doors as seamlessly as everyone else and cross the foyer with confidence. Would the air be cool? Would the theatrical boom of carefully edited trailers curdle in my ears along with the chatter of passers-by? Would I waltz up to the food kiosk and place my order without stuttering? What would I even have?

Now my stomach is audibly groaning. Clamping a hand to it, I turn my back on the cinema and all thoughts of eating. It's too risky. But popcorn, it's been so long since I had it, so long since—

Someone brushes against my shoulder. I'm being jostled out of the way as a group of five teenage boys swagger by, the stench of their cheap aftershave so thick I could choke on it. Grabbing the pointed tips of my elbows, I edge closer to the fringes of the car park, further away from the entrance to the cinema. I'm cold, but I can feel sweat gathering at the base of my neck, dripping down my spine.

Ignoring my body's protests, I pull up my hood. I want to see her. I want so desperately to look at her, to feel the fire of recognition burn in my belly. Would she know me too? The others had. Despair had glistened in their eyes.

Fuck. I'm not supposed to think about my brother. I need to think about her. Only her.

It's getting busy. More sweat. But I can't take down my hood. I can't risk someone seeing me, someone ending what I've started before it's even had a chance to work.

Time. It is always my enemy, always running away from me like a horse I can't control. What was my last meal? My thoughts are fuzzy as I try to remember.

I need to eat. To rest. And I can't risk doing those things here. What if she saw me and she knew? Or, worse, what if she saw me and looked through me, same as everyone else?

Feeling uneasy, I retreat to the bus stop. But I'll be back.

With the first film of the night set up, Beth had a moment to reflect. Whilst Colin had been kind about her tardiness, she knew better than to risk keeping it up. His kindness could surely only stretch so far; she needed to retain her former punctuality. She'd seen first-hand how even the kindest of people could twist into something sinister if pushed. And she needed this job, it suited her.

Beyond the little projection room, the audience sat in hushed silence as they gazed up at a vast screen and enjoyed a respite from their day-to-day problems for the next ninety minutes. Beth envied them. Sometimes she'd peer out from her perch and watch them, especially the teenagers. They were full of so much youth. So much freedom. Did they even know what they had? Or, like so many things, was it only once it was snatched away that they'd realise what was lost, long for it, spend a lifetime yearning?

'Damn.' Beth had let her mind drift. She packed up the first projector room and hurried into the next. Here, the audience wouldn't be able to forgo the slew of advertisements and trailers the cinema insisted on showing. Beth uncased the latest action blockbuster from Marvel and began feeding it into the projector. It was a simple process but still one that required great care. She handled every film case with reverence.

Woman, 29, dies in suspicious house fire

Film loaded, she let her thoughts carry her back to her laptop, to the headline she'd found from the small local newspaper. Something in Beth's gut told her that this was the Joanne Rowles she was searching for, that the woman who had been engulfed by a flurry of flames was somehow connected to the list. Their close ages. The nearby location.

It might all just be a coincidence. But then . . . what if it wasn't? She needed to know more, to find out for certain if this Joanne Rowles was the one at the top of her list.

Bridgnorth. It wasn't far. Her late grandfather would have described it as being an hour away, as the crow flies.

Thinking about her grandfather made Beth wilt. She could feel the energy seeping out of her arms, making her movements leaden. She'd only ever known him as an old man with a spritely wit. He'd had the heartiest laugh she'd ever heard, no family celebration was complete without him chuckling away at the head of the table. What would he say if he could see her now?

The projection room suddenly felt too small. With the film set up, Beth left eagerly, but she kept her steps along the corridor to her next destination slow. She looked at the film posters mounted along the walls which glowed in the dim light. So many stories, so many adventures. Beth wondered what the tag line for her own film would be. Or her own death.

Woman, 29, dies in suspicious house fire

Ultimately will we all be reduced to just one sentence? To a spattering of words upon a neglected headstone? What would Beth Belmont's read?

She stopped before a poster for a period romance movie. The lead characters were held in a loving embrace as, behind them, spitfire aeroplanes filled a sky coloured blood red by sunset. The tag line promised romance, adventure and heartbreak. Beth stared at the words, wondering what her story could boast.

Woman, 29, dies in suspicious house fire

What was suspicious about Joanne Rowles' death? And how could she be connected to Beth? She knew that she had to find out. The list was pointing her in a direction, guiding her. And though she hated bending to the will of others, Beth felt compelled to follow, her own curiosity too great to ignore. And Joanne's was only the first name on the list. But it was a place to start, a lead to follow. Maybe learning more about Joanne would shed some light about the other names on the list. About Beth's own name being on there.

Seven

Someone was screaming, the sound torn from them like flesh from bone. Pitched with panic, it punctured the night air. A desperate, haunting sound. Their screams carried through the thick shadows, growing in fervour.

There was fire. Ribbons of flame swept up from the floor, jumped up against the curtains, the bedcovers. Smoke was everywhere, clotting and consuming. Beth coughed. She breathed in the ash, the heat, felt it burn down to her belly. She coughed again.

The heat was unbearable. The sheets beneath her were scorching, devoured by the fire. A flame spat close by, pricked her skin. Beth opened her mouth to scream, but nothing came out. Instead, she choked on the smoke, feeling it curl its way down vital passages. Gasping, she blinked, eyes stinging. The house was on fire and she was still in it, about to be burned alive.

She drew in a final, ragged breath and the screaming stopped. Beth's eyes snapped open and the sudden darkness she found herself in was jarring.

'What the. . .?' Sheets clutched to her chest, she looked around. There were no tendrils of flames trying to claim her bed. All was dark. All was quiet. 'Shit.' Releasing a sheet, she pressed a hand to her temple. Here, the heat of the nightmare still lingered, her skin almost scalding to the touch. Snapping back her hand, she glanced at the other side of the bed, at the sleeping mound that was Josh. His chest rose and fell steadily. Clearly this was one nightmare which had not disturbed his slumber.

Quietly, Beth lowered her bare feet to the floor and tiptoed out of the room. The door gave a soft whine as it opened, but still Josh didn't stir. Out on the small landing, shadows clustered around her, dark and foreboding, so thick they seemed almost viscous, like oil. Reaching the staircase, Beth flicked on a light, illuminating her way.

Everything within her neat house was so eerily still, like the building was holding its breath in anticipation of something big. The absence of sound was unsettling. When Beth reached the kitchen, she was relieved to hear the distant hoot of an owl. At least she wasn't completely alone at this early hour.

She knew that she should sleep. She should creep back up the stairs, climb back into bed and curl up against Josh. But the nightmare had been so vivid. And there was now a new addition to the usual screaming soundtrack: fire.

Joanne Rowles.

Joanne who had died in a fire. The circumstances of her death both haunted and intrigued Beth. Like a moth lured to a flame, she wanted to know more. This woman was her age. Beth could have passed her in the street and never known, and now she was gone . . . just a headline in some local paper. Joanne's death was starting to feel as mysterious as the list.

Beth thought of the stranger's name with every careful step she took towards the lounge and her laptop. She tried to move with as much stealth as she could muster, acting like a burglar in her own home.

You're fixating.

Beth berated herself for letting Josh get in her head. Because that would be his assumption. The list . . . Joanne . . . she was just tumbling down a rabbit hole head first without any clear reason. But there *was* a reason. She and Joanne were connected. Beth had the piece of paper to prove it.

With the lights on, the lounge felt more welcoming than the rest of the house. The curtains were tightly drawn, concealing the darkness that lingered outside. Beth dropped onto the sofa and reached for her computer.

It felt mischievous to be awake, to be prowling around while the rest of the world slept. Like when she was a child and she'd steal her way downstairs after midnight for an illicit spoonful of ice cream. Back then, she didn't have to worry about waking her mother, who would be out until morning. Her siblings would also be unreachable until their alarm clocks shrieked in their ears come six in the morning. She had two older brothers, each equally wayward. When Beth had started junior school, Robert had been suspended from the local secondary for selling weed on the premises. Richard, newly seventeen, had been caught drinking and driving the weekend before Christmas. Drama was never in short supply back then.

Beth ignored the pang in her chest when she thought about her brothers. They had their own lives now, children and families.

The list drifted back up to the surface of her thoughts. Yes, she needed to focus on the list. With the click of a button, she called up the article she'd been reading when Josh came home.

WOMAN, 29, DIES IN
SUSPICIOUS HOUSE FIRE

She read on.

Joanne Rowles, 29, of Furbridge Lane, Bridgnorth, died in the early hours of this morning after a fire started in her home shortly after 2 a.m. Neighbours called local rescue services about the blaze, but when they arrived at the scene, the fire had claimed the majority of the first floor. Joanne was reported as dead at the scene from smoke inhalation. She was home alone at the time of the fire.

The cause of the fire is being treated as suspicious, with the fire department citing signs of arson at the scene.

A more thorough investigation is being carried out.

Beth's gaze slid over to the small digital clock in the lower right-hand corner of the screen: 2.10 a.m. The heat that lingered in her skin had quickly dissipated, causing her exposed arms to bristle uncomfortably.

'Joanne Rowles' death was not an accident . . .' So she was what . . . murdered? The skin on Beth's arms prickled, but she shook her head, resolved to be logical, not fearful. If Joanne was dead, then why was her name on the list from the woods?

Beth checked the date of the article. It had been posted just over eight months ago. Then she ran a quick search of the newspaper's site to find any subsequent articles about Joanne's death. There were none.

'Treated as suspicious,' she repeated the line from the article and chewed her lip. What could the fire services have found to make them suspect foul play? Had someone deliberately killed Joanne Rowles?

The same someone who wrote the list?

Her stomach clenched and bile burned up her throat. Sagging forward, Beth held her breath and waited for the sensation to pass. Eventually it did, leaving her forehead beaded with sweat.

'You might not even be the right Joanne,' she told her laptop, though not entirely convincingly. The only thing that tentatively connected her with the tragic woman from the article was her age, and surely that wasn't enough, was it? Was Beth grasping at straws? 'It's enough,' Beth told the shadows around her. Without this Joanne, she had nothing.

Overhead, a floorboard creaked.

Josh.

Beth quickly minimised the article and then closed her laptop. She scurried into the kitchen and began running the cold water tap just as her boyfriend's sleepy footsteps echoed down the stairs.

'Hey, babe.' He pushed a hand through the short bristles of his hair and regarded her with bleary eyes.

'I didn't mean to wake you,' Beth explained as she filled a large glass with cool water. 'I just woke up and was parched, needed a drink.'

'Another nightmare?' Josh leant against the door frame and yawned wildly, revealing teeth speckled with flashes of silver fillings. He had plump, sensuous lips which reminded Beth of soft velvet. The first time she saw him in the local nightclub, Passions, she knew she was desperate to kiss him, to taste him. Josh was confident, strong. Surrounded by a motley crew of mates, he'd walked through the club with an affable ease, shoulders back, head held high. But the glint in his eye told her that he was approachable. They'd kissed in that desperate, frantic way that people do when they let only their senses guide them. Josh was kind. Easily the kindest person she'd ever known. He invited her into his home, his life. He loved her.

Josh taught Beth that love was like a weed; it could spring up anywhere and grow in even the unlikeliest of places. And grow it did. She surrounded herself with Josh. His presence was so large, it didn't matter that hers was so small. He was always patient, always understanding, avoiding the topic of her absent family, missing friends, as though they shared some silent understanding. He accepted Beth as she was. Which was something she herself struggled to do most days. For that alone she placed him on the highest pedestal she could find.

'Yeah.' Beth gave a quick shrug. 'The usual.' She saw no need to mention the fire, not yet. Although her curiosity was ravenous. 'Doesn't one of your friends work as a fireman?' She tilted her head as the thought came to her.

'Umm.' Still groggy, Josh massaged his jowls. 'You mean Si?'

'Yeah, Si.'

'He's a fireman, yeah. Why, you want him to come do a house inspection?' As he began to wake up, a mischievous smile lit up Josh's face. Beth had always sensed that his smile could be devastating, in the way it broke down her walls, tried to burn a tunnel right through to her core with how it smouldered, made butterflies take flight within her. Whenever she was at the point of succumbing to her inner demons, her insecurities, he'd only have to give her that smile and she'd melt, lose all structure and just be malleable to his will. Josh's smile was a siren's call to lost souls. 'Or do you want me to borrow his uniform sometime?' he wondered slowly, smile widening.

Beth downed some of her water. She felt like she could still taste the smoke that had filled the air in her nightmare. 'Maybe,' she pouted alluringly.

It was time to be his perfect girlfriend, time to forget about what haunted her when she closed her eyes.

People always saw my brother before they saw me. Of course they did. How could they not? He stood out. Even without trying to, a blemish within a crowd. He was both striking and strange. I was always an afterthought.

The man in the corner shop, the bus driver, even our own family said his name first. Always. 'How's . . .' as though my well-being was secondary. And I wanted to hate him for it. I wanted to be jealous, wild with envy, as a young girl should have been. But I could never be mad at him. No one could. It wasn't his fault. None of it.

The stares. The remarks. The cruel comments uttered within earshot, he never set out to get them. How could he?

I learnt to be patient. Learnt to wait for people to react to my brother, then notice me. After the day our world was torn apart, I began to think that maybe, just maybe, it was my time to creep out from the shadows, to be the first name on everyone's lips. But like a record stuck on repeat, all anyone cared about was him. What happened to him. The fact that I had been there, had seen it all, didn't matter. At least not at first.

Morning sunlight burned through a gap in the curtains. Beth groaned as she felt its caress against her cheeks and rolled away to the other side of the bed, finding it empty.

'Mmm.' Sleepily, she fumbled for the crumpled sheets, feeling for Josh's long back. The distant hiss of the shower told her that he was already up and about.

Flopping onto her back, Beth shielded her eyes from the new day. It was still early, but the sun outside was goading, urging her to get up and out of bed.

'You need to be outside more.' This had been her mother's mantra during the long summer months, especially after Beth's brothers became obsessed with their Sega Mega Drive. 'You'll get square eyes,' their mother would chide. 'Get outside and enjoy the day, go on.'

For a time, Beth believed that her mother's insistence at them to go out and make the most of nature's splendour was out of genuine concern for her daughter's well-being. But she soon realised the truth of it. It was only later she came to understand that her mother wanted to enjoy her beloved day-drinking in peace.

'Honey?'

When Josh returned from the bathroom, the curtains were open wide, allowing the full force of the morning's brightness to penetrate the bedroom. Beth was at the window, admiring the way the light glinted off the roof of her car.

'Hey,' Josh came up behind her, warm hands settling on her shoulders. He smelt fresh – Lynx shower gel mixed with apple-scented shampoo. Beth liked him like this: when his skin was damp, and all the dirt and oil had been scrubbed away from beneath his fingernails. The moment he stepped on site for work, dust and debris would stick to him like a magnet. 'You sure you don't want to sleep in a bit? You had a rough night.' He massaged her shoulders as he spoke. Beth leant into the sensation. If she were a cat, this would be the moment she'd start purring, loudly. Though Josh's hands were rough, they were well-versed in how to caress a woman.

'I'll be okay.' The sunlight on her face felt so good, so rejuvenating. Within its blast, Beth hoped to burn away the remnants of her nightmare, of her worries.

'Good.' Josh kissed the back of her head and then stepped away from her. As he did, he took her good feeling with him. 'Well, I've got to get going. Make sure you're not late for work again today.'

49

'Mmm.' Now, the light outside was singeing her eyes, but Beth stayed at the window, waiting until Josh's van reversed out of their driveway. Still she lingered, unable to move out of the warming touch of the sun. A single question burned in her mind even brighter than the vast ball of fire and gas that hung above in a pale blue sky.

It looked like someone had killed Joanne Rowles. But why? What had a twenty-nine-year-old woman from Bridgnorth done to deserve such a brutal end? Beth wasn't sure she wanted to find out. But, as usual, her curiosity was leading her down a path from which there was no return.

And the other three names on the list. Who were they? *Where* were they? If Beth managed to track down Joanne, would that trail lead to them too? The names all surely had to be connected to one another. But how?

Eight

Beth was running. She hurried along the familiar woodland trail, slowing briefly as she passed the elderly lady with her excitable poodles who was always out at dawn. They yapped manically as she jogged by, straining on their leads.

'Magnus, Morticia, hush now,' the woman chastised them in a sing-song voice as she fumbled in her coat pocket for some biscuits.

Beth extended her strides once again. The sun warmed her bare arms as she passed through an open part of the woods. Here, the path had been scorched dry. A cloud of dust accompanied every footstep. Beth pushed herself to go faster. She rounded a tight corner and saw that ahead of her the route lay empty and clear.

Her iPod was just reaching the end of one of her favourite songs, Fleetwood Mac's 'Go Your Own Way'. Beth released her breaths in tight, carefully timed gasps. Her muscles were clenching. Soon she'd reach a point where she'd have to lower her speed. Sweat shone at the top of her back, on her forehead. But Beth knew she needed to go faster, needed to outrun the questions which kept snapping at her heels.

What had really happened to Joanne Rowles?

Had someone killed her?

Did that same someone leave this list out here specially for Beth to find?

Were there other lists out there? Like this one?

Were the other names now reading her own name, googling her, trying to find her?

A tree snapped in the nearby undergrowth and Beth's attention spun in its direction with hawklike intensity. Still running, she studied the shrubs and bushes that swelled at the base of tall, grand trees. Was someone watching her at that very moment?

More speed. She needed to run until the woods became a blur in her peripheral vision, needed to run until she felt numb, until her mind was too exhausted to keep bombarding her with unanswerable questions. The fog of fatigue. She needed it. Craved it.

The Fleetwood Mac track concluded and the iPod loaded the next song in her playlist. It was an old song, one which Beth hadn't listened to for many years. She wondered if Josh had added it to her library. But any curiosities she had about the song's origins were silenced when the tune got going. Tom Jones belted out a duet about burning down a house. Beth ground to a halt, one hand slamming against her chest as her knees buckled. As she bowed in the centre of the path, the song kept playing, the crooning Welshman jovially singing about fighting fire with fire.

Tears stung at Beth's eyes, but she wouldn't let them fall. It was just a song, just a coincidence. With a grunt, she straightened up, reached into her pocket and turned off her iPod. All she could hear was the chirping of birds and the rustling of leaves. Her heart was a jackhammer in her chest and she knew that she couldn't run the rest of the way home, she'd have to be satisfied with a brisk walk. Tightening her sweat-soaked ponytail, she set off, trying not to hum the catchy tune which had now infected her thoughts.

*

Why the running? Is it a hobby? A habit? Do you imagine that you're being chased as you race around the woods? At the very least, do you know you're being watched? Have you ever sensed me there, tracking your every movement?

Your house . . . it was so easy to get inside. I notice things, you see. Like when you and your boyfriend place a spare key under that little cactus in the tan plant pot. I've seen you do that. Don't worry, I didn't stay too long in your lovely home. Even though I wanted to. I was pushing things, I knew that. Like I pushed with the others. Only . . . I've learnt now to pull back. Not to leave the tap running, or random items out of place. And I put the key back where it belongs. So much magnolia. But I couldn't resist leaving a little something behind, something on your iPod. Just in case you weren't thinking about my note from the woods. Which you should be. It should be infecting your every thought in the same way it does mine.

Roger always said I was observant. At first, it was a compliment. But later he would linger on it, as though it were an excuse. He'd look at me with those pale, watery eyes of his and ask how I could have failed to see it coming.

'After all, you're so very observant.'

I reminded him that being observant isn't the same as being a fucking clairvoyant. But like so much of the stuff he said, it got under my skin. A parasite to which I became the unwitting host. How could I ever have seen what was coming? And even if I had, even if I'd known what might happen, there was no way I could have stopped it. No way. Roger didn't understand that.

But you would.

It's why you're running, isn't it? Why you sprint through the woods until your skin shines with sweat. You can run as fast as you fucking want, I'm not going anywhere. I'll wait. I'll be patient. This time . . . this time, I'm going to wait it out. You're going to do the right thing, I know you are.

'You can be so obsessive,' Josh had said when Beth had been consumed with suspicion about her neighbours.

He was wrong, of course. She wasn't obsessed, she was paranoid. Paranoia was like the plague: it came in and ruined everything. Wherever Beth looked, she saw signs that she was being watched, or that she was hated. For days, she walked around holding her breath, waiting for the axe above her head to drop. But it never did. And eventually she had to accept that a neglected greeting might really be just that.

'Not everyone has an agenda,' was something else Josh liked to add during that turbulent time. Again, she wanted to point out that he was incorrect. Everyone *did* have an agenda, it was just that very few people were brave enough to own up to it, most spent their lives feigning ignorance. Beth wasn't sure which was worse.

Back home, Beth put the shower on. It splashed loudly against the base of the cubicle and slowly filled the little bathroom up with steam. She was still in her running gear, hands clasped against either side of the white porcelain sink as she regarded her reflection with pained curiosity.

Her nightmares were there, held beneath her brown eyes in sunken shadows. Her paranoia was there too; a patchwork of lines around her mouth and across her fore-head. Was there beauty? If there was, Beth never saw it. When she'd finally worked up the strength to look into a mirror for the first time all those years ago, she still saw a frightened little girl. Now, that little girl was partially hidden by lines and ageing skin, but behind the eyes, she stood in plain sight, peering out in terrified awe at the world around her.

'It was nothing,' Beth sternly told herself before lowering her head and splashing cold water against her cheeks.

She was still thinking about the song, about Joanne Rowles. At least she'd died from smoke inhalation rather than being burned alive. That, Beth reasoned, was some small mercy.

Straightening up, she locked eyes with herself again. Droplets hung to her eyelashes and the tip of her nose, which in profile she was always told 'looked Roman'. 'I'm Beth Belmont,' she said loudly, squaring her shoulders and raising her angular chin. 'I'm Beth Belmont and I'm fine. I'm safe.'

Nine

'Will she come?' Ruby kicked out her legs and then swiftly drew them back in again, pretending she was on a swing instead of back on an itchy sofa.

'We've spoken about this.' The bespectacled woman was frowning behind her glasses, hand frozen mid-notation as she looked across at the young girl in the denim dungarees.

Ruby kicked out again, remembering how good it was to feel the wind against her bare legs. In here, there was no wind, just the arid air of the office, laced with stale coffee and cloying lavender perfume.

What time was it? She scoured the three walls within her line of vision, tracing the length of the walnut bookcases and the framed certificates which hung behind a nearby desk. There was no clock. Of course there wasn't. Everyone was conspiring to take time away from Ruby, to make her forget how many seconds, minutes, hours, days, weeks had slid by since she'd been pulled through the front doors thrashing and screaming, begging to go home.

'But you asked her, right?' Ruby cocked her head at the woman and tried to smile sweetly, remembering her grandmother's old adage: You catch more flies with honey than with vinegar.

Not that Ruby thought the woman a fly, but she wanted results. And fast. If they expected her to talk, then they needed to give her something in return.

With an exaggerated sigh, the woman put down her notebook completely and folded her plump hands in her lap. 'Ruby, do we really need to go over this again?'

'I just . . .' Ruby looked down at her kneecaps, which had become so knobbly, so fragile-looking. Alone in her room. She didn't eat right. When her meals arrived on a white plastic tray, her hunger was always replaced by loneliness. Would it be so bad to let her sit in the canteen with the others, just once? Ruby cleared her throat and dropped her hands into her lap, mimicking the woman's posture. 'You want me to talk; I want to see my mum. It's that simple.'

'If only it were.' The woman's lips lifted into a sympathetic smile. Today, she was wearing an unflattering shade of plum lipstick which washed out the rest of her face. 'I told you last time, when you requested a visit, that we spoke to your mother and she declined the offer to come here.'

'But it's been weeks. Maybe she's changed her mind. Maybe—'

'Ruby, I know this is difficult, but you need to accept your mother's decision.'

'Her decision to not see me?' Ruby felt the words breaking within her throat, getting clogged down by the mounting sorrow that had been festering in her stomach and was now rising like bile. How was it possible that her mother didn't want to see her? Was she too drunk? As Ruby sat talking to the bespectacled woman was her mum sprawled out on a very different sofa, caked in her own vomit? 'When you last asked her, she might have been drinking. My mum can be mean when she's had a drink. You should try her again, you should—'

A hand had been raised, plump and silencing. 'My job is to do what's best for you.'

'Right.' Ruby threw up her hands, abandoning her former pretence of civility. 'And a mother's job is to be there for her kid. Not once has she been here to see me. Not once!'

'Ruby?'

'Doesn't she miss me? Doesn't she want to see me?'

'You know that it's a complicated situation.'

'I'm her daughter!' Surely it was all simple; a mother's job, her duty, was to be there for her children. Linda Renton had numerous faults, but she tried to be a good mother, Ruby had always seen that in the heaving sobs that followed a night's bad drinking. As the vodka slipped out of Linda's system, the guilt returned. She once told Ruby that it was like choosing whether she wanted to stand on hot coals or sharp knives.

Rain splashed against the nearest window, soft and persistent. Today, the sun was not shining. The sky had darkened and, according to Dexter, a storm was on the way. Ruby wasn't sure she wanted to lie on her hard little bed and listen to nature rage outside. She didn't feel safe in her room, despite the locks on the door.

'Maybe . . .' Ruby shook her head in an attempt to clear her thoughts. Once again she'd brought too much emotion into the room. She knew that she needed to stop doing that. She wanted to show the woman in the other chair that she was calm, collected . . . mature. Maybe then they'd let her go home. Because this was all a test, wasn't it? 'My brothers . . .' Ruby rubbed at her eyes, knocking any tears that dared to present themselves back into their ducts. 'Maybe they can come and see me if my mum won't.'

'I don't think so.' The answer came swift and stern.

'But they're my brothers and—'

'The last time you saw them they assaulted you, do you remember?' The notebook was being retrieved. Ruby watched as the woman made a fresh imprint upon the open page.

'What, no, I—'

'Before you came here,' the woman ploughed through Ruby's mumblings, 'they assaulted you, broke your right arm in three places, dislocated your left shoulder and your jaw. Plus damage to your ribs. You spent four days in hospital before coming here. Do you remember?'

Ruby did and she didn't. The events which the woman mentioned existed in her mind like an old dream, or a movie she couldn't quite remember watching. Aspects of it were familiar – like the time in hospital and arriving here with a cast covering her arm. But had her brothers really done that to her? Weren't they supposed to protect and watch over their little sister? Why would they take it upon themselves to snap her little bones like twigs?

'It's in your best interest that we sever all ties with your family.' The woman ceased writing to once again peer at Ruby, plum lips sagging down at the corners as though she understood the gravity of the death sentence she was giving. 'Our aim in here is to help you heal, truly heal, and overcome what happened whilst learning to understand it.'

'I . . .' Ruby felt like she was alone on a deserted island, watching a boat full of her family and friends slowly drift out to sea, not even bothering to raise their arms and wave goodbye as they abandoned her.

'We're going to get through this, Ruby, I promise.'

'Sometimes . . .' she had to blink furiously to hold back tears. 'Sometimes my jaw still aches. Especially when I eat.'

'It will,' the woman nodded. 'But in time it will pass. All things heal, Ruby. Even you.'

Ten

The house was still. Beth kicked off her shoes and made for the kitchen, turning on lights as she went. Her limbs carried the ache of an eight-hour shift. With a groan, she reached for the kettle, longing for the warm sweetness of a hot chocolate before she headed up to bed. The clock on the wall rested just before the stroke of midnight. It had been a long day.

The sound of water boiling filled the kitchen and hall. Beth turned on more lights, and as she entered the lounge, she froze for a moment, saddened not to find Josh slouched in the corner of their sofa, watching a repeat episode of *Top Gear* on Dave with dead eyes. Then she remembered that hours earlier her phone had buzzed in her pocket, where she kept it poorly concealed, like everyone else at the cinema did.

Meeting the guys for drinks later, it's DB's birthday.
Will be a late one. Don't wait up. Love you x

That explained the stillness which had greeted her when she came in. Beth imagined her boyfriend three beers deep, surrounded by friends, laughing jovially. When Josh smiled, his entire face crinkled. And he had that infectious kind of laugh that could spread through an entire bar. Beth had been surprised the first time she'd laughed in front of him, having been quite certain that she'd forgotten how.

A click from the kitchen told her that the kettle had finished boiling. When she returned to the lounge, she had a mug of hot chocolate in hand. She moved to sit in the corner of the sofa she'd claimed as her own back in the furniture showroom two winters ago. Her free hand instinctively reached for the television remote. With Josh out, this was a perfect opportunity to enjoy one of her favourite Netflix shows – perhaps a couple of episodes of *Gypsy* – before bed. But, as though on autopilot, her hand drifted past the remote on the arm of the sofa and grabbed her nearby laptop. Moments later, it was open, screen glowing, and Beth was once again staring at the news story about Joanne Rowles.

They were the same age, divided by less than a hundred miles. At least they had been, before Joanne died. Beth scanned the article, taking in now-familiar words. She sipped on her hot chocolate but found it bitter to the taste.

She tried to find a corresponding Twitter profile, Facebook page, but there was nothing. Joanne Rowles was a ghost in every sense of the word. In the months that had followed her death, it made sense that any social media profiles she'd had would have been closed down. But that didn't help Beth, who desperately wanted to get a sense of the deceased woman, to at least find a picture of her. Maybe then she'd find a connection.

One a.m. came and went. Beth abandoned her drink, let it go cold, along with any thought of sleep. Questions pulsed behind her temple like a disturbed vein. Questions she couldn't ignore.

It was beginning to feel like Joanne Rowles was a dead end. Beth had found an address but nothing else.

The list. She didn't even need to look at it any more to be able to reel off the names. Her fingers began to type out the second person, Trevor Hoskins. Again, the name was completely unfamiliar, her mind devoid of even the dimmest glimmer of recognition.

Methodical. That's what she was being. If she was being manic, she'd google all of the names at once, drown in an ocean of information. Instead, she was being patient, collected. She was done with the first name. Now it was time for the second.

And you're the third.

Beth hit return and waited for the results.

Google presented her with names, social media profiles. A former jockey. Leaning forward, Beth scanned the data as her phone buzzed against the kitchen table. Like an alarmed bug, the sound rattled through the house.

'Dammit.' Beth slid her laptop from her knee and stalked back into the kitchen. Quietness and solitude pressed in on her from either side. But she ignored them both, instead reaching forward for the phone she hadn't touched in hours. She had a new message from Josh.

So sorry babe but DB has pulled us all into Passions.
I'll try not to wake you when I get in. Love you x

Beth could almost feel the thrum of the bass in the night-club through her phone. Was Josh now dancing drunkenly beneath neon lights?

There wasn't even the time to feel a pang of jealousy or concern. In less than a minute, Beth was back on her laptop, back to conducting her latest search. She drifted past the links that felt obviously incorrect: those of men too young or too old to be connected to her. She had a strange sense of purpose, as though she were following a trail of digital breadcrumbs that had been left just for her.

On page six of her search, she found an article that sucked the air out of her lungs. It was another story from a local newspaper, the *Telford Tribune*. Another little town just beyond the borders of her own county. Beth's hands seized up, feeling like they'd been plunged into a bucket of ice water. With some effort, she forced herself to open up the link. The headline made the frozen sensation in her hands seep further into the rest of her body.

LOCAL MAN PRESUMED MISSING
FOUND WASHED UP ON RIVERBANK

So did that mean . . .
Not daring to inhale, Beth read on.

Telford resident Trevor Hoskins, 31, was reported missing by colleagues six weeks ago. In the early hours of Tuesday morning, a body was found along the banks of the River Severn near Ironbridge. Police have identified the body as Hoskins.

Trevor Hoskins had . . . drowned? Beth read the article again. And again. The words blurred as her eyes became tired. Still she needed to keep taking it in.

Joanne Rowles had been killed in a house fire. Trevor Hoskins had been drowned in a river. Those were the first two names on the list. And the third was—

The lock in the front door turned so loudly that it shook through Beth like a gunshot. Panting, she clasped a hand to her chest and slammed her laptop closed, still reeling from what she'd just read.

'Babe,' Josh staggered uneasily over the threshold,

bumbling between illuminated rooms until he found her. 'You're still up?' He tilted his head and blinked at her.

'I . . . I figured I'd wait up for you.'

She felt cold, so cold. Invisible hands were holding her in an icy embrace. The pulse behind her forehead had gained in pressure, threatening to crack her skull open entirely.

Joanne Rowles – dead.

Trevor Hoskins – dead.

Beth Belmont – alive . . . for now.

And the other two names on the list. Where were they? Were they dead too? She tasted bile.

'Urgh, I'm knackered,' Josh wilted in the doorway. Whilst Beth was at work, he must have come home and smartened himself up, as his usual work clothes were gone. Instead, he looked polished, in a crisp blue shirt and beige trousers. It was his face that told the story of his night out – the bloodshot eyes and the slur in his speech.

'Okay, well, let's get you up to bed.' Beth welcomed the distraction and hurried over to her boyfriend, staggering back from the wall of stale beer that slapped against her when she reached his side. 'Oh, jeez,' she fanned a hand in front of her face. 'You smell like a brewery.'

'I feel like I drank one.'

'Okay, bed for you.'

'I need to piss.'

'Then bathroom first.'

Beth helped a drunken Josh stagger from the bathroom to the bedroom. She was about to help him undress when he collapsed on the bed like a felled tree. Any concerns were quickly silenced by the steam-train-level snores which began to vibrate through his body.

'Sweet dreams,' Beth quipped as she tried in vain to stuff his mass beneath the duvet. Straightening up, she froze.

Something about her own comment had unsettled her. She looked at the four magnolia walls of her bedroom. Did they hold the memories of all the nightmares she'd suffered in there? And now those nightmares were full of fire. What next – would she dream she was drowning tonight?

Rivers could be treacherous. She knew that, remembered how the Severn snaked its way through the lower parts of the county. When it rained heavily, the river had a tendency to break its banks and seep across nearby farmland like a slow-moving liquid invasion. On hot summer days, she'd hang out with her friends on a bridge that went over the river and they'd throw stones in, watching them sink into the murky depths.

No.

The word was sharp, like a dart. Beth flinched and drifted away from the bedroom, from the snoring hulk upon the bed, towards the bathroom.

Don't think about them.

It was an instruction she'd been giving herself for years so militantly that it felt embedded in the very fabric of her being. There were two things Beth Belmont didn't permit herself to think about: her past or her friends. Although they were arguably one and the same. For Beth, there was no safe route down memory lane.

Turning on the taps, she waited for the water to run hot and then splashed it against her face. Then she did it again. And again. Until her hands were becoming red and wrinkled. Withdrawing, she left the tap running and faced her reflection, where her cheeks held the sheen of the water.

What would it feel like to drown?

It was morbid curiosity that was guiding her frazzled mind. She'd heard before that when you drowned you felt an unbearable pressure in your chest. Who had told her that? Was it—

No.

Every thought held the potential of dragging her down into the depths of the past. She needed to go back to bed, to sleep, to try and find some sanctuary in slumber.

'Better to drown than to be burned alive.'

An echo from another life, Beth winced at the memory of it. Who had said that? Ollie? It seemed like something Ollie would say. But she shouldn't be thinking of him, even remembering his name felt like a betrayal.

'No.' Now Beth was berating herself aloud as she hurried back to the bedroom. Josh had not moved, he remained sprawled on his side, head turned and mouth open as wheezing snores creaked out of him. 'Just . . . no.' Beth flung back the sheets on her side, wriggled out of her uniform and let it fall to the floor. Not bothering to pull on her pyjamas, she crawled in beside her boyfriend in just her underwear. The cotton fabric of the bedding was soft against her skin.

Something shrieked outside. Probably a fox. The sound splintered the tranquillity of the balmy evening. In her bed, Beth lay on her back, wide-eyed, waiting for more screams of terror to join the sound of the fox in a horrendous wail. If she closed her eyes, she knew what was waiting for her on the other side of consciousness: more terror, more torment. And if she stayed awake . . .

Questions. So many questions.

Who killed Joanne?

What happened to Trevor? Was he really dead?

And most troubling of all – *what would become of Beth Belmont?*

*

I should be sleeping. My body is heavy with exhaustion, but my mind churns, each thought crashing against another. It was my own fault for going there today. Back to where it happened. Called back there like some mindless lemming, to stand beneath a leaden sky.

I can still feel the bumps from the bus ride rattling in my bones, still smell the acrid odour of piss radiating off the man slumped in the seat behind me.

'An object, focus on an object, hold it in your gaze until your mind starts to clear.' Those had been Roger's words. And I've become so very good at holding on to something, like the damp stain on my bedroom ceiling, cracked and peeling, which I watch until my eyes become dry and raw, until exhaustion shackles my wrists and pulls me under.

I'm trying to focus on the stain, waiting for my thoughts to quieten down. Grinding my molars together, I begin to count.

One, two, three . . . If I reach fifty and I'm still awake, I'll have to get up and pace around the bare floorboards, risk a splinter embedding in my sole.

I shouldn't have gone today. I'm too weak, too tired. But I did. I miss the smell of the flowers I took with me. If I could afford them, I'd have flowers in the flat.

Today, I'd taken carnations. So pretty. Almost like blossom. I try to pick a different kind of flower each time I make the trip. The smell of them in my backpack is always sweetly pungent, almost powerful enough to mask the odour of cider which still clings to the fabric. The base of my backpack is still sticky, thanks to that leaky bottle. And the prick at the store hadn't even apologised when I stormed back in, half the contents of the bottle dripping down my back. He'd looked at me and shrugged. Shrugged! Like it wasn't his problem. I explained how I could only afford the one bottle that week. Explained that I needed it. He'd just scratched his acne-laced chin and shrugged again. That's when I'd screamed.

'I'll call the police,' he'd threatened.

That was enough to make me leave. Just thinking about it makes my pulse go faster, thicker, in my veins. He should have given me a replacement bottle. He should have apologised. He should have—

Sleep. I need to sleep. But I'm still thinking about the bus ride. About the driver. How I could feel his resentment rippling off him in waves as he let me off at my stop.

But I got there in the end. The woods. Our woods. I was thinking of my brother as I looked around, as the trees whispered around me as though they knew my secret and were sharing in it.

The note I left. I turn on my side and regret not taking more time over it, over the penmanship.

But there hadn't been time to be meticulous. The handwriting, though rushed, is at least legible. I positioned the note in the centre of the pink petals, ensuring my message faced outwards, into the clearing, that it was prominent to passers-by.

People needed to remember.

'We'll never forget.'

Because, unlike the others, I won't. I'll keep coming back to the woods, keep leaving my flowers, my notes. Someone needs to remember, someone needs to be a warden for the past. I can't move on, find a new life, and I won't let them either. The lying. It's a parasite that grows. My brother . . . I wish I could see him, speak to him one last time. But he's gone. I can't save him from the past any more than I could save him that day. The truth. That is the legacy I want to leave. I owe him that. They owe him that.

You owe him that.

Why can't I sleep? I've taken the pills that sour-faced GP gave me. They do nothing except blur my vision. And the beast within my stomach is never still, it growls, it burns me from the inside out.

'It takes time,' the doctor had said, 'to find the right medication.'

Tablets. So many tablets. Ones that bloated my face, caused my concave stomach to swell, my legs to itch, my throat to dry up. Nothing took away the pain. Each time I stood on the scales at a check-up, the numbers dipped lower and lower. Now a stiff breeze could easily take me.

'You may need surgery,' the suggestion had been cautiously embedded into the conversation as my consultant drummed her fingers against her desk. I nodded numbly. I'm always numb. And cold. And in fucking pain. 'But there's a waiting list.'

I know how lists work. Someone like me, my name is never at the top of them. I could almost laugh at the irony of it.

Time. It has always been my greatest enemy. I just don't have enough of it. And I'm slipping away, bones held together by flimsy flesh. My body is hell-bent on destroying me and I don't blame it. And the way the doctor looks at me, I know she feels the same way. Sleep, she advises, will help me heal, grow stronger, bring solace.

But if I close my eyes, if I dream, then sometimes, sometimes, I see him. My brother. As I remember him: forever young. That is who I want to think of, not the putrid waste we all became. The truth is going to come out and then maybe, finally, once free, I can rest. I can repair. I can reclaim my withered body.

The television was on. She tracked its sound down the stairs, keeping her steps soft. She knew that she should be in bed. If she were found creeping around the house at this hour, she'd be punished. But the murmur of voices floated up to her like a lullaby, soothing and secure. She needed to get closer, needed to at least crack open the door to the lounge and see her mother on the sofa, bathed in the blue-tinged glow of the screen.

She was nearly there. She'd made it to the hallway undiscovered. Now she just needed to reach out and—

Hands. On her shoulders. The jig was up, now would come the inevitable punishment. She started screaming.

'Beth! Beth, wake up!'

She opened her eyes. The lounge was before her, dark and empty, containing only shadows.

'What the—' Words felt heavy on her tongue. The television was silent. But she'd heard it, she knew she had. And where was—

'Sweetheart, it's okay. I got up to pee and couldn't find you. You must have been sleepwalking again.'

'I . . .' Beth shook her head. 'Sleepwalking.' She repeated the word distrustfully.

'Look, let's get you back to bed, okay?' Josh still smelt of beer and e-cigarettes. Numbly, Beth let him guide her back up the stairs, each step sluggish. When she blinked, she felt the lines between reality and the past distort.

'Remember what the doctor said about your sleep-walking.' He tucked her up in bed and then shuffled over to his own side. Beth didn't even know what time it was. 'He said it happens during times of high stress.' Josh's mouth gaped open wide with a yawn. 'So is everything okay, babe, things all right at work?' He rolled onto his side and looked at her through red-rimmed eyes. The darkness in the room was easing, dawn was surely imminent.

A new day. But all the phantoms from the previous night still clung to the foot of the bed.

'No,' Beth was too tired to fight the truth. 'Everything isn't okay.'

'Oh?' Another yawn. How many precious hours remained before the alarm clock would shriek and demand they abandon their rest?

Beth breathed life into the paranoia that had gnarled itself around her like a poisonous vine. 'I think that someone is trying to kill me.'

Eleven

'You're being ridiculous.'

The sunlight was too bright in the kitchen. It gleamed off the chrome sink and the white cupboards. Beth winced as she looked at Josh, who was leaning against the little pine breakfast table clutching a large cup of coffee in one hand. A rich, oaky aroma filled the small room and Beth tried to concentrate on it, tried to breathe in the vapours. She wanted to focus on anything other than her boyfriend's thunderous expression. With eyes still shot through with red, he stared at her. His cheeks were laced with stubble since he hadn't bothered to shave.

'I mean, you know that, right?' he continued. 'No one is trying to kill you.'

In the dark it had felt safe to confide in him, to whisper her fears against the shadows that swelled around them. Cowed by the result of her late-night decision, Beth sat at the table with her fingers clenched around her own mug. Josh would not sit. He remained erect, back straight and shoulders set in a firm, hostile line.

'Beth, you're being ridiculous.'

Regret made her coffee taste too sharp, too sour. She should never have opened up, should have just clenched her teeth and kept her secrets locked up inside. When it was dark, Josh had pressed her for details, demanded to know what she was talking about. But now that the sun was shining, his interest had turned to disbelief. And frustration. She could hear it in every strained word he spoke to her.

'You really don't need to be going through this again. It's just a stupid list, it means nothing. Do you . . .' Josh sighed and averted his gaze towards the ceiling, just for a moment. Then his tired eyes snapped back towards her. 'Do you need to see someone about your paranoia again? A professional or something? I know you can get anxious and whatever, get a bit wound up from time to time, but—'

'I'm not paranoid.' Beth's protests grated against her. In her mind, everything made sense, it felt counterintuitive to try to explain her feelings to Josh, who didn't – who couldn't – understand, even if she talked herself hoarse.

'Beth, you're—'

'Five names are on that list and the first two are dead. *Dead*, Josh. And the third name on the damn list is mine. What am I supposed to think?'

'It could be anything.' He paused to drink deeply from his mug. 'You don't even know that the people you found online are the right ones. Besides, it all might still be a prank.'

'Died in a fire, drowned.' She released her mug to list on her fingers the ways that the deceased had met their fates. As she spoke, the sunlight felt brighter, began to burn. Beth wanted to rush around and close all the curtains, all the blinds, seal herself in the safety of darkness.

'Why?' Josh placed his empty mug into the sink and turned towards her, frowning intently. 'Why would anyone want to hurt you, Beth?'

'I . . .' She closed her eyes and reminded herself that this was a conversation she was never going to have. 'I don't know.'

'Exactly. Those deaths, I imagine that they're just some weird coincidence, a couple of freak accidents. It happens.'

'I don't know.'

'Look.' Josh came forward and stooped down to cradle her face between his large hands. He was so warm to the touch, as though there were fire in his veins. 'I don't want you fixating on this, okay? You'll drive yourself crazy. Bin the list, forget about it. Stop torturing yourself over nothing. Promise me.'

'I promise.' The lie came surprisingly easy.

'Okay, good.' He kissed her forehead, applying more pressure than usual. 'I've got to head off, will you be all right here today?'

'I'll be fine.'

'You sure?'

Mentally, Beth had already done a rundown of all the security measures in place in their little home. Every window could be locked, the front door had a deadbolt that was rarely employed. The side gate had a rusted lock that remained functional. Beth was safe at home, wasn't she?

Josh kissed her forehead again. 'If you need me, phone me. Just . . .' He stepped back from her, looking conflicted as he massaged the back of his neck. 'Don't freak out over this, Beth. Try to keep some perspective.'

'I will.'

'I'm serious. Don't go losing your head over this.'

'I won't.' She sounded so certain that she was at risk of convincing herself.

Ten minutes later and Josh was reversing out of the driveway. Another minute and he'd be leaving their cul-de-sac and turning out onto the A road that led him deeper into town.

Beth tugged down the blind in the kitchen with force. It was a relief to banish the glaring brightness of an early-summer morning. She was suddenly at odds with the season. Beth felt like she should be in the middle of a bleak winter, rather than a glorious July. She slumped into the lounge with her now cold coffee in her grasp. Usually, she'd be pulling on her running shoes and tying her hair into a high ponytail. As the sun crept ever higher in the sky, she'd sprint around the nearby woods until her entire body was covered in perspiration. But there would be no running today. Beth already knew that no matter how fast she went she couldn't outrun her current fears.

One burned.

One drowned.

Something had to link the deaths, the list. Beth was back on her laptop, focusing on Joanne Rowles again. The woman had barely left a digital imprint on the world. There was the news story and scant else. Except . . .

One article, buried deep in her Google search. It caught Beth's eye even though it was dated two years before the fire. Another piece from a local paper, this time notably less maudlin. With the click of a button, Beth was reading about how a local Co-op convenience store had raised two thousand pounds for a breast cancer charity. There was an accompanying picture with the story where the staff were gathered at the front of the store jovially clutching a novelty-sized cheque with the grand amount on. Beth scanned the names of those pictured and drew closer to her laptop. Third from the right was Joanne Rowles. Her head was tiny in the image, grainy, making it difficult to distinguish anything about her. Beth strained to see the face, struggling to make out any distinguishable features beneath a shock of bobbed black hair.

'So you're Joanne.' Beth looked at the woman behind the cheque, at her smile. Beth squinted at the hazy image in search of some recognition, but nothing was discernible, it was just too obscure.

One thing she could tell, Joanne looked like she fit in effortlessly with her colleagues, wedged in the centre of them all. Had they been shaken by her death just some two years later?

'How do I know you?' Beth asked the image as she dragged her cursor over towards the accompanying article.

Pictured were the staff from the Co-op on Bridgnorth High Street.

Now she had a location. Beth needed to go there. She had to hope that someone would remember Joanne Rowles and could shed more light on who she was than the internet was doing so far.

Twelve

'So, Ruby, how are you feeling this week?'

More rain. Ruby wondered if the weather now mirrored her feelings? The sun had refused to shine for days, hiding behind pewter clouds and letting dark shadows claim the world below. And that suited Ruby just fine. It was so grey in her room, her heart, why shouldn't it be grey everywhere else too?

'I'm okay.'

Today, she wore ripped jeans and an oversized Green Day T-shirt. Ruby hadn't bothered to tidy her hair. It fell in kinked waves down her back, the fringe she'd been trying to grow out now falling over her eyes. She looked how she felt – a mess.

'I was hoping we could talk some more today.' The woman in the armchair smiled as she lowered her glasses, letting them hang on their ornate chain. It was always the same room, always the same request.

Talk. Everyone wanted her to talk. What Ruby didn't understand was what they wanted her to say, they all knew what had happened. Her version of events was hardly going to make any difference.

'It's rained a lot lately.' Ruby nodded in the direction of the window, at the splotches of rainwater which landed heavily upon it and then meandered down the glass.

'It has, yes.' The woman penned a quick note. Ruby squirmed on the sofa. She felt like an animal at the zoo, like she was being studied, observed. And she didn't like it one bit. 'And how have you been feeling in yourself?'

Scared.

Alone.

Tired.

Frustrated.

There were so many feelings Ruby could thrust at the woman. Then she'd have to sit and watch as she quickly scribbled them all down, her plump hands tightly clenched around her fountain pen.

'I feel like I'd like to eat in the canteen again.'

'Eating in the canteen is a privilege,' the woman stated softly, 'one which has had to be revoked. We've been over this, Ruby. Once you start co-operating in these sessions, we can discuss your return to the communal areas. I don't want you sitting in your room all day, alone, but there has to be some incentive to get people in here to talk. You get that, don't you?'

'I'm co-operating,' the words released themselves like a whip. Ruby lurched forwards, hands clutching the sofa to hold her in place. 'I come here all the time. I'm doing what you ask. Stop punishing me.'

'Is that what you think I'm doing? Punishing you?'

'I'd hardly call this a holiday camp.'

'But this, our time in here, it's supposed to be a safe space for you, Ruby. Understand that any privileges that are withheld are done so for your own good.'

'Just let me eat with everyone else!' She was shouting. Something Dexter had always advised her against.

'Don't get riled up,' he'd tell her through the wall. 'Whatever you do, don't let them see you angry.'

Already the woman was adding to the plethora of notes. No matter how much she strained, Ruby was never able to

78

make anything out, the distance between them too great. If she could read the words on the pad, she imagined all too well what she'd be able to see.

Uncooperative.

Distant.

Difficult.

Isolated.

Was Ruby all those things?

'Once you're willing to talk about what happened that day in the woods, we can discuss your return to the canteen. I promise. How does that sound?'

Ruby pouted and said nothing.

'Maybe even the common room too,' the woman added gently, applying sugar to the carrot she was dangling before the young girl. 'I bet it'd be nice to sit on the sofas in there, play a bit of pool, watch some television.'

'I . . .' Ruby couldn't deny the allure of what the woman was offering. It would be nice to not spend her days alone, to be around people her own age. And television. Ruby knew she was woefully behind on *Dawson's Creek*. Perhaps she'd be allowed to sit in the common room on a Sunday when repeats of old episodes were often shown?

'Why don't we start at the beginning? Tell me how that day began.'

To say 'like any other' felt clichéd, but it was the truth. Nothing about that day had felt strange, there were no ill tidings written in the stars, like some Shakespearean tragedy, though that's what they'd all been walking into.

And where were they? The others? Thinking about them filled Ruby's chest with fire. Were they shut off from the world like she was? Or had they talked? And if so, how much had they said?

'So instead of going to school you went to the woods?' The woman was starting the story all by herself. Did she even need Ruby's intervention?

Truanting. Skiving. Playing hooky. There were many ways to describe what she'd done that day, but they all amounted to the same thing – she did something she wasn't supposed to. Instead of following her peers down her steep street and sidling up to the wrought-iron gates of her school for a morning of double maths, she'd skipped out, telling herself that life was too short to spend all day in class.

Only she hadn't said that, had she? It had been—

'Can you tell me why you chose to skip school?' the woman pressed.

Ruby raised a hand to massage the space between her eyes. She couldn't do this. She couldn't talk about them. It was all still so raw, so painful.

'I know this is difficult for you, Ruby. Let's take it one step at a time. So, instead of going to school, you went—'

'No, I'm done,' Ruby threw up her hands towards the ceiling. 'I just can't talk about it, I can't. Keep me locked up forever if you have to, but you can't make me talk. No one can.'

'You think this is for me?' the woman sounded confused. Gingerly, she laid her notebook across her lap and focused solely on Ruby. 'The reason we are here is for *you*. Ruby, this is all for you, to help you get better.'

Thirteen

It was raining when Beth pulled up into the car park beside the Co-op. Her windscreen wipers still swept back and forth as she peered out at the little store.

'You have reached your destination,' the satnav curtly informed her.

'Yes, I know.' Unfastening her seat belt, Beth leant forward and clicked off the device. It had taken just over an hour and a half to reach the Co-op, which meant that if Beth didn't intend to be late for work a second time that week she didn't have much time to conduct her investigation.

The sunshine had stayed back home. As she'd crossed the county line, ashen clouds had gathered overhead, making her journey feel even more ominous.

Outside, it still felt like summer. Despite the rain, a dense humidity hung in the air. Beth climbed out of her car and pulled up the hood of her lightweight jacket, which looked almost comical coupled with the denim cut-off shorts she'd pulled on earlier that morning. She made a mad dash for the glass doors at the entrance, which smoothly parted to grant her access.

'Okay.' Exhaling, she shook off the droplets of rain which clung to her and moved deeper into the store. Everything about it was completely ordinary, like the hundreds of other Co-ops scattered across the country.

Beth moved through the cereal aisle, trying to assume the

gait of an occupied customer whilst she was really scanning the staff present. There was an acne-ridden young man at the till and a woman stooped over by the refrigerator, stacking a shelf with yogurts. Beth changed the trajectory of her steps to approach the woman.

'Um,' nervously, she cleared her throat. What was she even going to say? She'd had an entire car journey to think through this next phase of her plan and yet she was drawing a complete blank.

Hi, so, the woman who worked here and died in a fire, know much about her?

Beth needed an angle, something to lead with.

'Can I help you?' Hearing the cough, the woman straightened, smoothing her hands down the front of her uniform. She looked to be in her mid- to late forties, greying hair pulled back in a loose bun. Deep laughter lines hinted at a kind nature. Her lips, glazed a fiery red, pulled into a patient line as she waited on Beth's response.

'I . . . uh . . .'

Present yourself as you want to be seen. It was advice Beth had been given in what felt like another life. It meant that if she wanted to be taken seriously she needed to act seriously. She cleared her throat a final time, buying herself a precious few moments to get her thoughts straight.

'This might sound kind of strange,' she began to wring her hands together.

Dammit.

She needed to be still, poised, not an irrational writhing mess.

The woman cocked her head to the right and said nothing. Clearly she'd heard her share of strange requests whilst working at the store.

'A relative of mine used to work here.' Beth managed to keep her hands at her sides. 'I mean, a distant relative.

I've been out of the country for a while and now I'm back and kind of wanting to know more about her.'

'Well, we have a big team here,' the woman had a thick Black Country accent. 'But I've been around for, oh, over ten years now, I should be able to help you out. What's your relative's name?'

'Joanne Rowles.'

Something in the woman changed. The corners of her ruby mouth dipped and new lines appeared in her forehead. 'Well, if you're a relative, you must know what happened to her. Awful business, truly awful.'

'I . . . I do know. That's . . . that's why I'm here. Since she's . . . gone . . . I kind of don't know how else to learn more about her.'

'Jo was a hard worker, I can tell you that,' the woman nodded reverently. 'She liked to keep herself to herself. I'm actually surprised you're a relative.'

'You are?' Beth squeaked out the question. Had her cover been blown after less than five minutes? How was she ever supposed to explain the truth to this stranger? That she found a list that had both her name and Joanne's upon it? The woman would think her crazy, would clam up and refuse to reveal any vital information she might know.

'None came to her funeral,' the woman was now lowering her voice. 'So sad. But you were out of the country you say?'

'I've been living and working in the States.'

When did lying become so easy?

'Ah, okay,' the woman nodded again. 'I guess that explains it. But Jo,' now she was drifting along the aisle, leading them to a quiet corner of the store, 'she was a quiet one. Like I said, kept herself to herself. Lived alone, never bothered no one. Her funeral was a small affair, only really those of us who worked with her showed up. No friends, no family.'

'What . . .' Beth pushed her hands into her jacket pockets to keep her from fidgeting. 'What was she like? I've not seen her since we were girls.'

'Hard-working, kind, quiet. Never once called in sick the four years she worked here. Jo was reliable, would happily cover someone else's shift.'

'What sort of things was she into? What sort of person was she?'

How does she connect to me?

'Now that I can't tell you,' the woman smiled sadly. 'Four years we worked together and not once did she talk about her life beyond this store. Figured she just valued her privacy.'

'Yeah, right,' Beth coughed nervously. 'I mean, she was like that growing up.'

'So what happened?'

'Excuse me?'

'For none of her family to show up to her funeral like that, I assume something must have happened.' The woman gazed at her patiently.

'There was a . . . feud. Big one. Guess no one ever really got over it.'

'What a shame,' the woman clicked her tongue. 'No one should be abandoned by family like that, no matter what they've done.'

'Indeed.' It was getting hot in the store, too hot. Beth could feel herself sweating beneath her jacket.

'I'm sorry I can't give you more information about her.'

'It's okay.' But it wasn't. This had been a dead end and heat and disappointment were spreading through Beth's body, making her skin itch. 'I mean,' she glanced hopefully at the guy behind the till point, 'maybe she was close to someone else here, maybe—'

The woman pressed a hand against Beth's lower arm. 'Sweetheart, I appreciate you want answers. You want to know who Jo was, but you'll find nothing here. She was too aloof. Best worker I've ever known, but she didn't let anyone in. She seemed . . . guarded.'

'Right . . . okay.'

'The scars from that family feud of yours must have run pretty deep.'

'Uh-huh, yeah.'

'Were you hoping to learn more about the fire?'

Beth blinked, the question almost knocking her off balance. The articles online made it seem as though the trail of investigation around the fire had run cold, that there was nothing more to discover.

'It was arson . . . right?' Beth frowned, trying to recall the information from the article. 'But no one was ever charged? No culprit found?'

'I guess since you're not from round here you wouldn't have heard, figured you'd have questions about it all.'

'Heard what?'

'People speculate, they talk.' The woman peered round Beth to check the surrounding aisle. They were still alone. 'My son, he works for the fire service and he was on duty the night they went to Jo's home.'

'So what happened to her?'

'Turns out the cause of the fire was the cooker. All of the gas burners had been turned on without a flame and then a lighter was left flickering on the countertop.'

'It was definitely arson then?' Beth pressed.

The woman sighed, the action sweeping through her entire body. With a slight shake of the head, she gazed

85

sorrowfully at Beth. 'The fire was deliberate all right, but it was set by someone in the house.'

'You said that Joanne lived alone?' Things weren't adding up. If Joanne Rowles lived alone, then had someone broken in and started the fire?

'Exactly.' The woman clasped her hands together and bowed her head. Raising her shoulders, she sighed again despairingly. 'There was no break-in. No evidence of forced entry. The signs were there, we just didn't stop to see them. She was always so alone, so cut off from everyone else.'

'Wait,' Beth uttered hotly, holding up a hand to the woman. 'You're saying that Joanne did this to herself *deliberately*? That she started the fire?'

'It's speculation at best. Like I said, people talk. No further investigation was launched into the cause of the fire. A terrible way to go. I still think about her often.'

Beth's head was spinning. Was it the heat in the store making her dizzy or something else? Pressing a hand to her temple, she forced her breathing to slow, to regulate. 'Could I maybe see a picture of her or . . . or something?'

Because there had to be something. She hadn't driven all this way just to learn that Joanne Rowles was supposedly responsible for her own death. How did that help Beth? It just left her with even more questions.

'I don't think there's anything. I could put in a request with HR for you to see her personnel file since you're family.'

'No, no, it's okay,' Beth replied a little too quickly. That kind of due process would require proof of her relationship to the deceased, proof she did not have. 'I was really just hoping to find out more about who she was.'

'Well, I'm sorry that I can't be of more help there, or even point you in the right direction. Are you going to visit her, while you're in town?'

Beth's eyes widened questioningly.

'She's up at the crem. I pop by her grave time to time when I go to visit my mother. Modest little plaque, but then from what little I knew of her, she led a modest life.'

'Right, the crematorium,' Beth nodded briskly. 'Yes, I'll make sure to swing by before I head home.'

'You do that.' The woman smiled kindly at her. 'Now you must excuse me, but I really should be getting back to work.'

Beth watched her amble back towards the refrigerator and the yogurt pots that still needed stacking. She waited for several moments to pass, absorbing everything she'd just learnt. Then she grabbed a Mars from the nearby shelf, paid for it at the till and hurried back to her car. The rain had eased, but the air remained pungent and humid.

I know who I am.

I'm strident in this more than anything else. It's what fuels me. In my weaker moments, when doubt is a toxin polluting my blood, I remind myself over and over of who I am, of why I'm still here.

The names. I've written them down several more times, attached them to my fridge door, tacked them above my electric fire, sellotaped them to the cracked mirror in my bathroom. I want to keep looking at them and keep remembering the truth. My truth. Her truth.

I know who I am.

But I also know who I should have been. And this is the knowledge which burns, the salt in all my old wounds. Working in a Co-op. At a cinema. Could that have been my future? Could I have put on a uniform every morning, brushed my hair, my teeth, and smiled at strangers as I served them? Is that what she wanted? I think she longed for more. Deep down, we all did, all dreamed of it but didn't dare hope for it.

They stole my future from me. They stole my brother's.

It's so fucking cold in this flat. Outside, the sun is burning hot and heavy, but this place is like a tomb. I'm by the fridge, staring down my most recently completed list of names, a pan in my hand full of cooled baked beans which I've been picking at for the last hour. They pop in my mouth like ant eggs and my guts swirl with the unpleasant memory of my brother destroying an ants' nest in our garden during a sweltering July afternoon. As all the little minions tumbled out onto the coarse grass, he gleefully pointed at the pearlescent eggs they were pushing with their tiny pincers, desperately trying to save them.

'Don't—' the plea was out of my mouth as an egg popped into his. Laughing, he crunched it between his teeth. And me, seven years old and knowing no better, copied him, grabbed a tiny egg and popped it between my teeth, enjoying the way he laughed when I did so.

I know who I am.

I'm sister to a dead brother. And these names . . . they won't bring him back. But they can release me. Freedom. From his shadow, from what they forced my life to be. It's all I've ever wanted.

Is she looking for them? Finding names on headstones? Is she afraid? She should be. They were.

I force down another spoonful of beans, wincing as I chew.

The radio played a Linkin Park song, the heavy guitars and pained voices filling her little car as it bounced along country roads on the return journey home.

Did Joanne kill herself?

The question plagued her at every junction, every set of red lights.

Did she really set her house up to burn with her in it?

It made no sense, no matter how much Beth swirled the thought around in her mind. No one would subject themselves to death by burning, it was just too brutal, too terrible. Someone had to have turned on all the cooker hobs, lit the fatal flame which torched the whole house. Someone who knew Joanne, who had access to her, as there weren't any signs of forced entry.

All Beth had learnt was that Joanne Rowles was quiet, a loner. And that was a connection. Beth also shared those traits. Aside from Josh, she had no friends, just her colleagues at work. Her world was small and she liked it that way, felt safe that way. But being quiet and introverted wasn't enough to warrant a target on someone's back, nor their name upon some strange hit list.

Was that what it was – a hit list?

Beth braked suddenly, jarring to a halt on an empty country lane. The rain was just a lazy whisper upon her windscreen. Breathing hard, she ran her hands around the circumference of her steering wheel, noting all the grooves, the bumps. Reality. She needed to ground herself in reality.

Death was stalking her. She half expected to see its shadowy mass in the rear-view mirror, gathering in the seat behind her, like the killer from some urban legend. But both Beth's car and the road beyond were empty, devoid of any other souls.

'I'm going crazy,' Beth told her reflection, digging her nails into the plastic of the steering wheel.

But the list was so very real, even Josh had seen it.

Trevor Hoskins.

He had drowned, been discovered washed up on a riverbank an hour's drive in the opposite direction. Had his death been accidental? Beth needed to know, needed to find out the truth of his demise before the author of the list caught up with the third name on it.

Fourteen

The projector whirred as the movie commenced. Beth peered out at the darkened theatre, at the images moving on the vast screen. An entire day had passed since her visit to the Co-op store where Joanne Rowles had worked and still she felt numb. Food had lost its taste, even her morning coffee proved insufficiently strong and failed to rouse her into a more reasonable state of awareness. Was this what it felt like to be hunted? Instead of sheer terror rushing through her veins, Beth was being overtaken by an empty sensation, as though she were almost disassociating from herself. This feeling wasn't new to her. She'd felt it before. When the punches and the kicks came.

Like in a dream, she drifted to the next projection booth, then the next. Echoes from distant movies became the soundtrack to her shift. In the space of a half-hour, she could move from a war-torn beach to New York in December. This was the greatest gift her job gave her: escapism.

There was the darkness. The numbness. But the names. They marched through her like an army that never slept. A parasite that gnawed at her, the names refusing to let go, refusing to be dismissed.

Trevor Hoskins.

He was next. Beth's thoughts kept circling back to him, wondering who he was, why he died.

Trevor was close. She knew the river that had taken his life. If she could track him down like she tracked down Joanne, then perhaps—

'Hey, everything all right in here?'

The door to the projector room was thrust open, bringing with it cooled air and the scent of stale popcorn. Beth turned, reel in hand, to face the figure clutching the handle and staring at her.

'Oh, Colin, hey,' her words came slowly as though she were speaking through treacle.

Trevor.

Trevor Hoskins.

Her thoughts were incessant, distracting.

'The 3D isn't lining up in screen five, you need to take a look at it.'

Beth had to remind herself how to nod. 'Right, yes, okay.'

Five. Screen five.

Trevor Hoskins.

'You all right, Beth, you seem a little out of it?'

Drowned. Washed up on a riverbank.

'I'm . . .' She blinked, embarrassed that she looked as spacey as she felt. 'I'm a little tired, that's all.'

Colin straightened, rolling back his shoulders and tilting his head to the side as he regarded her with interest. Could he see the numbness within her? Did he know what caused it? Beth's skin began to burn. Was there to be more kicking, more punching? She swallowed and tasted copper.

'Well, try and take it easy if you can. But first, screen five. Had a couple of complaints already, so let's get it sorted as quick as we can, okay?'

'Okay.'

Feelings were returning, pricking like needles. Beth finished up and then hurried towards the projector room for screen five. There was a crimson glow along the corridor and she slowed her pace just briefly to bask in it, to remind herself that here she was safe, here she could blend into the shadows and be unseen. Bundling herself into the little room above the fifth screen of the theatre, she slammed the door and leant against it, breathing hard. She could feel the wetness of her fear against the underside of her hands. What was she doing? Was she afraid of Colin?

Had he written the list?

Of course not. Colin was kind, sympathetic. He didn't judge the holes in her CV like other managers had done.

Screen five and another adventure courtesy of Marvel. Beth quickly realigned the film in the projector so that the 3D effect was seamless. Even up in her little tower, she could hear the muffles of appreciation and relief ripple through the audience. Beth wanted to linger with them awhile, to join them as they stared up at the screen. But without specialist 3D glasses the image from the projector just appeared blurry to her eyes. Beth scowled at it from her little peephole. All she wanted was to see things the same as everyone else, to not be plagued by fears she couldn't control.

Trevor Hoskins.

The list was real, which meant that so was the potential threat it held. Beth needed to learn more about the second name on it.

All she wanted was to go home, to fold herself into Josh's embrace and hide within the four walls of their happy life, their safe life. Because Josh would always keep her safe, wouldn't he? He knew her. He loved her. At least the bits he could see.

Home. It's a strange word. Does it mean where you sleep? Where you feel safe? Where you belong? I slam closed the front door of my home. It rattles in its hinges. Like so much else around me, it is cheap, unsteady.

'This place will be good for you,' Roger had insisted.

'How?'

'You can make it your own.' He'd proceeded deeper into the flat, ignoring my question. 'All it needs is a little TLC to spruce it up a bit. Maybe a lick of paint, some nice curtains.'

A lick of paint.

Some nice curtains.

He might as well have been telling me to recreate the Sistine Chapel on the ceiling. I'd heard about that place from school, about the beauty of it, the splendour. And, like an idiot, I'd sat there thinking to myself that one day I'd go, one day I'd see it, oblivious to the chains already coiling around me.

'Seriously, this place could be . . .' his smile fell as he turned back to face me. 'Homely,' he concluded with an apologetic tilt of the head.

'Yeah,' I scoffed as I shouldered my way past him, 'this place could be a real palace some day.' Already I could feel the dampness in the air, the cloying presence of mould. Pushing my teeth together, I thought of Roger's home, with its driveway and double garage. With its double-glazed windows and ivy growing up the left side of the house. Now that was a home. It was solid, grand, proud. This . . . four yellowed walls and a kitchen full of empty cupboards. This was just a different kind of prison.

'You're going to make something of yourself,' he said as he came over and placed his hands on my shoulders. I knew he didn't mean it. How could he?

'Sure.' I shrugged him off. 'I'm going to be a fucking rock star.'

'Mind your language.'

'Why?'

'Because you want to be well-spoken, it'll help people get to know you. To like you.'

'To like me?' I'd laughed at the suggestion. 'Should I be making friends?' He was backing away from me as I shook my head vigorously. 'No, I'm done with friends. I don't want any more fucking friends.'

It was almost one in the morning and Beth had learnt several things.

One: Trevor had worked in a large branch of B&Q before he was reported missing.

Two: his death wasn't being ruled as suspicious, something she discovered when she visited the website for West Mercia Police, who oversaw the Telford area in which Hoskins had lived and worked.

So now Beth had another destination, another store to visit. Was this going to be just another dead end?

Overhead, a floorboard creaked. Josh must have climbed out of bed after disappearing up the stairs an hour ago, openly dubious of Beth's insistence that she was doing some necessary work on her laptop, completely unrelated to the list. Her boyfriend had given her a long, level look, mouth twitching like he wanted to speak. Then he'd shrugged and slumped his way up the staircase which ran through their magnolia-hued house like a spine, clearly too exhausted to enter into a fresh argument.

Her internet search yielded no picture of Trevor, just a few sporadic details about his life and, more notably, his death. Like Joanne, he appeared to be something of a ghost online. Did that mean he too was a loner?

Being an introvert isn't a real connection.

Beth knew this, trusted her own logic on it. But still . . .

With a click of a mouse, she drifted to the Facebook home page, where she was immediately invited to set up a profile. Biting her lip, she closed the window. Then she went through the same process for Twitter and LinkedIn. It would be so easy to form an online identity, to join the world of social media. So easy and yet . . .

'It means nothing.' With force, she closed her laptop and stared at the little apple logo on it. So what if Joanne and Trevor were as allergic to online engagement as she was? Many people chose to abstain from social media for good reason.

You're afraid.

The little voice in her head taunted her.

'I'm not,' Beth scolded as she left the living room, killed the lights and began to traipse upstairs.

You've every right to be afraid.

She froze halfway through her ascent, one hand tightly clutching the banister. Her cinema uniform was crumpled, her hair tumbling out of the bun she'd pulled it into earlier that morning. Even the modest amount of make-up she was wearing was now fading. The day was done, Beth should be heading up to bed excited for a night of sleep and respite from the worries of the everyday world.

But all she'd find in the darkness was more screaming, more terror.

You can never stop being afraid.

This time, she didn't object to her thoughts, she just shuddered and continued up the stairs. Tomorrow was a new day. Another chance to face her fears.

Fifteen

'I'm leaving.'

Ruby heard the words through the wall and said nothing. She sat on the floor with her back against the hard plaster, the cool of the linoleum beneath her seeping into her skin.

'I said I'm leaving,' Dexter repeated, his voice rising.

'I know.' Her response was so weak, so strained. Would he be able to tell that she'd been crying? The wall between their rooms was thin enough to permit her to eavesdrop on the conversation he'd had the previous day, the one where he was informed of his imminent departure and told to pack. He'd warned her that day was coming and yet Ruby had refused to accept the truth, kept telling herself that in the end he'd stay.

'They're coming to collect my stuff at three.'

Three. Ruby's head instinctively rose to search for a clock, even though it was futile. Time didn't exist between the four walls of her 'bedroom'. Did Dexter have a clock? Was this yet again some privilege that was being withheld from her?

'So how long do you have left?' She raised a hand to swipe the back of it against her eyes. It came away damp.

'An hour or so.'

Was that it? In just sixty short minutes, Dexter would leave and by the evening someone else would be in his room, making it their own, lamenting the small window and the bare walls.

Time could be devastating. Ruby was learning that on a daily basis. A second could change your life just as much as a decade could. And now Dexter was leaving. More change, more departures. She squeezed her eyes closed and felt a tear prick her eyelashes like juice from a lemon. It stung.

'I was hoping to see you before I left,' Dexter continued. 'But you're never in the canteen, or the common room.'

'I'm still not allowed out of here.' She swallowed hard.

'So you're still not talking?' Was that judgement in his voice or concern? Without being able to read his expression, it was difficult to discern.

Like most of the boys there, Dexter had his hair cropped short. A deep-set scar from a childhood bout of chicken pox crinkled beside his right eye. There was a danger to him, like a wolf puppy who had the potential to be kind and lovable but also harboured a taste for the wild.

'I've tried.' Ruby looked up at the ceiling, at the cracks that fed across it like erratic marks on a map.

'Not hard enough.'

So it was judgement. Ruby could imagine Dexter on the other side of the wall cradling his knees against his chest just as she was. Only instead of despair etched into his young features, there was sadness and frustration.

'I tried, really I did.'

'Don't you want to get out of here one day? Don't you want to eat with other people, to watch the television?'

Ruby sighed and ground her hands into fists. She so desperately wanted those things. And the sun, more than anything she wanted to feel it warm her face. But if she talked, what then? She'd either be condemning or liberating herself and Ruby didn't know which way the chips were going to fall. No one had really laid it out to her, she'd just been bundled from the hospital to here.

She needed to see her mother, she'd know what to do, how to proceed, what to say. Only—

Thinking about the last time she'd seen her mother was just too painful. Ruby winced, feeling pressure in her chest as though someone were performing an autopsy on her while she was awake – cracking apart her ribcage to peer at her heart as it was still beating.

'In here, you can only rely on yourself.' Dexter was speaking as loudly as he could, ensuring that his advice made it through the centimetres of cinder blocks between them. 'No one is coming for you, Ruby. If you want out, then you've got to talk.'

'Is that why you're getting out?'

'No, I just ran out the clock. I'm eighteen now, remember? First thing tomorrow, I'm going to go and buy a lottery ticket.'

'Good luck with that.'

'I talked to make it easier on myself while I was here.'

For a moment, Ruby was preoccupied with massaging her chest, checking that all the muscles and ligaments were still holding together.

'I'm not sure talking will make things easier,' she finally replied, getting breathless. The pain in her chest was still there, even though everything looked and felt normal.

'Trust me, Ruby, it will. No matter what they think about what you say, they have to let you out, they have to, this isn't a fucking prison. You talk, you get to leave your room. That's how this place works. So just bloody talk, talk yourself hoarse if you have to. I don't want to be out there picturing you still locked up in here.'

'But that's how it will be, you're the one getting to leave, remember?'

'You'll be eighteen one day too.'

'That feels like a lifetime away.'

'Then talk,' Dexter was now delivering it as an order. 'Make all the days you have to spend in this shithole feel a bit shorter. Last night, it was pizza in the canteen, and the decent stuff, too, not the cardboard crap they feed you at school.'

School.

Ruby craned her neck to peer up at her distant window. She could see blue, which meant that it was a nice day, that the sun was shining. Had the school holidays concluded? If she talked might she be given a calendar as well as a clock? Was that too much to hope for?

'I'll talk.' Ruby kept staring at the blue beyond her tiny slither of a window.

'Good. That's good.'

'I'll talk just so that I don't have to spend every hour of every bloody day in this stinking prison cell.'

'I think they prefer to call them bedrooms.' Dexter sounded like he was smiling.

'Same difference, right?' Ruby smirked.

'Pretty much, yeah.'

'Enjoy your life beyond here.'

'You too, Ruby Renton. And who knows, maybe our paths will cross again someday?'

Ruby was opening her mouth to respond when she heard muffled sounds on the other side of the wall: a door opening and a new voice speaking. His departure was coming early. It was time for Dexter to go. She didn't call out goodbye, instead she remained on the hard floor, gazing up at the slice of blue perfection she could see beyond her window and praying that one day she'd once again know what it felt like to be free.

Sixteen

The sun had decided to come out. It warmed the tarmac which spread across the car park like a blackened ocean. Beth stood beside her car, one hand on the bonnet, beneath which the engine still hummed from its hour-and-a-half-long journey to this branch of B&Q, lodged within a large retail park between Mothercare and Harveys. More cars surrounded her, glistening in the sunlight like exotic jewels. It felt good to feel the heat on her back, the sting in her eyes as she squinted towards the entrance to the store. One way in. One way out.

Trevor Hoskins had been deemed missing before dead. Beth inhaled, tasting the burning rubber which lingered in the air.

Will there be answers here?

She figured that there better be as she pushed off from the car and made for the glass doors granting her passage into the air-conditioned interior.

It was busy inside. Shoppers idled behind trollies overloaded with plywood and tins of paint. Despite the cool air pumping into the store, she'd carried the heat of the afternoon in with her. Her legs prickled with sweat beneath the acid-wash jeans she'd pulled on, even her bare arms were clammy as they extended from her Ramones T-shirt.

Unlike the Co-op, which had a modest floor space, this store was vast. High white ceilings and polished floors swept away from her in every direction. Tall aisles crammed with everything from door handles to garden wrenches spilled away from her. Given her task, the scale of the place was instantly intimidating. Where was she supposed to go to learn more about Trevor Hoskins? To the bathrooms display? The plants outside? Would her lie about being a relative even float here? Somehow she doubted it.

For twenty minutes, Beth just drifted. She weaved between aisles, paying fleeting attention to the goods that she passed. There was now an orange basket clasped within her left hand, its contents consisting of a pack of duct tape, a wrench and a ball of twine.

'What am I doing?' she asked herself, entering the paint aisle. From there, she ambled towards shelves storing long planks of pine and timber. She breathed in their woody aroma, it reminded her of the way the hutch from her childhood had smelt. Pine dust and mildew. She'd owned guinea pigs once, Flotsam and Jetsam. They were both tan, which made it difficult to tell them apart. Beth had loved them dearly, doting on them when she came home from school, sneaking them treats from her lunch tray – pieces of carrot and pepper. But, like so many things in her childhood, the guinea pigs weren't meant to last. One morning, she went out to freshen their water and food bowls and found their hutch empty.

'Rats,' her mother had stated, with the barbed acidity with which she always spoke. 'They must have got in during the night.'

But even at ten, Beth's powers of deduction were strong. There was no sign of forced entry, just an empty home where once her precious pigs had lived. As she stood on the dew-clad grass, blinded by her own tears, she sensed foul play. Her brothers had done this, some cruel prank perhaps. And her mother . . . of course she would protect them. They were her boys, the apples of her eye.

'They didn't leave me with stretchmarks and prolapsed parts,' she'd sneer at her daughter.

Yes, the boys were always favoured, always protected.

With a gasp, Beth released her overly tight grip on the basket and realised that she'd dotted her palm with crescent-moon-shaped crests of blood.

'Dammit.' She wiped her hand against the back of her jeans and hurried out of the aisle. As she passed a display for fertiliser, her eyes locked onto the customer service desk. Was that where she wanted to go? Turning back, she took a moment to align her thoughts.

There were questions which needed to be asked, questions about Trevor. What was he like? Did he have any friends at the store? Why did he go missing? How long was he missing for?

'Hi.' Somehow her feet had dragged her over to the desk before her mind felt ready.

A young woman looking to be in her early twenties glanced back at her from behind heavy-set lashes, her lips painted so richly red that they looked like velvet.

'I . . . um.' Beth's fingers flailed in the air as they sought for something to fidget with. 'A relative of mine used to work here and I'm looking for any friends he might have had.'

So far the lie had a hundred per cent track record of success, which meant that, flustered, Beth chose to go with it again.

'Uh-huh.' The girl eyed her with obvious boredom, long nails clacking against the countertop of the desk. Her name tag read 'Stacie'.

'If, um, you know anyone who might have known him, could you point me in the right direction—'

'Name?'

'Uh, sorry?'

'Name,' Stacie deadpanned her repeated order. 'Of your relative.'

'Oh, right, yeah.' Beth clasped her basket tightly and breathed deep. 'Trevor. Trevor Hoskins.'

Stacie's eyes suddenly widened with interest. 'The drowned guy?'

'Uh-huh.'

'He your cousin or something?'

'Um, yeah. Second cousin. We weren't all that close.'

'Okay.' Stacie cocked her head to the side as she delved deep into her thoughts. 'I think he worked in the stockroom. Shift work. Nights.' The tapping of her nails quickened. 'He must have hung around with FP and Clive. They've been working here since, like, forever. I'll see if FP is about, don't think Clive is, he only works nights.'

An announcement was made over the tannoy – could Frank Parker come to the customer service desk.

Beth waited. The minutes crept by excruciatingly slowly. She considered attempting small talk with Stacie, but the girl was already riffling through a stack of nearby papers, clearly in no mood to chat. Beth's shoulders sagged with relief. Speaking with strangers was definitely not her forte. Once she'd discussed the weather and any recent dramatic news events, she was spent. Not like Josh. He had a natural affinity with people, he could chat to anyone, any time, about absolutely anything. If he were there now, he'd be ignoring Stacie's subtle signs to be left alone and chatting away about the store, the sunshine, even his favourite football team.

A pang surged through Beth. She missed Josh. Moreover, she hated lying to him. There were already too many lies that made up the foundation of their relationship, why keep putting wood on the pyre?

Because one day it'll all go up in flames anyway.

With a wince, Beth scolded herself. Things weren't like that with Josh. He was strong, stable and had been by her side for years. He held her when she trembled in the night, stroked her forehead to help lull her back to sleep. She could—

'Lemme guess, you just wanted to see me, needed your daily FP fix?' A man in a faded blue uniform with slicked-back ginger hair was sauntering towards the desk, bringing with him a pungent cloud of Old Spice.

'Please.' Stacie rolled her eyes and pouted simultaneously. 'This customer was asking after Hoskins.'

FP clocked Beth and his posture instantly changed. Gone was his casual demeanour, instead his spine straightened, shoulders pushing back. His fingertips nervously grazed his jawline as he looked between Beth and Stacie. 'She got questions about Trev?'

'She's his cousin.'

'Really?' FP's green eyes narrowed suspiciously. ''Cause I worked with Trev three years straight and he never mentioned any family. Only his mother.'

'We were . . . estranged.' Beth glanced about, aware that a bustling store was hardly the most discreet place to be having this conversation. 'There was a family feud. I've only recently moved back to the UK.'

Shoulders relaxing, FP seemed appeased. 'Ah, well, that makes sense. Explains the lack of family at his funeral.'

Beth frowned. Just like the notable lack of relatives at Joanne Rowles' funeral. And if Beth died, she already knew that her own mother wouldn't show. Why would she?

'I . . . um,' she tried to pick up the thread of her enquiry. 'I just wanted to know more about him. It had

been a while since I saw him, years, and then to learn
what happened to him was just so . . . awful.'

'Such a tragedy.' FP's head drooped and his hands found
their way into his pockets. 'Trev was a good guy, a bit
of a loner, sure, but decent enough. Never missed a shift,
was obsessed with *Red Dwarf* and *Blackadder*. Most of his
jokes revolved around them.'

'The police said he'd gone missing?' Beth ventured,
keen for more information about the weeks leading up to
Trevor's death.

FP nodded. 'Uh-huh, sure. No one was all that
surprised, truth be told. Trev was kind of, you know,
paranoid. Always thought someone was after him. Got
real bad the weeks before he disappeared, he wouldn't
even walk to the bus stop alone. Something had spooked
him for sure.'

'Any idea what?'

'Nope.' FP shrugged regretfully. 'Sorry. Trev was pretty
private about stuff, I could just tell something was bothering
him. Then one day he just didn't show for his shift, had
left his flat and, poof, just gone.'

Beth forced herself to look concerned instead of scared.
She needed to keep playing the role of the inquisitive
distant cousin.

'Three weeks later, they find him next to the Severn.'

'They say he drowned?'

FP reached for Beth's shoulder and guided her towards
the back of the customer service desk, clearly keen for more
privacy. 'I hate to tell you this . . .' he'd lowered his voice,
'. . . but your cousin was troubled, deeply. Sure, he was a
great guy to work with, but you could see in his eyes that
something was eating away at him. I think when he went
missing, he was being, you know, like a cat.'

'Like a cat?' Beth repeated, not sure she'd heard him correctly.

'Uh-huh, like a cat. He'd gone away to die.'

'So you think,' Beth had to cough against the bile suddenly climbing up her throat, 'you think it was suicide, his drowning?'

'Yeah, 'fraid so. I mean . . .' FP pushed his hands back into the depths of his pockets, '. . . maybe someone was after him, maybe his paranoia was legit. I guess now we'll never know. They cleared out his flat some months ago, but his mum is still about. I assume you'll be popping by to see her?'

'His mum?'

'Yeah, only place he ever went beside work was to visit his mum at her old people's home. She was kept at some place thirty minutes from here. Lemme think,' FP tapped his work boot against the polished floor of the store. 'Sunnymead, that's it. Nice little place. Shame they wouldn't let the old girl attend the funeral; she's so weak these days, you know, from being so sick.'

'And Trevor was close to his mum?'

A coarse grunt escaped through FP's lips. 'Just a bit. Gave her most of his wages, went there every other day. Doted on her. Guess he was an only child or something.'

'Um . . .' Beth shook her head, knowing she needed to appear to be aware of this. 'Yes, yes he was.'

'Well, yeah, go see her. Sure she'll be glad to have some family pop by.' FP's gaze flicked towards Stacie and his smile broadened. 'I'm not in a hurry to head back to the stockroom if you'd like some company out here.'

Stacie's styled eyebrows plateaued into a flat line. 'Trust me, I'm fine.'

'Well, thank you,' Beth looked earnestly at FP and then Stacie, 'for your help, thanks so much.'

'Any time,' FP clasped her on the shoulder, giving a brief squeeze, and then began to stride away, whistling a soft tune to himself as he went.

'Anything else I can help you with today?' Stacie asked in a monotonous tone.

'No,' Beth began to back away from the desk, 'I'm good, thank you.'

Flicking on the switch beside the door, I wait for the bare bulb above my two-seater table to hum itself to life. Above me, a floorboard creaks. Then another. Mrs Norris is probably en route to take a piss, she has about fifty of them a fucking night these days. Burning with resentment, I drop my empty backpack to the floor and stomp over to the kitchenette, yanking open the nearest cupboard. Something scurries towards the darkness of the far corner. A spider. Large. I've instantly lost my appetite.

'Dammit.' I slam the cupboard shut and kick off my worn trainers, feet throbbing. How far have I walked today? A couple of miles? Who knows. It's not like I have one of those fancy tracker devices like she does. I've seen her checking it as she bounces around the woods in her expensive trainers, hair sleek as it swishes in its ponytail. She doesn't need the sheen of sweat upon her skin to make her glossy. When she runs, she's neat, tidy, arms pumping primly at her sides. Sometimes she stops, presses her hands to her knees and then glances at her left wrist. At first, I figured she was checking the time, but now I'm pretty sure she's monitoring her steps, her heart rate. If she hits her targets does she reward herself somehow? Does she go home and let that boyfriend of hers massage her feet, run her a hot bath?

My own body aches. I think of the boxy shower cubicle in my bathroom, of the grime crusted around each tile. I could turn it on, make the water as hot as I can bear it and stand beneath the weak flow, pivot as I wait impatiently for my hair to become wet.

She probably has a power shower. Or one of those waterfall wet rooms I've seen on television. Showers that promise the sensation of being in the rainforest. My shower makes me feel like I'm being pissed on by some drunk.

I could use a drink. But my last few quid for the week was spent on the flowers. It was a gamble. I know it was. She might not even go there, to those woods. She might just keep jogging around her beloved route near her pretty little home, bouncing around on the memory-foam soles of her fancy shoes. But then if she does go, there needs to be something there, something to greet her.

Voices. Rumbling, gently, like distant traffic. Mrs Norris must have turned on her television. If I strain, I can probably make out what she's watching, but I don't have the energy to eavesdrop, not tonight. I walk the short distance to my bedroom and collapse on my bed, gazing up at the ceiling, at the stain. I think of her, wrapped in the arms of someone who cares, someone who loves her. Does he hold her tight as she sleeps? Do they wake up wrapped around each other, smiling like couples do in films? I reach for my spare pillow, clutch it to my chest.

'Patient,' I remind myself, mouth widening into a yawn. 'Be patient.' Change was coming, I could sense it. She was going to make things better. Either by her own will or by force. I can't let things fall apart. Not again.

There wasn't time to get to Sunnymead in the same afternoon, so as soon as Beth got home, she phoned the residential home to make an appointment for the following day. She said she was a distant relative of Mrs Hoskins. The woman on the other end of the line was quiet for several seconds before asking, 'You mean Trevor's mother?'

'Yes, yes, that's her.' Beth was moving around the kitchen as she spoke, preparing dinner. It was just past five, leaving time to eat and then dash out to work.

'Most visitors come between two and four,' the receptionist told her.

'Okay, yeah, that's fine.' It meant having to drive straight to work afterwards, but Beth could manage that. Just. It was going to be tight.

'And your name?'

'Beth Belmont.' The kitchen was beginning to smell like spaghetti bolognese, which made Beth's stomach growl appreciatively. Now that she had a plan of action, the numbness had subsided and she felt alive, invigorated. Trevor's mother would have to know more about him than his colleagues did. If there was a connection between the names on the list, Beth was going to find it. And soon.

'Okay, Beth, you're all booked in for tomorrow afternoon. I'll let Sheila know you're coming, I'm sure she'll be delighted.'

The dial tone droned in Beth's ear as she stood over the bubbling pot of minced meat and tomato sauce.

Sheila.

It was the first name she'd heard which had the slightest sheen of familiarity to it. She shivered with unease.

Seventeen

At night, I see them. It used to be just my brother. He's in the woods, staring at me, not saying anything. Then the grass beneath his feet turns to blood, an ocean of it, and I'm trying to run away, but instead I'm sinking, thrashing about as I drown. I always wake up in my bed, pillow to my chest, bathed in sweat, my heart a jackhammer in my chest. But as weeks turned to months, then years, the nightmares began to shift, to change. Instead of them being only about my brother, Roger was there too. Maybe there's an irony to that. I'm not sure.

Now, when I start to sink, a hand grabs my wrists, yanks me up. For a moment I'm happy, smiling at the prospect of salvation. But as I slide above the glassy surface of the bloodied water, I see him. Roger. His big hands wrapped around my slender wrists, squeezing tight, as though he could snap the bone, like it was made of glass. He wears a wolfish grin and I'm screaming. The sound shatters the nightmare, returns me to my damp bed. I keep screaming. Sometimes I shove my face into my pillow to muffle the sound. Not that Mrs Norris can hear me.

'Dreams are just the mind's way of processing trauma,' was the explanation Roger used to give me, back when I'd actually open up to him. But I've been processing this shit for decades and nothing has changed.

If my brother was still here would that help? Would that change things?

I realise that I'm barefoot in the centre of my flat, the rough fibres of the carpet making the soles of my feet itch. It's dark out, the street light outside glowing like a false moon. I must have been sleepwalking.

Approaching the window, I hold my wrists up to the light, turning them over to behold the thick scars that sit raised and angry, pulsing as my body remembers the weight of Roger's touch in my dream.

'Beth?'

As she opened her eyes, she instantly felt the dampness upon her cheeks. Scrambling to sit up, she hastily fought to wipe away her tears.

'Sweetheart, are you okay?'

Even in the fragile early-morning light, Josh's concern was obvious; gathered in the creases that rippled across his forehead. He reached across the bed and let his fingertips graze Beth's arm. She shuddered at his warmth, her whole body feeling like ice.

'You were shouting,' he spoke gently, carefully. 'You kept shouting stop.'

Beth opened her mouth and tried to control the clammy pressure of her tongue. The nightmare had yet to leave the room. She could feel its presence stalking along the magnolia walls, circling her like a serpent determined to strike again. 'I,' with a cough, she found her voice. 'I don't remember, I must have been dreaming.'

The lie was easier than the truth. A part of her was still rooted to that terrible spot in the woods, still feeling the sun on her back as her world fell apart. How many times had she visited that scene? For how many years would it gnarl around her subconscious like a poisonous vine?

'It must have been some dream,' Josh leant in close and left the whisper of a kiss upon her lips. 'You were properly thrashing about.' She felt him studying her.

'Weird, huh?' Beth self-consciously tucked a strand of dark hair behind her ear. If Josh had theories about her nightmares. He kept them to himself. Occasionally he'd pry, try and lift the veil on the darkness which tormented her so. But Beth knew better than to let him in. Some things were just better left unspoken.

'You sure you're okay? You seem to be having your nightmares more often at the moment.' Things weren't playing out as they usually would. He was still watching her, eyes crinkled with concern. 'You're not still thinking about that list, are you?'

Beth flinched. 'What? No! I mean . . . nightmares. I have them. They're normal for me, remember? Don't . . . don't get me stressed about it.'

'I'm not, I'm just . . .' he looked hurt.

'Please, Josh, I'm fine.'

'Right. Whatever.' The mattress shifted as Josh climbed out of bed, stretching his arms up above his head. Sleep still clung to him, causing him to yawn widely. 'You got much planned for today?'

'Just work,' Beth replied flippantly.

And a visit to a residential home.

But the latter part needed to be left out since she couldn't explain it to Josh, not rationally. He'd surely see through any lie she told and know she was still chasing ghosts on the list.

'Well, I need to shower.' He sauntered out of the room and Beth was left alone to watch the sky turn pink and then golden. Her ears still throbbed from the power of the screams within her dream.

People were always looking to place blame for what had happened. Like everyone made a choice that day. One thing none of us ever had was choice. I see that now. And he saw it back then. He was so much smarter than anyone knew. They saw him, how he was, and they put him in a box. Perhaps it made them feel bigger, to make him so small.

But to me he always stood a hundred feet high. Words meant nothing. No matter what they called him, what they said, it didn't change how I felt. He was my brother. And then I lost him.

'Sticks and stones,' our mother would hiss at me whenever I moaned about kids at school being cruel. What did she know? In our world, abuse wasn't just a cursed word on a forked tongue. It was a slap, a punch. A kick in the ribs. And those will break your bones. In our world, not even the innocent were safe.

Rain tracked her progress to Sunnymead, which didn't surprise Beth. So far, the entire summer had felt reassuringly British. One day of glorious sunshine would be followed by four of grey skies and endless drizzle.

The residential home was tucked off the side of a surprisingly long A road, which felt Roman in design. Beth parked and darted over to the entrance and the glass doors, which sighed as they parted and granted her access into a welcoming hallway. The decor was dated but cosy: wallpaper adorned with roses, coupled with plush armchairs that bore just the right level of use to appear worn but still comfortable. To Beth's right, there was a small partial opening, beyond which she could see desks forming the foundations of a chaotic office space. As she lingered, taking in her surroundings, a uniformed nurse appeared in the opening, her smile bright.

'Hi, can I help you?'

'I'm . . .' Beth nervously pulled on the sleeves of her coat that were spattered with raindrops. 'I'm here to see Sheila?' she delivered her response as a question rather than a statement of purpose. Not that the nurse seemed to mind. She nodded and produced a clipboard.

'If you can sign in please.'

'Yeah, sure.' Beth took the board and carefully wrote her name in cursive and then a scribbled signature: Beth Belmont.

'Thanks, Miss Belmont. I'll just buzz you through. Sheila is in the day room waiting for you.'

An interior door within the entrance hallway sang like the surgeon's game Beth had played as a child, where the patient's red nose would shine bright if you made a mistake. The sound was jarring and her hands quickly reached for the handle to the secondary door, which released her from the seal between outside and the main part of the home she was now standing in.

The smell greeted her first – stale but also sweet. Burnt toast swirled with cinnamon, lavender and settled dust. And . . .

Beth's nose crinkled and she raised a hand to her mouth to suppress a cough.

Ammonia. It was there, thick and pungent, residing just beneath the lavender. After a few moments, her senses accepted that they were being assaulted and the odour became less offensive.

Beth looked around at the corridors that twisted away from her, at the chairs gathered in every spare corner and appeared to be pinched from her late grandmother's home. They were chairs with long backs and wooden spindles for arms. Chairs that were plush with fabric but still formal, concerned with function over style. Doors dotted the walls still covered in the same faded rose pattern. Beside each brass-numbered bedroom was a little noticeboard, where photographs were placed, images of loved ones, Beth presumed.

As she drifted along the corridor, she saw beaming

brides and laughing babies. The occupant of the room had condensed their life, their worth, to the contents of the little noticeboard beside their brass number to represent who they were, who they had once been. And Beth was fascinated. So many weddings, so many cherub-faced children. Clearly the residents of Sunnymead derived their joy from their loved ones, their families. Her footsteps became heavy, as though the burgundy carpet had turned to tar. These displays of love, of devotion, were too much. She should never have come here, she should—

'Hi, are you lost?' A slim blonde in oversized scrubs had materialised before her without Beth noticing. With a start, she snapped her attention away from the walls and tried to seem present.

'I'm looking for the day room.'

Wrong.

Why didn't she just say she was looking for the exit? Why prolong this torture? Her gut was already clenching, telling her that she was making a mistake.

'Follow me.' The blonde smiled kindly and turned on her heel.

Beth followed and, after several paces, they reached a glass-fronted room that was much larger than any of the others. Chairs and sofas were gathered together in little clusters, there was a piano in the far corner and a flat-screen television on the adjacent wall. A second glass wall boasted a view of outside, of the green Shropshire fields that rolled away into the distance.

'It's much nicer when the sun is shining,' the blonde explained as she opened the door and guided Beth inside.

'It's still pretty nice,' Beth noted. There was just so much . . . light. It burst in through every window and, despite the drabness outside, the large room felt bright.

'Are you Sheila's visitor? She's just over there.' The blonde subtly pointed towards the far right corner where a small grey-haired woman was bundled into a hard-backed chair, legs tucked beneath a tartan blanket, her face turned towards the nearest window and the rain splashing against it. 'It's nice for her to have a visitor. No one has been since her son died.'

Trevor.

Beth's heart threatened to fall into the pit of her stomach at the mention of him. She was still searching for what connected them, had hoped that his mother would be able to offer some further insight, but now that Beth was here, and could see the frail form of the old woman in the corner, she began to doubt that she'd be able to tell her anything relevant.

'Thanks,' Beth kept her reply breezy and tentatively approached the woman in the corner. 'Sheila?' Carefully removing her coat, she settled herself in the nearest seat. Sheila kept her gaze towards the window, towards the rain. 'Sheila, hi,' Beth was raising her voice slightly, doing her best to be heard. 'You don't know me, but I knew your son and . . .'

Instantly, the woman's head pivoted in Beth's direction, like a dog that had just been shown a bone. Her blue eyes, held within the wrinkled depths of her face, were bright with interest.

Beth recoiled for a second. Those eyes, that bright blue. She knew them . . . didn't she? In another life, when they'd been shrewder. But the face around them was severely decayed by time and further toil. Sheila's cheekbones were razor sharp, her skin almost grey and so terribly thin, stretched too tight over her crumbling features. Hesitant, Beth glanced over her shoulder, eyeing the exit.

'You knew my boy?' The rasp of her voice told of the years spent sucking on cigarettes.

'Umm . . . sort of.' Beth clasped her hands together and turned back towards Sheila, smelling the brisk odour of Dettol and Germolene which clung to the old woman as though, instead of perfume, she doused herself in a chemical cocktail each morning.

'He was a *good* boy.' Sheila drummed heavy on the 'good'. 'I don't care what anyone says about my kids, they were good, I tell you. He . . . he was a *good* boy.'

'I'm sorry about what happened to him,' Beth offered sincerely. Her chair squeaked beneath her as she shifted positions. 'You mentioned kids? I thought your son was an only child?'

'Hmm, I forget what I can and can't say these days. I don't care any more. The cancer is going to take me soon anyway. I keep fighting it, it keeps coming back. One of us is going to give in sometime soon and I'm old. And tired.' Sheila narrowed her eyes, faded eyebrows flattening. She cocked her head in a birdlike manner and scrutinised her guest, old hands covered in papery skin pulling tight on the blanket that shrouded her lower half. 'You're pretty.'

Beth blushed a little. 'Um . . . thanks.'

'I was pretty once,' Sheila kept staring at her, 'back when my life was my own. I had this blonde hair, permed, always permed, and my nails,' she released a hacking cough as she peered down at her frail hands. 'I used to have such lovely false nails and big, thick lashes. I turned heads on my estate.' Her blue eyes again pinned Beth. 'You look familiar.'

'Oh,' Beth blinked in surprise and eased back from her eager stance, 'I do?'

'Hmm,' Sheila openly continued her visual inspection, casting her eyes over Beth's long damp hair, strong jawline, tired gaze. 'Yes, I've seen you before.'

'N-no, you're mistaken,' Beth could hear the quake in her voice.

Blonde perm. Thick lashes. Talons for nails.

Red. Always painted red.

She was going to be sick. She needed to leave. This couldn't be the Sheila she was thinking of . . . could it? She didn't dare steal another glance at the woman to check. It was time to go. But she'd come so far, her visit couldn't be in vain.

'I wanted to ask you some questions about Trevor.' Beth clasped her hands so tight the blood ceased to flow to her fingertips. She was here with a purpose. The old woman was mistaken, she had to be. There was no way she could be the former blonde Beth was thinking of. No way. Because that would mean—

'Trevor?' Sheila croaked.

'Yes, Trevor Hoskins, your son.'

'No,' Sheila was shaking her head. 'My son's name is Ollie. Ollie Turnbald.'

All of the air was sucked out of the room.

'Wh-what did you say?' Beth struggled to lift her voice above a squeak. But she needed to speak, had to speak. Already her heart was starting to freeze within her chest – how long until vital oxygen ceased being pumped around her body and she collapsed, lifeless, to the floor? Did shock truly have the power to kill?

Her tongue grew thick in her mouth, throat constricting.

No. No, it wasn't possible. It couldn't be.

'Ollie. Ollie Turnbald,' Sheila repeated proudly. 'That's my son, that's the only name I'll ever know him by.'

'No,' Beth was so cold, on the verge of freezing. She was surprised not to find a puff of vapour accompanying her strained words. 'No, that's impossible,' she told the old woman with certainty. 'There's no way you could know that name.'

Eighteen

'I'm ready.' Ruby wasn't sure about the truth of her declaration, but she made it anyway.

'You are?' The woman with the glasses lowered them to peer at her with her natural vision.

'Yep.' Slapping the sofa around her with the underside of her hands, Ruby tried to seem overly co-operative, excited even. 'I'm ready, this is it. Today, I'm going to talk your ears off. Because that's what you want, right?'

'Why the sudden change of heart?'

Already Ruby could feel herself deflating, sinking down against the fabric of the sofa like a blown-up remnant of a birthday party now useless and forgotten in a corner. She had been ready earlier, so very ready. That morning, as she'd showered, she'd mentally prepared herself for what was to come, for what she needed to say.

'I thought you wanted me to talk,' Ruby declared hotly, crossing her arms against her chest.

'I do,' the woman insisted softly. 'But only if you're sure you're ready to. So, tell me, Ruby, why now? You've been here for over two months and never wanted to open up before.'

'Yeah, well,' Ruby gave a nonchalant raise of her slim shoulders. 'I figured I might as well start talking. I'm sick of being in my room all the time, sick of eating alone.'

'You want to get out more. Have some more space.'

'Exactly,' Ruby nodded. 'Like I said, I'm sick of being alone.'

'Are you sick of the nightmares too?' The glasses were back in place upon the tip of her nose and the woman was dividing her attention between Ruby and her notebook.

'Nightmares?' Bile rose in Ruby's throat. Had they been watching her sleep? Once, she'd asked for some sleeping pills, just once. Was that somehow enough to label her as having night terrors?

'I can't promise that they will stop if you talk about what happened,' her tone became more serious, 'but opening up should definitely help.'

'Look, I just want to go in the canteen, the common room.' Ruby crossed her arms against her chest.

'You'd like some more freedom. That's normal and understandable. If we start talking today, I'll definitely hold up my end and make sure your privileges are restored, how does that sound?'

'Great.' And it really did. Ruby wasn't sure how much longer she could keep staring at the same four walls. She wanted to see people, to hear laughter, even tears. Loneliness was a carcass on her back that she was keen to cast off. Dexter leaving had reminded Ruby how truly alone she was.

'Okay then, Ruby, whenever you're ready, let's start talking about that day.'

'Do you know that when I'm in here, time grows wings?' Ruby offered with a nervous laugh. Because it did. In this formal room. An hour felt like ten minutes, whilst back in her cell of a bedroom. an hour felt like a lifetime. Was that something to do with relativity? If only she'd paid more attention in science.

'You're stalling,' the woman noted flatly, hand drifting across her notepad as she scribbled something down. 'Don't stall, Ruby. You'll feel better once you've opened up.'

'Fine.' With an exaggerated sigh, Ruby uncrossed her arms and let them fall to her sides. She looked towards the spines of the numerous books neatly lined across the shelves, scanning their unfamiliar titles. She told herself that she was just telling a story, that the words she was about to speak didn't belong to her, didn't define her.

'I've told you before that the day started like any other.' Wasn't that how all stories started? It was a quiet day until the storm blew in? Her best friend, Annie, she was smart, she read books for actual pleasure. She'd say something about how the start of a story was establishing the equilibrium. And when that awful day began, they were just six kids skiving, six kids thinking they knew better than the adults in their world.

'You went into the woods?' The woman was spurring her on, keen to keep the momentum in the story.

'We went into the woods and everything changed.' Ruby kept staring at the thick spines of distant books, wishing she could tell any other tale than her own.

'Tell me what happened in the woods.'

'But you already know.' Pressure was building behind Ruby's eyes, tears that desperately wanted to cascade down her cheeks in a waterfall.

'I know,' the woman's voice was soft, sympathetic. 'But I need to hear it from you.'

'He said it was just a game,' Ruby hiccupped against the sobs she was holding inside, 'and we believed him. We always believed him.'

Nineteen

'They think I'm crazy.' Sheila scratched against the blue-veined back of her hand with yellowed nails. 'But I know my boy. I know my son.'

With great effort, Beth forced her teeth to cease nervously knocking together so that she could speak. 'No. Trevor. Your son's name is Trevor. Trevor Hoskins.'

Out. She had to get out now. Alarm bells were ringing in her head, deafening her.

A laugh that was more like a cough escaped through Sheila's thin lips. She shook her head, her once-permed grey hair grazing the collar of the thick knitted navy cardigan she wore. 'That's not his name.' Her blue eyes narrowed. 'You know that.'

Beth felt dizzy. Sick. She clutched tightly to the arms of the chair she was sitting in as though she were suddenly on a roller coaster, about to surge down a precarious dip. 'N-no,' she stood up and swayed on her feet, staring at the old woman like she was looking upon a ghost.

'I know my Ollie.' Sheila kept scratching the back of her hand, kept staring intently at her visitor. 'And I know he was a good boy. He came here, didn't forget his old mum. Didn't keep away. Such a *good* boy. Always marched to the beat of his own drum, but that don't make someone bad.'

It was getting difficult to breathe. Could you drown in mid-air? Beth's chest was tightening, her lungs wedged within a vice that was ever turning, ever constricting. The room was beginning to spin. Was this how Trevor felt in his final moments, when, beneath the murky waters of the Severn, he could no longer breathe, his body tightening excruciatingly as it was deprived of precious oxygen?

Only he wasn't Trevor. Not really. Not truly. He was—

'And you.' The hand that had been scratching whipped into the air and now a long nail was angled in Beth's direction like a deadly arrow. 'I know you.'

Beth was staggering back from the corner and the chairs, hands raised in submission. 'Please, I'm just . . .' she gulped for air.

'Ollie Turnbald.' The finger remained pointed, raised. 'That was my son's name and I shan't forget it. Not now, not ever.'

She couldn't hear the name spoken again. Beth turned her back on the old woman and ran towards the glass doors, but her steps weren't taking her there swiftly enough. She needed to get out. The glass-walled space had become a cage. Drawing in heaving breaths, she clumsily gripped at the door handle, twice lacking any friction. Finally, she kept her hand in place long enough to push down and she was released.

Was Sheila watching her harried departure? Beth didn't turn round to check. She powered down the corridor, past all the doors with their little noticeboard shrines. Now she could see the thorns on the vines that twisted beneath the roses in the wallpaper and the ammonia in the air was seeping into her skin. If she didn't get out soon, Beth was either going to vomit or faint.

If any of the nurses on duty threw her confused looks, she didn't notice them. Like a rat in a maze, she was focused only on the reward of freedom, scurrying back along her tracks until she saw the familiar outline of the chairs within the entrance vestibule. Beth sprinted up to the glass doors and paused briefly to wait for the flat tone of the buzzer which meant release. One more gateway, one more obstruction to go.

'Oh, Miss!' a voice was calling her back, chipper in tone.

Beth sucked in a lungful of dry air and stopped. She could feel her muscles fighting her decision, keen to keep thrusting forwards. The car park was in sight, glossy with rainfall. She was so close.

'You need to sign out.' The nurse in the opening was producing the same clipboard Beth had signed less than twenty minutes earlier.

'Oh, um, yes, of course, sorry.' Flustered, Beth gripped the board and the proffered pen and scribbled her name.

'Leaving so soon?' the nurse enquired as she took the board back into her possession.

'Yeah, there's a family emergency.' Beth wrung her hands together, certain she looked like someone in a suitable state of panic for such a lie.

'Oh dear, nothing too serious, I hope.'

'Me too.'

Beth was at last free to pass through the final set of doors. As she did, the rain hit her. During her time inside, it had grown in ferocity. Large drops smacked against her skull, quickly soaked through her clothes. And without her coat she was vulnerable. Running to her car, Beth thought of the garment still on the chair back in the day room. There was no way she'd be going back to retrieve it. She couldn't be around Sheila.

Once in her car, she locked the doors and placed her hands against the steering wheel. Gasping for breath, she felt her face begin to burn. It was as if there suddenly wasn't enough air in the entire world to satiate her.

'*You're having a panic attack*'.

It had happened before, but this time Beth wouldn't allow it to end with a blackout. Keeping her hands on the wheel, she tried to recall what the doctors had told her.

'*Deep, steady breaths.*'

But she was still gasping manically, still flailing.

'*Slowly now. In . . . and out.*'

Each breath was laboured and uneasy.

In.

Out.

In.

Out.

Wasn't she supposed to be breathing into a paper bag or something? But she had nothing similar to hand. Beth could only rely on her mind to settle herself.

In.

Out.

As her cheeks burned, her breathing finally slowed. Her heart quietened from a drill to a hammer.

'Fine.' Beth sagged forward to let her forehead rest against the centre of her steering wheel. 'You're fine. It's okay.'

Rain pattered loudly against the roof of the car, like a dozen pairs of tiny hands clawing to find a way inside. The sound settled in Beth's bones and drew forth tears, which merged with the raindrops that already spotted her cheeks.

Oliver Turnbald, known to those closest to him as Ollie. It was a name Beth knew all too well, a name she'd spent what felt like a lifetime trying to forget.

Twenty

'Double maths, that was what I was missing.' Ruby picked at the ends of her nails as she spoke. Her heartbeat latched on to the ticking of a nearby clock, matching it in rhythm.

'Because you played truant that morning.' The woman behind the glasses pursed her lips and made a hasty note upon her pad.

Ruby pulled at the skin around her nail. 'It wasn't like we planned to skive. We'd even made it to the school gates. But then . . .' She didn't want to go back there, to that day, to that memory.

'There were six of you?'

'Yes. Six.' Ruby sighed uneasily. 'Mostly, we hung out after school, since we were in different years and that. But we all walked in together, since, you know, we lived on the same estate.'

'So who decided not to go into school that morning?'

'I don't know.' She did, but she wasn't about to say his name, let it taint the calmness of the ordered office. 'Somehow we ended up in the woods. The plan was to just mess about for a bit, maybe go on the tyre swing there and, well . . .' Ruby stared fixedly at her blunt nails, unable to look over at the bespectacled woman, 'smoke,' she uttered quietly. 'We often went to the woods to smoke.'

Another note was scrawled across the notepad, the woman in the plush armchair no longer even feigning discretion when she annotated their meetings.

'So going to the woods during school hours that day, it wasn't a unique experience for you?'

'No.' Ruby began to dig the ends of her nails into the soft flesh of her palms. 'I skived a lot.' Her teachers were forever lamenting her poor track record, the dark path she had set herself upon. Ruby wanted to scream at them that she had no choice, that her world wasn't like theirs: full of order and routine. Her world was chaos. She and her brothers lived day to day, existing between their mother's hangovers.

'You went to the woods, and then what?'

Ruby's voice became dreamy, detached. 'The sun was shining, I remember that. At least it was at first. The clouds rolled in later. But as we walked through the woods, I felt the sun on my back and it felt good.'

Because for a moment it had been good, hadn't it? Instead of sitting in her stuffy maths classroom, Ruby was out in the world, the wild. The air smelt of damp earth and moss, instead of chalk and sweat. Algebra had no place in their lives anyway, at least that's what her brothers were always saying.

'We weren't alone.' The recollection sent a dizzying shiver down Ruby's spine. She unclasped her hands and realised that they were trembling. 'When we went into the woods, we weren't alone.'

'Someone followed you?' In her chair, the woman made one final quick note and then leant forward, eyes widening behind the lenses of her glasses with interest. Her blouse was the colour of fresh blood and Ruby hated looking at it.

'Yeah.' Tensely, Ruby smoothed her hands over the rough fabric of her jeans, lingering over the hole in her kneecap. Touching the frayed edges, she recalled catching the garment as she'd hurriedly clambered down a tree during a far less eventful visit to the woods. 'Someone followed us.'

'And who was that?'

Ruby winced and closed her eyes. The woman knew. The whole damn world knew. What had happened in those woods had become public knowledge, whipping through town faster than any plague ever could. 'You know.' She could feel the corners of her mouth dipping in sorrow. She'd thought she could do this, that she was strong enough to return to that day, but she was wrong. 'You know who was there.'

Had she said enough? Would she perhaps be granted access to the canteen but not the common room? She looked up, eyes pleading with the woman in the scarlet blouse not to force her to delve deeper into that dark day.

'Pretend I don't know,' was the advice given. 'Pretend I've never heard this story before. Because, really, I haven't. What I'm interested in is your story, Ruby, no one else's.'

'I don't know if I can carry on.' Because that was the truth of it. Already Ruby could feel her legs locking up, the muscles tightening with reluctance even though she was sitting perfectly still. If only her body had reacted in such a way back there in the woods, if only she'd turned round when she had the chance and walked away from it all.

'I know this is hard.'

The ceiling. Ruby snapped her head up to stare at it. Was the sun shining outside? Did it even matter any more?

'If I carry on, do you promise I'll be allowed into the canteen and the common room?'

'Ruby.' The woman put down her pen and drew her eyebrows together. 'What I'm trying to learn is why the things that happened, happened. If you can offer me your perspective on that, then by all means you'll be granted access to both the canteen and the common room. Does that sound fair?'

No more eating alone. No more endless afternoons tracing a small square of sunlight along the length of a bleak grey wall. Ruby wasn't sure if it sounded fair, but it certainly sounded appealing.

'We were in the woods, we'd just made it to the tyre swing and the tree trunks near it we used as benches.'

'The six of you?'

'Yeah, the six of us.' Slowly, Ruby lowered her gaze, hands still resting on her knees. 'We were just laughing and joking, passing a cigarette around, when we saw him.'

'And where was he?'

'At the treeline,' Ruby recalled with unease. 'He just kind of lingered there for a moment, staring.'

'And what did you think?'

Ruby could still see the wild look in Ollie's eyes when he'd clocked their visitor. It still had the power to chill her to her core.

Clearing her throat, she tried to sit up as straight as possible, hands pressing into her kneecaps. 'I thought that we were in trouble.'

Twenty-One

'Six,' Beth hissed the number to herself as rain kept pattering against her windscreen. 'Six.' She felt on fire yet freezing, her stomach plunged to the soles of her feet as though she were standing high up on some epic precipice and any wrong step could send her plummeting to her doom. 'Six.' Leaning back, she gripped the steering wheel tightly, using it to anchor herself in an upright position.

The number was important. Dubbed the Stirchley Six by the papers, it was important, crucial even. Because on the note from the woods there were only five names written. Where was the sixth one?

'Dammit, dammit, dammit.'

Already Beth had lingered in the car park for too long. What if Sheila had remembered how she knew Beth's face and was now informing one of the nurses within the home of the connection between her visitor and her late son? Would she sound like a rambling old woman or would the nurse's smile drop as she recalled the story which had flooded the news during her youth? Beth couldn't risk hanging around to find out. Shaking out her hands, she prepared to leave.

'I signed my fucking name.'

'Stupid,' she grunted through gritted teeth as she erratically reversed out of her spot, tyres squealing. Really she was in no state to drive, but what choice did she have? Like an animal being chased, she had to get away, had to run.

After merging back onto the A road that ran parallel to Sunnymead, Beth began to pick up speed. She glimpsed at the marker on the dashboard as it broached sixty miles an hour, then seventy. Still she felt fear nipping at her heels, feral and sharp. How far was going to be far enough? Was anywhere going to be truly safe?

Home.

Beth longed for the comfort of the small house she shared with Josh. She wanted to run through the front door, bolt it shut and then hurry to the bedroom, where she could burrow beneath the duvet and hide away from the world. Because someone knew the truth. Someone other than Sheila, and this person had written a list, had left it for Beth to discover.

Because they knew.

It was a battle not to cry. Beth began hiccupping as she flew up the road, her car's engine groaning in protest. She overtook a tractor, surging past it with reckless abandon. Did it even matter if the police caught her speeding? Did anything matter any more?

Someone knew the truth about her and what terrified Beth was their intentions. Were they seeking to destroy her? Hurt her? Kill her?

Five names on a list. The third one is yours.

And the first two names were gone, dead. Was Beth next?

Joanne.

Beth thought of the black-haired woman in the picture she'd found online. If only she could have seen her more clearly, maybe she'd have realised that she was . . .

One of the six.

Hot tears were sliding down her cheeks. But then who was Joanne, really? And the others, who were they? And Ollie, with his crooked smile, Ollie was . . . gone.

Slamming down on her left indicator, Beth knew she had to stop and saw an opportunity in an upcoming lay-by. Pressing hard on her brakes, she pulled off the road and killed the engine. In the seconds that followed, she sat, breathing deeply, reminding herself that she was still in one piece, still very much alive.

'Everything is going to be okay.' Her voice was shaking as she uttered the mantra she so often had to call upon. Only now it had truly lost its potency. How could she ever hope to be okay when someone knew the truth of their identities? 'Fuck.' Balling her hand into a fist, she punched the central panel of her wheel and felt her knuckles ache from the force. Then she screamed, the sound bouncing back at her within the enclosed space of her car. To anyone driving by, she must have looked crazed, possessed. Or deeply distraught. The latter was most definitely true.

Ten minutes passed, each sliding by as though coated in treacle. Beth waited them out, waited for the shaking in her bones to ease, for her breathing to level into a calm plateau. She wasn't going to achieve anything if she remained on the verge of hysteria. Finally satisfied that she was in a more reasonable state, Beth reached into her jeans pocket and found her phone, grateful that she hadn't left that back in Sunnymead along with her coat.

Her first instinct was to call Josh, to weep to him down the line about how terrified she was. But what could he do? And how could he even hope to understand what she was going through when she'd so carefully concealed the truth even from him for all these years?

No, there was a more pressing call that needed to be made. There was someone who could confirm what had become of the Stirchley Six, someone who might be able to explain why there were only five names on the list.

Perhaps there was no connection at all, other than a bizarre coincidence? The hope for such a conclusion fluttered in Beth's chest like a caged butterfly.

Stoically, she found the contact hidden deep in her phone, the person whom she had never intended to speak to again. But choice had been taken from her. Had the list done that? Beth wasn't quite sure, not yet.

Three rings. They dragged by – too long, too melodic. As Beth waited for someone to pick up, she watched the rain falling on her windscreen, at the tiny death of each droplet as it met the glass with a soft splash.

Six.

The number burned through her. Had six somehow become five? Could that have happened? And what then? What if her worst fears were confirmed?

Six.

'They're going to kill me,' Beth whispered to the ghost of her reflection in her windscreen. She was about to spiral into dark thoughts when the ringing stopped and her call was answered.

Twenty-Two

The following five minutes were a jumble of names and dates and though she'd provided one side of the conversation, Beth could scarcely account for her participation in the call, as though she'd been dreaming.

'Glenda,' she'd managed to pant out, chest heaving. 'Glenda Roberts, please.'

'One moment, please hold.'

As Beth waited, dark thoughts circled her like vultures. *What if Glenda isn't there?*

What if there's no one who can help?

Her lungs felt too large for her chest, her eyes too wide for their sockets. Was she having another panic attack? The rain continually pattered against her windscreen, providing a gentle soundtrack to her chaotic free fall.

Hang up.

Again and again, she urged herself to end the call, to drive home without glancing in her rear-view mirror, to leave the past behind.

Just hang up.

Instead, she was inviting the past back into her life with open arms, extending the olive branch herself. But why? Was she really that afraid? Was it really worth—

'Hello?'

Time crumpled in on itself and all the years that had stretched between this moment and their last meeting condensed into a single heartbeat. Beth still knew her voice, would know it anywhere.

'Glenda, is that . . . is that you?' With her free hand, she ran her fingertips against the armrest of her door, fighting the desire to step out into the rain and run, leaving her phone and her past dropped in the mud.

'Yes, who is this?'

Glenda had retained the confident warmth in her speech that Beth had once responded to so well. She wondered if the woman was still sat in the same office, still wearing the same long skirts and tortoiseshell glasses. Or had time claimed her too, forging deep rivets within the corners of her eyes and adding inches to her waistline?

'It's . . .'

Breathe. You're okay.

'Beth. Beth Belmont.'

Silence.

As the conversation plateaued, Beth pressed a hand to her temple and cowered behind the wheel of her car. What had she been expecting, that Glenda would be glad to hear from her? That she'd respond to Beth's name as though finally reconnecting with a long-lost daughter or friend?

'Beth?' The surprise was there, in the gasp which accompanied the utterance of her name. 'Is everything . . . Are you . . . are you all right?'

The tightness in Beth's chest strengthened. How much pressure could her lungs take before they simply ceased working due to stress?

She pushed her words out, delivering them over the discomfort. 'I need to know about the six.'

Josh.

He came to linger on the edges of her thoughts and Beth wanted to lean up against him, feel his strength beneath her palms, hear the steady beating of his heart. But she'd been hiding behind him for far too long. Now she needed to stand alone, to face her demons for herself.

'Beth, I—'

'I need to know what happened to everyone.' She was gritting her teeth and seeing the list in her mind's eye, a slip of paper so purposefully left, so carefully manufactured. Her thoughts reeled like they'd been tossed onto the waltzers at the fair. So many damn questions. Who had sent it? And why? Would Glenda know?

'We shouldn't be having this discussion on the phone.'

Beth was silently nodding in agreement, barely daring to breathe.

'You need to come by my office. Do you remember where it is?'

How could she forget?

'Yes,' Beth squeaked.

'Can you come tomorrow at three?'

'Umm . . .' Work. Did she have work? Did it even matter any more? The appointment with Glenda would take precedence over all else. Beth had to know the fate of the six. Had to know if the threat she perceived within the list was real. 'Yes, three is fine. I'll be there.'

'Okay.' Glenda wasn't saying goodbye, perhaps there was still something she needed to say. 'And Beth?'

'Yes?' She felt like a girl again, lost and terrified.

'Take care.'

The line went dead and Beth stared absently at the falling rain.

I remember being young. I remember the conflicting sensation of feeling infinite and claustrophobic in my small life all at the same time.

When I turned thirteen, I thought I knew everything. I thought I had it all figured out. I wanted to be a model. A model! It'd be hilarious now, if it weren't so fucking tragic. This boy from my estate, year above, would hold my hand when no one was looking and the last weekend of the summer holidays I let him feel me up under my dress as we hung out under the rusty swings at the park. His hands had been so cold and they'd shaken the whole time.

Her uniform itched, the fibres feeling laced with tiny shards of glass. Beth kept scratching at herself as she hurried across the car park that bordered the grand multi-screen cinema.

It was early evening and the rain that had fallen over Sunnymead had not followed her home. Here, the air was thick and heavy, laced with an electric tension which hinted at the prospect of a storm.

Though her steps were quick and light, Beth's progress across the car park was slow-going. She kept turning, kept twisting to look back over her shoulder to see if she was being followed.

Empty cars glistened in the early-evening light, vacant and innocuous. But Beth feared what dwelled within their back seats, their shadows. What if someone was watching her at that very moment? What if the author of the list was smiling, enjoying the cat-and-mouse game they had created as they watched Beth clawing at her flesh, head pivoting round like a bird cowering from the hawk passing overhead?

The interior of the cinema lobby offered little comfort as Beth pushed her way through its glass doors. Cool air was being blasted throughout the building and it swept down to greet Beth, but she ignored its icy caress. Still she was scratching her arms, leaving red lines upon her pale skin.

A group of teenagers were gathered at one of the ticket machines, loudly deliberating which film they were going to see. Beth was relieved when they continued to conduct their debate as she walked by, not pausing to stare at her. The sensation of being watched stalked her like a shadow. As she ascended the escalator, Beth tried to glance at every person around the popcorn stand, everyone milling about the lobby, engrossed by their phones as they waited upon their friends or dates.

She was searching for someone who, when she locked eyes with them, she'd find staring straight back at her. And then the terrible thought would flicker through her mind like a doomed falling star:

Do they know?

Because someone knew. They had to. And how far had that truth travelled?

'Hey, Beth.'

Gregg Peters, still plagued by his teenage acne even though he was in his early twenties, raised a hand in greeting as she approached the ticket booth. She was almost at the darkened interior of her beloved screens. Soon she could slip amongst the shadows, darting between projector rooms without the stressful burden of worrying about being seen.

'H-hi, Gregg,' Beth put on her most polite smile.

'Think it'll be a busy one tonight?' Clearly an afternoon spent manning the ticket booth had made him lonely. Beth wished she was the kind of person who could stall her own progress through the cinema to engage in some friendly chat. Perhaps they could discuss the weather, how it had rained heavily in one county, yet over here things were dry. Maybe Beth could comment on the films currently showing, which ones she'd seen, which she'd enjoyed. To anyone else such a simple exchange would be easy, second nature. But not to Beth.

Maybe in another life.

Still smiling nervously at Gregg, she thought about the woman she might have been, the one who'd led a normal life, the one who didn't wake in the night almost deafened by the sounds of screams. Who would that woman be? Would she be confident, friendly? What job would she have? Which dreams would she pursue?

'Ah, I'll let you get to it,' Gregg dismissively waved a hand in her direction. 'I know you're not one for chatting, Beth.'

And he was right, she wasn't. But now the comment felt like more than just a flippant remark, it felt like an astute observation, made by someone who might have been watching her too closely.

It's just Gregg.

Beth was scratching again, dragging her nails deep against her flesh. Gregg Peters drove a run-down Fiat and seemed to only listen to Fall Out Boy. In the summer months, he reeked of sweat and Joop and always ate a large bag of popcorn on his break, no matter what time of day it was. She *knew* Gregg. Didn't she? At least in the same way he knew her. Only—

He doesn't know you. Not the real you.

'I'm . . . I'm running late.' Now she was almost sprinting along the corridors, wishing the shadows that swelled along the plush walls would swallow her whole. If Gregg knew the truth, how would he greet her? With disdain? Indifference? Or worse . . . with hatred?

Hate had the ability to make even the kindest men cruel. Beth threw open the door to the projector room which needed her attention and scrambled inside. Her ribs had begun to ache, still holding the pain of rejection even after all these years.

Approaching the film reels, it felt good to give her hands something to do, to stop them assaulting her bare arms. Still her uniform itched like an ill-fitting second skin.

This isn't you. This isn't real.

'This *is* real,' Beth sternly assured herself as she began to lace the delicate reel into the projector. 'This is my life.'

She was Beth Belmont, projectionist, girlfriend of Josh. She lived at 18 Sutton Gardens beside the Arden Woods. In her free time, she liked to run. She was a person, a fully rounded person who was just living their life.

Five names on a list. The third one is yours.

Only someone knew enough to join the dots on a decades-old puzzle. The fear that now writhed inside her like a foul serpent, was that what had plagued Joanne and Trevor? Were they really who she suspected they could be? Or was this just paranoia at play?

Josh had not been afraid of the list, perhaps because he'd been able to see it for what it was – nothing.

Beth's hands shook as she loaded the film reel, the room filling with the mechanical whirr of rotation as the lights in the theatre dimmed and the screen lit up. Tentatively, she approached the little porthole which peered out into the large theatre. All members of the audience were hidden in darkness, the commanding boom from the screen drawing their attention.

'I'm Beth Belmont,' Beth whispered to herself as one trailer fed into another. 'And I'm real.'

It was dark when her shift ended. An ebony sky was pierced with distant stars that shone like tiny diamonds. But Beth failed to notice the heavenly beauty above, her gaze solely focused on the dwindling number of cars around her. As a new engine grumbled to life, she'd turn, startled, hoping to glimpse the driver, but instead being blinded by the glare of headlights.

Am I being followed?

The thought wouldn't leave her. It had snapped at her heels as she hurried between projection rooms, it had sat beside her as she nibbled on her sandwich during her break. Eating had become a futile effort. Beth had no appetite. It had drained away along with her sense of security.

Beth reached her car and paused beside it, taking in the surrounding area with the scrutiny of an FBI detective. If she uttered the name – *the Stirchley Six* – to her co-workers, young as they were, would they understand the meaning? Or would certain things always remain in everyone's minds, no matter how much time passed, left in their memory like a brand, a scar that never faded?

Her appointment with Glenda Roberts was now just over thirteen hours away. Beth knew where she had to go, could find her way to the small offices nestled in the centre of town even blindfolded. How many times had she trod the path to Glenda's building? Dozens? Hundreds? Once, their appointments were daily, then weekly. And when monthly turned to biannually, Beth felt like she was finally breaking free, finally making progress.

With a creak, her car door opened. Glenda would know the fate of the six and then, armed with that knowledge, Beth would be able to decide just how much danger she was actually in.

I try not to think about my mother. Not even at Christmas. Not even on her birthday: 15 October. I wish I could just erase the date from my fucking memory. But it's always the worst shit that sticks. I forget to buy batteries for my clock, but that bitch's birthday – I'll remember that till the day I die. Where is the justice in that?

She never cared about me. Not truly. She cared dutifully – she fed me, clothed me, bathed me when I was dirty. I don't think she ever loved me. Not really. It was like her heart only held so much capacity for love and my brother had taken up all the available space before I was even born.

You understand. I know you do. It's part of what drew me to you, made me want to seek you out. You grew up like I did; like a weed grasping at any slip of sunlight that came your way. We had to grow up fast, else we risked not growing at all. Because our mothers, all their love, their glow, it was lavished on their boys. Their precious, golden boys. Did they loathe us for our youth? Our looks? Were we a constant reminder of what was slipping away from them, of all the doors which had now closed? We came second, you and I. And it wasn't fair, especially in a world where we were already fighting against the odds.

We know what it is to be eclipsed by a son.

I wanted so badly for my mother to look at me like she looked at my brother. In her eyes, he could do no wrong. Which made me crazy. But she thought he was a saint. He could sneeze and she'd applaud how well he'd done it. I think it drove my dad away, the blind adoration of it all, in the face of the real situation. Especially the blind part. Not that I blame her for loving him, I was just as besotted and always defended him. But I wasn't supposed to divide myself, my loyalty, my love. She was. She had two children. She was supposed to love them both.

My dad never had any trouble spreading himself around, he left us and kept making more and more children, like it was some sort of sick hobby, like he'd fucked it up the first few times and was trying to improve on past efforts. Last I heard, there were the twins and another baby on the way. Different mothers. He must be a magnet for dumb women. Like, truly, what do they see when they look at him? He's a deadbeat on the dole, divorced, probably balding by now. Yet desperate bitches keep lining up to carry his seed.

I guess he was handsome, once. He gave me his height, his green eyes. But he's as dumb as he is attractive. I remember asking him to help me with my homework when I was seven, a reading assignment. He'd taken the book I'd passed to him and thrown it against the wall, shouting at me to do my work on my own. Afterwards, once he'd skulked off to the pub, my brother dropped my book in my lap, along with a tissue. That's how he was, no words . . . just actions. He didn't hug me, didn't tell me everything would be okay. But he understood pain. But he'd do something nice and move into the next room as though it hadn't happened, just like that. Drifting. He was always drifting. But he was the current, and he was carrying all of us along with him.

Twenty-Three

'Ollie saw him first.' Ruby could feel the weight gathering around her words. Clearing her throat, she forced herself to keep talking.

'And what did he do?' The woman sat in her plush chair with her glasses perched on the end of her nose. She was as calm as ever, pen clasped between thick fingers as she remained poised and ready to document the ensuing conversation. Ruby envied her elegant perseverance. Her own body was engulfed in a tsunami of negative emotions and she could easily just get swept away, could just sit and hide behind a waterfall of tears.

But that would get her nowhere. If they saw her break, she'd just be returned to her 'bedroom', to solitude. To once again move beyond those tight four walls, she needed to talk, needed to give the woman what she so wanted to hear – the truth.

'Ollie . . . he was, he was mad.' Ruby bit her lip and trembled as she let her mind return to that terrible place, to that day out in the woods. Ollie had shot up like a weed over the previous months and now he was tall and full of misplaced energy. He was constantly tapping something: his foot, a pen, his tongue against the inside of his cheek. He was never still. His mousy brown hair had been shaved close to his head, too close, revealing freckles and moles previously hidden from sight. Like most of the older boys at school, he raided his dad's bathroom cabinet, drowning himself in Old Spice or Brute most mornings. But despite his best efforts, Oliver Turnbald was still a boy, the fluff that had sprouted on his jawline and upper lip barely requiring the weekly shave he loved to boast about.

'Did Ollie often get mad?' Fresh notes were being written down.

Ruby scoffed at the question. To ask if Ollie often got mad was like asking if it rained much in England. The answer was a resounding – of course. It was how Ollie maintained control, not just at school but across their estate. Spindly built as he was, those knuckles of his were pure bone and full of feral force. Twice, Ruby had seen him split open another boy's nose, hot blood pouring forth as anguished screams filled the air.

Two doors. That was all that separated Ruby's cramped terraced home from Ollie's – number six and number eight. And, every morning, he'd wait for her by her crooked garden gate, cigarette in hand, a lazy smile pulling on his lips.

'Come on, Ruby Tuesday,' he'd say. 'Let's get this fucking day out of the way.'

So when Ollie suggested going to the woods that day, Ruby had immediately obeyed. Even her brothers respected him, despite his being several years younger than they were. Ollie was the Artful Dodger of the estate, charismatic and cruel, with an ability to round up all the other misfits until they were outcasts no longer, they were a group.

'Ollie could get mad.' Ruby clenched and then released her hands as though just talking about the ringleader of her former friendship group made her embody his restlessness.

'So what did he do that day?'

'He . . .' If she listened closely, she could still hear Ollie's voice lifted above the birdsong, the whisper of the wind through the leaves. His words were a whip, cracking and cruel. 'He told him to leave.'

'In those exact words?'

'No.' Ruby bowed her head and wished she could leave herself, wished she didn't have to relive what was about to happen. 'His words were a lot . . . ruder . . . than that.'

'I see. And did Caleb leave?'

Ruby wanted so badly to cry, to tug her knees against her chest and rock herself back and forth until her arms ached. She couldn't, wouldn't, think about Caleb. Simple Caleb Walters, with his moon face and thick black glasses. Caleb who would cry if someone glanced his way and occasionally start screaming randomly in the middle of assemblies. He had only his sister to fight his battles. She was his fierce, loyal protector. But she couldn't be there all the time. And when Caleb was vulnerable, the bullies swarmed in.

'He didn't leave.' Ruby looked towards the bookcase, the clock on the wall, anywhere except the corner where the bespectacled woman sat. She could hear the whisper of pen against paper. More notes. More potential condemnation. Ruby had been worn so very thin by it all. 'Ollie shouted a couple of times,' she recalled uneasily, 'told him to fuck off back to school.' The obscenity made her blush. Had she uttered it at home, either her mother or brothers would have struck her hard and fast across the face. Ruby whimpered involuntarily, the gentle burning in her chest that accompanied every breath rising to a fierce heat. Would she wear the wounds of what they did to her forever? Did she deserve such a fate?

'I know that this is hard.'

Did she? The fire from her chest travelled up to her eyes. Ruby dared to hold her interviewer in a heated gaze.

What she was doing was beyond hard, it felt like she was slowly committing suicide, aware that in the end there was going to be nothing but endless, empty darkness.

'So what happened when Caleb refused to leave?' the woman pressed, keen to complete her annotation of events.

'Annie knew.' Ruby thought of her pale friend whose face always wore a serious expression. She would have liked this office, would have wanted to browse through the collection of books that lined one wall.

'I'm never going anywhere,' she'd state bluntly to Ruby, 'but at least within stories I can live a thousand different lives.'

Like the rest of them, Annie was desperate to escape. But unlike the rest of them, she had the intelligence and foresight to understand that it would never happen. They were all doomed by their birthrights, by the small town's failing economy around them, by their families' lack of funds and ambition. Annie's mother didn't work, she lived off benefits and spent her days chain-smoking. Ruby secretly felt that was time better spent than her own mum, who basically lived down the off-licence. Across their estate, it felt like all the adults had just given up, too weary and worn to try and fight for a better life. Ollie and the others would kid themselves, would talk up grandiose schemes of how they were going to make their money, make their escape. Annie didn't dream beyond her books. She knew what was coming, felt the pull of the tide which would eventually drag them all under, long before anyone else did.

The woman in glasses ceased writing. 'What did Annie know?'

'What was about to happen.' Ruby swallowed and dragged her gaze up towards the ceiling, reminding herself not to cry. 'Annie was always so smart. Of course she knew. She saw Ollie's face, the anger building.'

'Did she say anything?'

'She whispered to me that we had to get Caleb out of there.'

'And then what happened?'

Ruby shook her head, still refusing to cry. 'Ollie . . . he . . . he'd taken charge then. He moved towards Caleb before any of us could stop him.'

'And what did he do?'

The words haunted Ruby every night, delivered by a boy but sounding like they belonged to the withered soul of a broken man – a man twisted by time. He'd turned to face his friends, smiling to reveal a newly chipped tooth from a fist fight, and placed one hand on Caleb's slumped shoulder.

'We're going to play a game,' he told them all.

Twenty-Four

'I found this in the woods.' Beth's fingers behaved like they were being flooded with an electrical impulse, shaking involuntarily, as she slid the scrap of paper across the table.

She was back in Glenda's office, back in a place where time hadn't performed its usual act of erosion. The desk was still the same; thin pine wood barely visible beneath all the stacks of papers and books haphazardly strewn across it. Filing cabinets stood shoulder to shoulder along an entire wall, each drawer boasting a letter of the alphabet. A single strip light overhead bathed the small room in an unflattering garish glow, the glass panel in the now closed door revealing the mottled shadows of people drifting by in the corridor outside.

A flat-screen computer. It chirped softly, placed on the left-hand side of the messy desk area. Beth briefly glanced at it – the only new addition to the office. The walls were the same sad shade of egg-shell blue, the ceiling tiles mottled brown with water damage.

This was Glenda's 'real world' office. The one she resided in beyond the institute, the one Beth had visited for so many years when she was finally granted freedom. Only freedom had never felt like the right word. Were you ever truly free if you remained clad in chains? An open door was useless if you could barely get through it.

'What is this?' Glenda reached for the paper with one hand, fixing her glasses in place with the other. Still she smelt of lavender. But unlike the office around her, Glenda had changed. Her chin had acquired several new layers, her hair, now pulled back in a tight bun, was streaked with silver and her lips were thin and puckered with lines. Beth watched the woman's face fall with fear as she read the names upon the piece of paper.

No, she thought. *Please, no.*

But as she watched Glenda's reaction, she knew she'd been right, that her fears were all valid. The older woman continued to peer at the now dog-eared slip of paper, its white corners curled and its once fairly smooth surface creased. But the ink still held, even though Beth had spent hours staring at it, draining it with her gaze.

'You found this in the *woods*?' An air of incredulity accompanied the question, which set Beth's nerves from fearful to angry. It wasn't like she was lying. Why would she?

'Yes, I was out jogging and saw it on the ground, beneath a tree trunk.'

Glenda was silent, pulling her lips into such a tight line that they went completely pale and all but disappeared into the sagging creases of her ageing face.

'There's five names on it,' Beth leant forward in her blue chair, hearing the plastic creak. 'But there were six of us. So it can't mean what I think it can. And the first two . . . I mean, it's Ollie and . . .' her voice was threatening to break. 'The first two names on the list. They're dead.'

Glenda remained silent.

'Did you know?' Beth stared across the desk, unblinking. 'Joanne Rowles died in a fire, Trevor Hoskins was found drowned in a river.'

'I knew.' Slowly, with careful deliberation, Glenda put the list down. Her hands, now unoccupied, floundered momentarily in the air before coming to rest upon the cluttered surface of the desk. 'Everyone involved in the case is made aware of any . . . updates. But nothing about those deaths seemed . . . suspicious to those of us aware of their true . . . identities.'

'You think they both killed themselves?' Beth had to clutch at her chair to stop herself surging forwards. Surely her former friends had been targeted by whoever wrote the list? Why couldn't Glenda see that? Accept it? Was it somehow easier to believe that their deaths had been of their own design? Did Glenda see justice in that?

Heat began to creep up Beth's neck. She hadn't come to the office to be judged, she'd come to seek solace, reassurance.

'Beth.' Glenda removed her glasses with a flourish, letting them hang upon the chain she still wore around her neck. Her eyes were watery. Straightening in her chair, Beth kept her hands firmly at her sides, refusing to hold them in her lap, refusing to embody anything of the girl she had once been. She'd even arrived in her uniform, had done her best to smooth out the creases in her shirt, as though she was trying to prove something, as though she wanted Glenda to look at her and see only the woman, not the girl. 'When did you find this? Has anyone contacted you or—'

'Five names. Why not a sixth? Tell me I'm wrong, Glenda. Tell me that I'm not connected to the names on that list in the way that I think I am.'

The clock on the wall ticked by the following six seconds. Beth died on every stroke of its hand, her desperation for the truth engulfing her.

'I need you to tell me I'm wrong!'

'You never knew what happened to Annie Harvey.' There was something strange in Glenda's tone, something beyond remorse that Beth couldn't quite place. 'No one knew and we fought to keep it that way.'

'What happened to Annie?' Beth's breathing was quickening, the walls beginning to advance towards her. Smart, wise Annie who had a lust for books which their lacklustre school library could never fully satiate. Where was she now? Had she finally done the impossible and escaped the shackles they had all unwillingly forged for themselves in their misspent youth?

'She . . .' Glenda bowed her head reverently. Respectfully.

Beth's uniform began to itch, the starched fabric roughly rubbing against her skin as though it had suddenly turned to scouring pads. 'She what?'

'A year after it happened, Annie, she hung herself. In her room. Our intention was never to tell you, never to tell anyone.' Glenda was still gripping the list, still eyeing it with frightened desperation. 'But this,' her voice dropped to a strained gasp. 'This changes everything.'

Twenty-Five

So six were now five. Or rather, three, assuming everyone else on the list was still alive. Beth shrank down in her chair as her stomach plunged to the floor.

'And you really found this in the *woods*?' Still Glenda's voice carried that lilt of disbelief. Beth wanted to scream, but if she opened her mouth she risked vomiting.

Joanne Rowles
Trevor Hoskins
Beth Belmont
Harry Jensen
Rebecca Terry

She thought of the list, of the names so carefully etched upon the slip of white paper. Trevor Hoskins was Ollie Turnbald, but she'd known that before entering Glenda's office, had known that the moment his grieving mother, Sheila, declared the truth about her deceased son.

It all pointed to the grim reality that someone *knew*.

'You say there have been no additional threats?' Glenda's mouth remained puckered with concern as she looked between Beth and the list.

Additional threats.

So she'd read the list the same way Beth had – as something written with dark intent. Two were already dead. And Beth . . . was she next?

'Just . . . just the one note.'

Beth wanted to be outside, she wanted to be standing on a hilltop with the wind roaring past her ears, almost deafening her. She wanted to look to the horizon and see it dip and disappear in a curve of green grass. She wanted to feel free. The office felt too small, too much like a box. A prison.

'I mean, I don't know who could have done this.' Glenda was now frowning, peering at the list like a counterfeit twenty-pound note she knew better than to trust. She held it up to the light, the canyon of concern between her eyebrows deepening. 'Everyone involved signed NDAs very early on. The contracts were watertight. My responsibility was always to you; each of you had your own appointed counsellor to avoid bias.'

None of this information was new. Beth had always been aware of Glenda's role, of their connection.

Annie.

In her mind, her friend was still a girl, shrewd and wasted on their little town. Had she been staying at the same institute when she took her life, secured in a separate wing to Beth to ensure that their paths never crossed?

'I think that this changes things.' Glenda's gaze delicately drifted towards the slip of paper now resting beside her, as seemingly innocuous as a fallen feather. 'This . . . list . . . does suggest that you're being targeted.'

'Joanne Rowles, who was she?' Beth needed to know, needed to put a name to the blurred outline of a face she'd seen in the Co-op photograph.

Glenda leant back, her shoulders more stooped against her frame than they used to be. 'I'm not sure that—'

'Who was she? Tell me!'

'Vikki. Vikki Tate.'

Ollie's sometime girlfriend. Beth looked at the faded blue carpet of the floor, head throbbing.

Vikki Tate had once been a bleached bottle blonde who painted her lips bright red every morning and laced her eyes with far too much kohl liner. Like the rest of the group, she hailed from the same run-down council estate, but Vikki had a currency worth even more than Annie's sharp mind – she was pretty. Pretty in that obvious kind of way. She had pale blue eyes and was well developed for fourteen, verging on buxom.

Beth had always envied her: the way she walked, swaying her hips just so; the way her hair was always brilliantly bright and poker straight. Even the way Vikki clutched her cigarettes between the tips of her fingertips, oozing sophistication. But, like the rest of the group, Vikki was ultimately flawed, and they all shared at least one glaring imperfection – their blind devotion to Ollie.

Vikki and Ollie were like a teenage Bonnie and Clyde: dangerous and unpredictable. They'd been sleeping together since they were thirteen and Beth used to think they were so mature, so knowledgeable of the wider world, whilst she at twelve still felt very much like a child.

'Vikki Tate.' Beth said the name and went cold. It had been well over a decade since she'd breathed life into it. Now, the name felt foreign on her tongue, burning against her taste buds. The woman from the Co-op, she'd been described as a loner, with dark, short hair. Where had the brave Vikki Tate gone? She'd been fearless, brazen. Beautiful. All that Beth had found at the Co-op was a shadow.

'You have made so much progress.' Glenda gestured across the table, palms turned towards the tiled ceiling. 'I don't want this list to undo that, Beth. You've come on so well, no longer needing our appointments. You have a job, a life.'

'So did Vikki.' Beth picked at the tips of her nails. 'So did Ollie.'

'Look, Beth—'

'They had jobs. Lives. Both of them. I—' Biting the inside of her cheek, Beth took the plunge, knowing that Glenda would feel like she'd already gone too far, already disturbed too much of the past. 'I went looking for them. After I found the list.'

'What? No!' Glenda was shaking her head manically. 'Do you have any idea how *dangerous* that is, Beth? How destructive it could be to you? I don't know where this list came from, who wrote it, how they learnt what they did, but I implore you to cease digging up the past. Let sleeping dogs lie.'

'I'm next!' The words snapped out of her like a bullet. 'Five names on that damn list and the third one, it's me!'

'I'll call the police.' Instantly making good on her gesture, Glenda reached for the phone on her desk, hastily wedging the receiver into her hand. A plump finger was about to press down on the first button when Beth stood up, her chair skittering back from the sudden force and crashing down onto its side.

'No! No police.'

'But, Beth,' Glenda cocked her head at her guest, receiver still clutched in her grasp, 'you may be in very real danger. I can't tell you where that list came from. I can only tell you that whoever is behind it has access to some highly confidential, highly sensitive information and we need to sort that. My priority here is you. Perhaps it is time to move on before any of this gets out. We can relocate you and—'

'I gave up one life,' Beth felt the aching pressure of tears building up behind her eyes and she blinked repeatedly to push them back. 'Don't make me give up another.'

'Oh, sweet girl.' Glenda put down the phone and began to get up, her chair grinding against the worn fibres of the carpet as she pushed it back from her desk. 'I'm not saying give up on this life, but . . . this list. The fact that the knowledge of your new identity is somehow out there puts you in danger.'

'Danger? But you think Ollie and Vikki . . . killed themselves.'

'Someone knows your real name,' Glenda said gravely, 'someone outside of those committed to protecting you.'

'Can you be sure?'

Glenda looked dispirited. 'Sadly, no. That's why we need to keep you safe. Please, Beth, let me call the police. Let me do my job, let me protect you.'

'And the others?' Beth ventured. 'The final two names on the list. Are they . . .' She grasped for the right word. 'Are they okay?'

'As far as I know, they are fine. But, Beth, don't go looking for them, don't go digging up the past; it's important that you only look forwards.'

'But someone is digging it all up,' Beth replied fiercely, 'someone is leaving . . . notes . . . names . . . someone is trying to . . . I don't know . . . hurt us all, somehow.'

Glenda reached for her desktop phone once more. 'I think we need to involve the police.'

'N-no. No police. I can . . . I'm fine. I'll be . . . fine.'

'Look, I—'

Beth's hands slammed against the desk and Glenda flinched. 'It can't get out.' Her throat felt tight, her words strangled. She could feel sweat running down her back, gathering behind her knees. 'If . . . if the police get involved then . . .' She closed her eyes and imagined the damning headlines, the walls of her perfect home crashing in on

158

her. 'Please, Glenda,' the tips of her nails scraped against the wood, 'no police, not yet. I can't risk . . . I can't risk being . . . exposed.' She pressed her chin to her chest and released a shaky breath.

'I understand, I do.' Glenda was staring at her. 'My job has always been to protect you. But, Beth, it's my duty to call the police over this and—'

'No,' Beth was shaking her head, hands now balled into fists. 'Please, no. My life . . . I don't want to lose it. Not over . . .' she gestured towards the list.

Glenda puffed out her cheeks and frowned. 'Any more threats. Any more notes, calls, anything strange at all. *At all*, Beth. Promise me you'll call the police yourself. Right away, don't hang around.'

Beth hesitated.

'Promise me,' Glenda ordered. 'I'm just looking out for you.'

Don't say it.

'I care about you.'

Beth had to leave. She couldn't risk being embraced by the big-hearted woman who had nurtured her for so many years. She knew she wasn't strong enough to endure feeling like the girl she had once been. The room, so small, growing ever smaller. Beth had to get out.

'I just needed to know what became of us all.' She hurried back towards the door as Glenda froze beside her desk, eyes downcast with sadness. 'If those names were . . . were *our* names. I needed to know that. Thanks.'

'I'm here for you, Beth!' Glenda called out as Beth fumbled with the door handle before finally thrusting it open. 'You don't have to be afraid. It's okay. I'll always be here, Ruby. You need to keep being strong, can you do that for me?'

Out in the corridor, Beth drew in a deep breath, knees buckling. Had she imagined the final part of Glenda's goodbye? Because no one called her that. Ever.

Ruby Renton was dead.

I wanted a family. A big one. I wanted to find someone to love me. Get a nice house, a dog. The whole clichéd dream.

I wanted a future. I deserved one. So did my brother. But that was stolen from both of us that day. I keep trying to pick up the pieces, turning around in circles. Nothing sticks. No one stays. How can they?

So tell me your secret. Why does your boyfriend stay? How have you trained him to look past what you are?

Do you think your boyfriend loves you? Or does he just love the lie?

I'm in the woods again, watching the little house with the neat front door. But the past is stirring within me like the leaves skittering across the ground. I keep remembering my brother. I keep remembering you.

I liked you. And back then there were so few people I could say that about and mean it. Now . . . now there is no one. How can that be? The girl who could have been a model, the girl who French-kissed a boy two days before her twelfth birthday, how can she have ended up alone?

There was so much shit my mum neglected to tell me. She was always too busy running around after my brother, worrying about him. It wasn't surprising when my dad left. Just . . . sad. Like a rotten bridge finally collapsing, and you're there, watching pieces of wood drop into the water, knowing that your way across is gone forever. He replaced us so quickly.

My brother . . . he didn't understand. Couldn't understand. It was up to me to be strong for us both.

The woods are quiet, so I quickly stand up and shake out my legs, jeans hanging low over my hips. Nothing fits properly any more.

'You should dress for your build,' Roger had advised.

My build. I had scowled at him before hurrying from his office. I needed to leave before he offered to buy me more things, more clothes. I was getting tired of providing the kind of payment he demanded.

Beth should have been driving home. She should have taken a sharp right as she exited the small car park opposite Glenda's office building, but instead she veered left. For a while she just drove, letting instinct and ghosts from the past guide her.

Thoughts of Vikki and Ollie spun around her mind like a twisted carousel. The two of them kissing, fighting. They did both in equal measure. At fourteen going on fifteen, they were the oldest members of their little clique, closely followed by Jacob Rowlins who was also fourteen but had an August birthday.

Pausing at some traffic lights, Beth realised that Jacob must now be Harry Jensen, the name beneath hers on the list. What was he doing now? And where was he? *How* was he? The Jacob she remembered had thick black hair and pale grey eyes, a quiet confidence and a stillness which she always found calming, especially against Ollie's turbulent nature. When not in his faded school sweater and trousers, Jacob lived in baggy jeans and T-shirts of bands his father had once loved, like AC/DC and The Clash. He was musical. In better circumstances, he might have owned an instrument, like a guitar, but all his family could afford to give their eldest son was a second-hand portable stereo, which he took everywhere, loading it with mixtapes he'd made in his bedroom.

Beth had spent so many nights beside a campfire or sitting on a rusty swing at the neglected park outside of their estate listening to Jacob's tapes, letting herself become drowsy to the swelling sounds of The Smiths and Tears for Fears.

'You need to record something modern off the radio,' Vikki would urge. 'Like The Spice Girls or summat.'

'Modern music is shit.' Jacob rarely spoke, but when he did, it was laced with profanities, even during school. When his dad was arrested for selling drugs, he punched a hole in his bedroom wall and then covered it with a torn poster of The Cure.

Beth couldn't help but like Jacob. She'd been harbouring quite the crush on him, even though it seemed like he would always treat her like a surrogate little sister.

'When your tits come in, he'll see you,' Vikki had promised. But Beth had been underdeveloped for twelve, growing upwards instead of outwards, all bony edges and no curves.

Annie and Beth were the youngest of the group, both still in year seven. Kate Turnbald was the year above and the final member of the once infamous Stirchley Six. For a time, it was rumoured that Kate was sleeping with Jacob, but Beth refused to believe it was true. Kate had brown hair cut in a harsh bob, green eyes and severely angular features which made her seem permanently pissed off. If it wasn't for the spattering of freckles across her cheeks, she'd look older than thirteen, more like sixteen. And she was tall, almost as tall as her brother.

As serious as Kate could sometimes be, she was also kind, sneaking Beth numerous hand-me-downs over the years when she grew out of clothes, saying she wanted them to go to someone 'who would appreciate them'.

There was greenery beyond Beth's car now, endless fields of it. She'd pulled out of town and was now winding her way through country lanes, slowing to pass by a tractor shuddering along, casting hay into the breeze like confetti. The sun was out. It painted the world in a warming glow and to the objective eye the view was serene. But Beth realised where she was heading and felt a knot begin to twist within her stomach as she headed left at the roundabout.

Why wasn't she going home? Home was safe, stable. Josh might even be there. She could fold herself into his arms and breathe him in until all the dark thoughts went away.

But memories were a rip tide dragging her back, pulling her under. Thinking about the others made her feel like a little girl again. Despite all her best efforts over the years, her past wasn't a world away. Quite the contrary. It existed just so slightly beyond reach, like a box of biscuits on the top shelf. Accessible if you went up on your toes and stretched as hard as possible.

That's what Beth was doing now – overextending herself. And she was so close, her fingertips almost grazing the box. Only when she did snatch it into her grasp, it wouldn't be full of sweet treats. She was delving into her past, heading to a place that was rotten and rancid.

Turn back. Go home.

She passed a sign marked Stirchley and knew she had to venture on. She'd come this far, she needed to see things through, needed to finally accept what had happened all those years ago.

Twenty-Six

Beth's car bounced along a small dirt track which veered away from the main road. Branches scratched at the windows, dragged along the side of the vehicle, like long, gnarled fingers. She was fenced in by hedgerows, sunlight glinting off her windscreen and glaring into her line of vision.

Turn back. You can still turn back.

Just a few more rotations of her worn tyres and the track was opening out into a small makeshift car park. Beth turned into the nearest space and slammed on the brakes. Cracking her door, she allowed the sounds of the woodlands to filter in. Birds were singing, wind danced through leaves like the whisper of silk through a ballroom. Dirt crunched underfoot as Beth climbed out. Beneath her car bonnet, the engine was still hot, causing the metalwork of the car to audibly pop.

It was a beautiful day, the sky clear and blue. Closing her eyes, Beth tilted her head upwards and felt the full flush of the sun's warmth bloom across her cheeks. She didn't need to open her eyes again to find her way into the woods. Several feet away, there was a rotting stile. Once she crossed that she'd be on a narrow path which fed like a tributary through the woodlands towards the main route at the core.

How many times had Beth wandered amongst the grand oaks and lean beeches? Hundreds? Thousands? If she were to cut a path directly through the woods from where she was currently standing, she'd reach a dilapidated estate crammed full of two-storey houses, wedged together like uneven teeth, with tiny windows and overgrown gardens. A place that had once been home.

Just leave.

There was danger in the air. Beth could almost taste it. She felt like a wounded seal waiting for a passing shark to sense the blood in the water and come for her. Was that why she had come here, to be judged? Did she want people to throw words at her like arrows? Or did she just long for some sort of closure?

Despite the heady warmth of the afternoon, Beth dipped back into her car to grab the grey hooded jumper she always kept draped across the back seat. Zipping it up all the way, she concealed her uniform and then tugged up the hood, shrinking back beneath its protective shadow. It was unlikely anyone would recognise her, but she wanted to be cautious. After all, someone knew enough to have written the list. If they knew her new name, she bet that they knew her face too.

As Beth clambered over the stile and delved deeper into the woods, voices reached her on a warm, lazy breeze. She could hear children laughing, the brilliant rise of their mirth lifting above the treeline like bubbles. Were they on the tyre swing, or at least a new version of it? Were they kicking out their legs and gazing up at the endless ocean of sky above them, feeling infinite, feeling free? When darkness came would they huddle around the crackling flames of a campfire and tell ghost stories? Was Beth now a part of those stories, something to fear?

The thought settled in her stomach like a block of ice. Beth tugged on the sleeves of her jumper, grateful for its protection as she trudged towards the heart of the woods.

It took her less than ten minutes to reach the open section where the treeline hung back to permit a perfect lawn of green grass to spread out, unencumbered by shadows. Had she really got there so quickly? Back when she was younger, the woods seemed much larger in scale. Now, she was confident she could traverse its complete breadth in just over twenty minutes.

'Please, just stop.'

An echo from the past came out to greet her. Beth shuddered at the desperation her own voice had once held. The raw fear. Then screams, so many screams. Clamping her hands to her ears, Beth tried to ignore them, but they bounced around her brain, heckling her.

'Jesus, no,' Beth could barely speak, barely stand. Her knees were shaking with the need to buckle, to let her fall against the soft grass and just lie there, curled up, until the sun dipped low in the sky and velvety shadows swept out from the treeline. But then something caught her eye, something so surprising that it anchored her back into the moment, helped her regain her balance.

Carefully, she removed her hands from her ears and picked her way across the open space, to a grand oak on the far side from whose thick branches she had once swung upon a swing. Against the base of the trunk was a bouquet of flowers, dog-eared by time but still not more than a week or two old. Pink rose petals were curling in on themselves, their tips tinged brown. The plastic paper binding the bouquet had been bleached by the sun, as had the little note tucked amongst the offering, but the writing was still just about legible. Beth knelt down and strained to read what it said.

We'll never forget.

Something meant as a tender offering winded her. Beth straightened and staggered back as though pricked by one of the rose's thorns. Instinctively, she turned round, searching for someone watching her. Who had left the flowers? Was someone still mourning Caleb? Still visiting the place where he died? Still clutching on to the past?

The screaming returned, rising to a piercing hum powering between Beth's eardrums like an electric current. She was wrong to have come here. Memories grew thick all around, like weeds. If she reached out a hand, she could almost touch the ghost of her former self and the terrible, awful thing that had happened when—

Beth was running. She didn't even know when the impulse grabbed her. It was as though those seconds had been erased from her mind, consumed by sheer darkness, and now she was sprinting through the woods, back towards the sanctuary of her car. She didn't dare look back.

Twenty-Seven

'Ollie said we were going to play a game.' Ruby tangled her hands together in her lap, forming an awkward basket.

'What kind of game?' the woman in the armchair asked gently, delicately. But she knew full well what kind of game, the whole damn world did. So why torture Ruby now? Why make her relive the worst day of her young life? She could feel the poker heat of her own unshed tears pressing against her hazel eyes, growing in pressure and determination to be set free. But she couldn't cry, could she? Wouldn't that be giving in, giving everyone what they wanted? She needed to stay strong, needed to keep control of her emotions.

'Look, lady—'

'I've told you before, Ruby. You can call me Glenda.'

No matter how many times the woman insisted, the request never sat well with Ruby. Adults were always Mrs this or Mr that. To call someone older by their first name seemed, well, disrespectful. If Ruby's mother were there, hearing her call the bespectacled woman Glenda, she'd slap her young daughter clean across the face, making sure to leave a red mark to remind her of her insolence. But her mother wasn't there. Nor was she coming. Time had made Glenda's prediction about that true.

'Okay, Glenda,' she tried the name on her tongue and it felt strange, like biting into an exotic fruit for the first time and your taste buds not knowing how to react. 'Something you need to know about Ollie Turnbald – wherever he went, whatever he did, he always had three specific things on him.'

'Which were?'

Ruby swallowed. So many times she'd relived that day in her mind. She wished so intensely, as though she might burst or spontaneously combust, that Ollie had forgotten part of his holy trinity that day, that his pockets had been uncharacteristically sparse. But, of course, they hadn't been. Ollie would never leave his home without his beloved items, let alone the estate entirely.

'Ollie always had some cigarettes, a screwdriver and razor blades.'

The reasoning behind the cigarettes was obvious, Ruby knew she didn't need to explain those.

'He used the screwdriver to do a bit of B&E, bust into a car now and then.'

Whenever Ollie broke the law, he wore the most assured grin, promised his friends that everything would be fine. And up until that terrible day, it was. The police suspected he was trouble, but he was too young, too quick to have anything tied to him. A life in prison always seemed like an inevitability for someone like Ollie, but he didn't seem fazed by the dark prospect.

'They need to catch me first,' he'd state confidently with a wink. And he had protection in the form of more than just the contents of his pockets. Their estate was a sprawling net of families which came together to lock their secrets in and keep any dangers out. But Ruby had learnt first-hand how this wasn't a perfect system. When a father struck his wife or his kids, it was seen as a secret, not a danger. Each time Ruby's own mother passed out in the pub or outside the offy, it was another secret to be kept, no one dared comment that the booze-riddled woman was an unfit mother, a danger to her brood.

'And the razors?' Glenda asked mildly. If she were offended by Ollie's choice of possessions, she was doing a good job of hiding it.

'The razors he'd put between his knuckles before punching someone.' Ruby sank against the fabric of the sofa as she remembered seeing Ollie's bony fist connect with someone's face in a firework of blood. He'd laugh, savouring the gruesome spectacle of it and the ensuing fear that he'd instilled in his gang. Despite his young age, Ollie had quickly grasped that if people feared him they'd follow him and he worked diligently on his dark reputation.

'But that's not what he used the razors for that day in the woods.' Voice still level, still mild, Glenda sucked in her cheeks and gazed at Ruby expectantly. Was she asking a question or making a statement? Ruby couldn't tell, so she pressed on.

'He told Caleb to leave. Shouted at him to fuck off, but Caleb just stood there.'

Glenda released a silent breath. 'And that made Ollie mad?'

'That made Ollie very mad.'

Caleb Walters was slow. Ruby would later learn that he was severely autistic, but back then, in their neighbourhood, no one used such terms. He was tolerated by teachers and abused by other students. Normally, the abuse was only ever verbal, but Ollie had struck him a few times when his patience had worn out, which happened pretty quickly. In the aftermath, there would be an assembly where students were urged to be more considerate to their peers and then the matter was dropped.

It wasn't just Ollie who singled Caleb out. Pretty much all of the boys at school did. He became a punching bag for their teenage frustrations. If a football match went wrong, they'd lock Caleb in a toilet stall and laugh when he wept for his mother. If a girl rebuffed them, they'd throw his backpack and all of its contents into the mud, their cruel cackles ringing out across the yard. Caleb was the perfect target for them because he couldn't fight back since he simply didn't know how.

There was only little Suzie Walters who fought her brother's corner. Wiry, with a shock of red hair she always wore in a long plait. She was young, same age as Ruby, but what she lacked in size, she made up for in spirit. She'd spit on the boys who threw punches at her brother, bite them sometimes, feral in her desire to protect him. But she couldn't be everywhere, all the time. And for her efforts, the school often suspended her for poor conduct. The system was broken, rigged to be unfair.

Ruby could almost choke on the sadness of it all.

'So the game Ollie proposed, what was it?'

'He . . .' she could hear her voice breaking. 'He thought Caleb would dob us in for skiving. I'm sure he just wanted to . . . to scare him a bit.'

Was that really what she thought or was she just denying the darkness which was in Ollie's eyes as he plucked the razor blades from his trouser pocket and handed one to each of his friends?

'I call this game "piggy squeals",' he told them, eyes never leaving Caleb's frightened face. 'You want to play?' Ollie asked the boy, who nodded, eyes wide with fear and confusion. 'Okay, well, the rules are simple – just don't scream. The more you scream, the more we cut you. Got it?'

Ruby remembered Annie's hand finding her own as they followed their friends to form a menacing circle around Caleb. She'd known what her friend's grip meant, that they needed to get out of there before things got out of hand, but where to go? And to leave would signal betrayal in Ollie's eyes and both girls had seen first-hand what he'd done to those he deemed not on his side. He made life easy for Ruby on the estate, kept a brotherly eye on her and made it so she could walk to the Spar without fear of harassment. To lose his protection would be social suicide. But terror was plastered on Annie's face and surely mirrored in Ruby's own expression – whichever way they went, they were damned.

'This game sounds fun,' Vikki was instantly at Ollie's side, smirking cruelly at their victim.

'So, what . . .' Kate turned over the blade she'd been given, admiring its sharp edge, 'we just cut him and hope he doesn't squeal?'

Ollie's mouth lifted into a vindictive smile. 'Exactly. Each squeal gets a fresh cut.'

'What did you make of this game?' Glenda wondered, tone flat, eyebrows held in a firm line.

Ruby searched the net of lines around her eyes for those etched by judgement but couldn't find any. Was this truly a safe space? Could she describe what happened next without being viewed as evil?

So many words were later attached to the Stirchley Six: sick, sadistic, satanic. Ruby read them in the headlines that flooded the country as they peered out at her from newspapers in harsh black and white. She became hated, vilified. One awful act had damned her for life.

'The game seemed stupid,' she admitted openly. 'And dangerous. But it was Ollie's idea and we never argued with Ollie.'

'Why not?' It was a simple question and, looking back, Ruby wished she'd followed a different path that day, that she'd kept hold of Annie's hand and told Ollie that he was being cruel. But what then, would the game have turned on her? Would she have been the one who bled to death out in the woods?

'Like I said, we never went against Ollie.' It was growing cold in the small office. Ruby sank deeper into the sofa, fantasising that the fabric could somehow shift into quicksand and swallow her whole. Shame burned across her icy skin but left no scars in its wake. Ruby scratched at her arms, bit her tongue to fight against the urge to cry.

Ollie had struck Caleb first. As fast as a viper, he'd swiped at the scared boy, leaving a ribbon of red across his pudgy cheek. And Caleb had screamed, he'd wailed as his eyes bulged in terror.

'Ah, you know the rules,' Vikki stepped forward keenly, blade in hand. 'You scream, piggy, you get cut.'

And so Caleb had suffered a second slashing. Then a third. And a fourth. Still the boy kept screaming, tears causing the blood on his face to run in crimson rivers down to his chin. Ruby wondered why he didn't just run away, why he didn't just turn from this menacing gang and flee? It was as though he completely lacked the fight or flight response and was trapped in the moment, at their collective mercy.

'Ruby, come on.' Ollie jabbed her in the back, forcing her to stagger closer to Caleb. This was typical of his leadership skills: keen to ensure that everyone had blood on their hands so that the guilt was collective for the group. In the past, she'd stood beside him as he handed her stolen goods out of a car, had stashed money and cigarettes beneath her mattress when the heat in his own house had become too much. Ollie ensured that someone else was always complicit in his sins.

Caleb wouldn't stop screaming. Ruby peered at the treeline behind him, expecting someone to come running any minute to see what the ruckus was about. Only no one came, the woods were empty. Everyone else was in school or at work, tucked away in the regimented formality of their lives, which kept them safe, kept them away from situations such as this. Why hadn't Caleb just gone through the gates that morning? Why had he followed them into the woods? Did he just want to play, to belong? To be part of their ill-fated group?

'Christ, Ruby.' Ollie clamped his hand around her wrist and guided the razor between her fingertips. He slashed at Caleb's arm, exposed in the polo shirt he was wearing. And Ollie cut deep, applying too much pressure, but Ruby wasn't strong enough to hold him back. The blood which oozed out from the fresh wound was dark.

'Look, enough,' Annie raised her hands and her voice. 'Just leave him be, Ollie.'

'He knows,' Ollie raged, turning on her, lips held in a snarl. 'He knows how to get us to stop playing. He just has to stop screaming. Don't you, piggy?' Now he was once again facing a tormented Caleb, who couldn't stop howling, couldn't stop crying. Ollie, Vikki and Kate were no longer taking turns. They dragged their razors across the screeching boy's skin with cruel indifference as Annie, Jacob and Ruby stood back, stunned.

'Jesus, Ols, just stop,' Jacob's voice suddenly boomed like thunder over their heads.

Ollie seemed to snap back from insanity and withdrew his hand, blade bloodied, letting it hang at his side as he breathed heavily. But whilst he wilted, Vikki lunged. She dragged her razor across Caleb's inner arm as the boy wailed and shook.

Ruby was the first to gasp. The blood that was gushing from this freshest wound was coming out thick and fast, dark in colour, almost like tar. And there was just so much of it. It quickly soaked Caleb's wrist and dripped down to his fingertips.

'Fuck,' Vikki uttered as she exhaled.

'Holy shit,' Ollie pressed a hand to his temple, 'how deep did you cut, Vik?'

'She must have hit an artery,' Annie sounded so detached, Ruby wondered how long it had been since her friend had mentally checked out from the macabre scene? Clearly it was the only way she could cope with the unfolding horror before her.

'An artery?' Ollie was looking between his friends, his face contorted with a mix of fear and anger. 'Fuck!'

'We need to get the hell out of here.' Vikki threw her razor blade into the grass and Kate did the same.

'We can't just leave him,' Jacob insisted, gesturing to the boy who was now on his knees, staring at his weeping wrist as though it were a phantom limb, mouth still open in a mournful cry. 'He needs to go to a hospital.'

'And where does that leave us, eh?' Ollie was instantly upon him, grabbing at his friend's collar and drawing him close. 'Caleb will sing like a fucking canary when an ambulance shows up and we'll all be done for. Vik's right, we need to get the fuck out of here before anyone sees us.'

'Ollie,' Ruby spoke up, tasting the salt on her lips from her tears. 'He's losing a lot of blood. We need to call an ambulance.'

'Ollie?' there was a tremor in Kate's voice. 'Ollie, what do we do?'

'We need to call 999!' Ruby cried desperately.

'The nearest payphone is, like, twenty fucking minutes away!' Vikki said in a scolding tone, grabbing Ruby's hand and relieving her of the razor she'd been holding on to.

Ruby had been holding on too tight, letting her fear press the sharp edge against her inner palm and now she felt the heat of her own blood trickling between her fingers.

'Ollie?' Kate was glancing between her brother and Caleb, green eyes wide. 'Tell us, what do we do?'

'We leave, now.' Vikki shoved Ruby by the shoulders and then turned back to snatch at Annie's hand. 'He'll be fine. Some dog walker will soon find him dazed and whimpering and he better hope to God he doesn't rat us out.' This final comment she threw over her shoulder towards Caleb.

'Okay, let's go.' Ollie grabbed his sister's hand and pulled her along, eagerly sprinting away from the clearing, jostling Jacob with him.

Ruby glanced back at the fallen boy now alone in the grass, bloodied and howling, but Vikki didn't let her stay like that for long.

'Don't be a little bitch,' the older girl hissed. 'Ollie is saving your life right now.'

In reality, he was ruining it. But Ruby wasn't to know. Numbly, she ran after the others, raced out of the woods and turned her back on Caleb Walters, a decision which would haunt her for the rest of her days.

When Ruby finished speaking, for a moment Glenda just stared, pen poised atop her notebook. But she wasn't writing, she was gazing intently at Ruby. Finally, she broke the silence which had grown between them. 'Do you know what happened after you left?' Still there was no judgement in her voice, the question was just open and honest, searching.

Ruby hung her head. She knew, but she lacked the strength to say it.

'Caleb Walters was eventually found by a dog walker, some two hours later. He had bled to death alone in the woods,' Glenda stated softly.

'There,' Ruby screamed the word, felt the fire of her sorrow upon her cheeks as she wept, unable to hold back the tidal wave of tears that had been gathering within her. 'There's your truth. They killed him. I killed him. I'm a fucking monster and everyone knows it!'

The group had been seen leaving the woods by a nearby farmer and it was only when the news broke of Caleb's tragic demise that the weathered old man had put two and two together and realised the gang's involvement.

'Ruby—'

'I just wish I could take it back.' She hid her head in her hands, knowing full well that there was no escape from how she was feeling. There never was. Her shoulders quaked as she sat on the sofa, feeling the warmth of her tears in her palms as she'd once felt the slick oil of her own blood. 'I wish I'd never played that dumb game. I wish I'd never followed Ollie Turnbald into the woods.'

'But you did,' Glenda's voice was still soft despite all the harshness which spewed out of Ruby. 'And that's why you're here now, Ruby. Because you can't go back, you can only go forwards.'

Twenty-Eight

Her heart was racing. Beth sat drooped behind her steering wheel, chin dipped against her chest, panting. She could hear the nightmares of her past still screaming behind her. Though the sun was still shining, her body was covered in a cool sweat.

We'll never forget.

The declaration from the mouldering bouquet in the woods felt as though it had been branded upon her irises. She could have written the statement herself. Because although she could run, could hide, she could never, ever forget.

It is a nice house. I have to give you credit for that. It is neat and new. The white frames on the window, the finish on the door, glistening in the sun. And the brickwork, yellow and orange. All so tidy. The side gate is bare, fresh pine. Has that boyfriend of yours not got around to painting it yet?

Such a lovely little house. Inside, it smells like vanilla. Vanilla! As though you live in a fucking gingerbread house in some fairy tale. And you get to live there. How lucky for you. You've really landed on your feet, haven't you? Even more so than the others.

And right by the woods! Perfect for you to go jogging every morning. Is that what you thought before you moved in? Did you imagine yourself running through the trees, hair swinging behind you? I bet you didn't look at all those shadows, at the way the woods curl around your property. I found the most desirable spot. Away from the path. Away from all the footfall of joggers, dog walkers and teens looking to get high come dusk. I sit cross-legged at the base of a great oak and from here I can see the front of your house. I can see your clean front door, the gravel driveway. I can watch you come home from work.

You have a car. A car! How much did that set you back? But he always leaves first, doesn't he? The boyfriend. He loads himself into his van and off he goes. You bounce your way around the woods and then leave much later for your shift, uniform usually starched and clean. Your routine is so predictable.

At night, yellow light glows from your front windows and I watch you at the sink, on the evenings you're not working, hands soapy as you throw comments over your shoulder. You smile a lot. Those slatted blinds you have offer little cover. Especially at night. That's my favourite time to come and check in on you as all the houses burn bright and brilliant, the woods a blanket of pure darkness I can wrap myself in. And no one sees me. All these weeks and no one even knows I'm here. Least of all you.

But I've told you now that I'm here. You found my note, I know you did. So why not make yourself known? Why not change things? I thought you were different to the others. I thought you were brave, maybe even good. Don't let me be wrong. I hate so badly to be wrong.

Sometimes you seem so close, I could reach out and touch you. All I'd need to do is leave the base of my tree, scramble over some leaves and dirt and then mount the fence which separates our two worlds. I could waltz right up to your lovely front door and press the bell with my grimy finger. Don't think I haven't thought about it. I have. A lot. Or I could come in again, pluck that little key out from under the plant pot and turn the lock myself. I imagine the look of shock on your face when you see *me. And then what? Would you invite me to stay for a cup of tea, pretend to be civilised? Do you think we could do that, sit across a table from one another and make nice? Pretend that no one died that day in the woods? Shall we find out?*

Two hours later, Beth used her elbow to push open her front door, both hands burdened with shopping bags. Staggering inside, she made for the kitchen, planting the bags on the table, plastic rustling.

'There.' Dragging the back of her hand across her forehead, she stood back and took a moment to let her breathing regulate itself. No matter how much oxygen she greedily drank in, she felt like she was still panting, still caught up in a race she couldn't hope to win.

'Beth?' Josh appeared in the doorway still clad in his oil-stained polo shirt and work trousers. He glanced at the laden kitchen table and frowned. 'I thought you were working tonight. What's all this? Why have you been to Homebase?'

'I . . .' A hand remained at her brow, flittering back and forth across it like a nervous tic. 'I called in sick.'

That had happened, hadn't it? It hadn't been some weird hallucination she'd had down one of the aisles of the local hardware store? No, Beth was certain she'd made the call, could vaguely remember the flow of the conversation as she stood, phone cradled between her chin and her shoulder, eyeing up the deadbolts on display.

'Are you not feeling well?' Josh advanced towards her, destroying the distance between them in a single stride. He placed a hand on her shoulder and noticed the once smart, now crumpled attire beneath her hoody. 'How come you're in your uniform?'

'I was going to go to work,' that was very much true, 'but then . . . I don't know . . . I started to feel sick.'

Hunted.

She felt hunted, like the poor souls in that science-fiction movie, *Predator*, which Jacob used to like. Fear and desperation made for a stomach-churning concoction. As Beth had weaved her trolley around Homebase, she'd kept glancing over her shoulder until her neck ached, certain that someone was following her, that someone knew her darkest truth.

'Okay, well, maybe you should head up to bed and rest. I'll make dinner tonight.'

'No, no rest,' her voice was clipped and shrill. 'First I need to make everywhere safe.'

'*Safe?*' Josh came down hard on the word. 'Beth, I—' he broke off when she began emptying out her plastic bags.

She'd bought two new deadbolts: one for the front door, one for the back. Window alarms. Extra locks for the windows. A new padlock for the side gate. A small axe. A small sledgehammer.

'What the hell is all this stuff?' He picked up the axe first and turned it over in his thick palms, a look of concern never leaving his face.

'I'm just making everywhere safe.' Reaching out, Beth snatched the axe back into her possession and returned it to the pile on the table. To an outside observer, it would have looked as though she were under siege, or preparing for the zombie apocalypse.

'This . . . this is ridiculous.' Josh kept pawing through the pile, picking up deadbolts and placing them back down as he shook his head. 'Our house is perfectly safe, Beth.'

'It's not.' Grabbing one of the deadbolts, she moved past him and advanced towards the front door. She held it up against the plastic frame, judging how it would fit in place.

Josh was behind her, grabbing her wrist and withdrawing both her hand and the heavy-duty lock. 'Yes, it is. We have locks. And bolts. An adequate amount of them. What's got into you? Has there been a break-in locally or something?'

Beth felt her muscles clench as she considered this. 'Yes.' She knew it was the easiest avenue to go down, the most plausible explanation for her current behaviour. 'Number five was broken into last night.'

'Really?' Josh scratched at the trace of stubble along his jawline. 'I didn't see any police there this morning.'

'They arrived after you'd left for work.'

Why had lying always come so easily to Beth? Had practice made perfect? The words slipped so effortlessly from her tongue that she almost believed them herself.

'What happened? What did they take?'

'Broke a window round the back. Turned the place over, emptied all the drawers, wardrobes. Took a couple of laptops and phones. It's a real mess over there.'

'Shit.'

'Mmm,' Beth slapped the deadbolt against the front door once more, eyeing it with interest.

'I guess that's the risk we take, living so close to the woods. Anyone can jump one of the garden fences at the back.'

'So will you help me with these?' Beth demanded tersely. She needed to feel safe, secure. Her home had stopped being a sanctuary the second she found the damn list. 'And I want to order a couple of security cameras online.'

With a sigh, Josh took the deadbolt from her grip and placed it several inches higher, using his free hand to test the surface of the front door. 'I'm not sure fixing this place up like Fort Knox is the best solution.'

'Then what is?' There was heat in the question. Beth kept seeing the list in her mind, only now the picture swung to the note on the dying flowers as well.

We'll never forget.

Someone was still holding on too tightly to the past, refusing to let go, even as their palms bled from the pressure. Is that what had tipped Joanne and Trevor over the edge – the knowledge that even after all this time it still wasn't over?

Who was now set on hunting them down, one by one? Did someone want revenge for Caleb? His mother? Sister? Is that what this was?

'Sweetie, you should rest.' Josh pulled the deadbolt away from the door and let it hang by his side. 'You look exhausted. Go to bed, I'll bring you some tea and toast. Okay?'

'How can I rest when I don't feel safe?' She was shouting. Sweat ran in a river down her spine as her fury turned to fire against her skin. She had thought the woods were safe. Each morning, she eagerly pulled on her running shoes and took off, enjoying the burning in her muscles and lungs as she powered through the foliage. Now someone had taken that, had soiled it. Where would they strike next? Her home? Would she have to witness the four walls of her little end terrace come crashing down around her?

'Beth, calm down.' Josh's voice had hardened. He was speaking to her like she was an obstinate toddler throwing a needless tantrum. 'Go on up to bed, sleep. There's no need to get yourself worked up over all this. Number five is on the corner and, like I said, we've already got more than enough—'

'I'm scared.' It was a truth she'd been living with since that day when she'd fled the woods alongside the others. Back then, it was a familiar feeling, like when she'd wake in the night and hear her mother stumbling around and shouting downstairs. Her bones would lock, muscles tightening as her body slowly began to freeze. But after the incident in the woods, the fear she'd known paled in comparison to the potency of the terror she felt now.

When news of Caleb's death broke, there was no assembly for her and her friends to attend, where they would be urged to treat one another more kindly. There was just the uniformed officer at her door late one night the following week, the disgusted look on his face as he explained to Beth's mother her daughter's involvement in the tragedy, that she was going to be taken away for further questioning.

She spent ten hours at the police station, explaining what had happened, lacking the energy to even try to lie. Back then, it wasn't a skill she'd had to acquire. And they'd never known they were coming, never had time to prepare. Ollie had been so certain that no one had seen them in the woods, could link them to the crime.

The murder.

The first time Caleb's death was labelled as murder, attached to words like 'homicide', Beth felt like she'd been pushed off the top of a roller coaster and was just plummeting down to earth without any sort of safety harness.

Finally, the police released her, on temporary bail.

'We'll need you again,' they warned. As Beth climbed out of the taxi and looked at the home she'd grown up in, she saw her brothers waiting for her by the front door. Their expressions were far from welcoming.

'Don't be scared.' As Josh touched her shoulder, Beth flinched. Old pain flared in her chest and she crumpled back against the door, like a puppet released from its strings.

'I . . . I . . .' she tried to hide her face in her hands.

'Hey, Beth, come on now,' Josh's voice became softer, more soothing, as he crouched down beside her. 'Don't freak out over this, it's a break-in, that's it. You've nothing to fear. I'll always protect you.' His warm fingertips stroked against her forehead and then reached for her chin, urging her to drop her hands.

She gazed at him and saw the fierce loyalty that shone behind his eyes. But even the closest bonds could snap like overused tendons, Beth knew that. With a sigh, she wilted against him, exhausted.

The chase was still in her bones, her blood. A part of her wanted to keep running, to sprint away from her home, her life, until she had nothing left to give. Then she'd collapse in a heap on some street somewhere and wait to be scooped up with the morning waste. Because that was all she deserved, wasn't it?

Yet love had found her, had enveloped her in its soft embrace. Josh was scooping her up and helping her up the stairs and into their bedroom. Soft evening light painted a pale oblong across the bed and the air was reassuringly warm, tinged with cologne and perfume. It smelt vaguely like her mother's room used to – full of all the adult delights off limits to children. Except Beth's room lacked the oppressive musk of liquor and smoke, the scent of a night out, which had once clung to everything her mother touched.

'You rest.' Josh was drawing back the duvet and helping her out of her clothes. 'You'll feel better after a good night's sleep. I'll wander down to number five and try and get a better understanding of what happened, might make you feel better to be more informed.'

Panic stabbed through her, causing her eyes to fly open wide. 'No.' Beth shook her head against the pillows. 'Don't leave, Josh. Stay in the house, please.' She sounded crazy and paranoid. But she was both of those things, what point was there in fighting it? With Josh home, at least he should act as a deterrent against the author of the list. It was when she was alone that Beth would need to worry . . .

'Okay, baby, I'll be right downstairs if you need me.' Josh leant in close and kissed her lips. As he moved back, silhouetted against the light bleeding in through the thin bedroom curtains, Beth felt the connection between them stretch, but remain intact. Three years they had been together. Josh respectfully kept his questions about her estrangement from her family to a minimum. He accepted Beth as she was: a shy woman who worked in the shadows at the cinema. He never tried to scratch beneath the surface, to pick at old wounds. Because Josh was trusting. It would never even occur to him that she was lying. Did that make it all worse, to have spun him a tale for so long?

As Beth lingered on the cusp of sleep, she was reminded of the Shakespeare quote she'd learnt at school, before she was pulled out of the education system:

A rose by any other name would smell as sweet.

Surely that meant that she was Beth by not only name but also nature? Josh *knew* her, didn't he? This wasn't an act, it couldn't be. So much of her life was a lie, but not all of it.

Curling onto her side, Beth reached for her pillow and grabbed a handful of the case in her hand. She could hear Josh's footsteps disappearing down the stairs.

We'll never forget.

Beth squeezed her eyes closed as she started to cry.

Twenty-Nine

Entering the canteen was like passing through a waterfall of sound. Metal forks scraped against plastic plates, chairs clattered upon linoleum floor tiles and voices hummed like a hive of angry bees. Ruby lingered in the doorway, taking it all in.

On the far wall were the food counters, where the dish of the day, spaghetti bolognese, was sitting beneath heating lamps and issued to the waiting line of youths by women in hairnets and white coats. Long tables stretched away from the back wall, bordered by stiff blue chairs, like the ones they'd had at Ruby's school. The ceiling was high and vaulted, kind of like a cathedral, with strip lights hanging between the beams, shining light across the collection of lost souls sitting stooped over their dinners.

'Snooze you lose.' A short, waif-like boy with blond hair that fell into his eyes shoved his way past Ruby and carried himself with quick, determined strides over to the hairnet-clad dinner servers. Reluctantly, Ruby followed. Despite the rich aroma of cooked meat filling the large space, she wasn't hungry. Her stomach felt as though it had shrivelled in on itself, turning from a melon to a tiny prune in the hour since she had left Glenda's office.

'I think we're done for today.' The woman had replaced her glasses on the end of her nose to bid her farewells. 'You've made great progress, Ruby. I'll make sure that you're allowed in the canteen tonight for dinner.'

Before, Ruby had felt utterly trapped by the four walls of her bedroom, but now she longed for their caged comfort. She was dwarfed by the sudden enormity of the canteen, by the medley of voices which tangled together in an undercurrent of indecipherable words. If only she had a friend there, could spot a familiar face. But the rest of the six weren't in this facility, she knew that now, felt foolish for straining to find them in a sea of strangers for as long as she had.

'It's dangerous to keep you all together,' Glenda had explained. 'I'm sure you understand.'

Ruby understood all right. The Stirchley Six were currently public enemy number one. They made headlines in every newspaper, their names were on the lips of every television presenter. And people hated them with a passion usually reserved for the demons of history, like Hitler, who Ruby remembered learning about in school. There were even schoolyard chants springing up – little girls would skip rope and sing sweetly about the awful Stirchley Six. She'd once glimpsed them on a news report, singing in their angelic tones such sinister, hateful words.

'How many years should they serve?' they'd asked and then with each rotation of the skipping rope the sentence would rise. 'One, two, three, four—'

'Pasta or rice?' The face beneath the hair was as lumpy as the dinner she was serving. Pinching thin lips into a tight line, she stared impatiently at Ruby.

'Umm . . .' Somehow she'd drifted across the canteen and grabbed a plastic tray which she now held between her clammy palms. 'Pasta.'

The tray was snatched from her grasp and food was unceremoniously dumped into some of the vacant compartments. As it was slid back over to her, Ruby gripped the sides of her tray, hands shaking, unable to look the server in the eye. Muttering words of gratitude, she hurried away from the warmth of the heat lamps and surveyed the long sweep of tables to her left.

At school, she never had to wonder where to sit. It was an unwritten rule that whichever member of the six entered the canteen first, they held spaces for all the others, a rule which all other students acknowledged, for fear of soliciting Ollie's wrath. Ruby had always found such safety in belonging. Even her brothers approved.

'With Ollie taking you under his wing, no one will ever bother you,' they'd told her. And Ruby had felt more than reassured, she'd felt emboldened. She'd walk along the school's corridors with Annie, shoulders back and head held high. Even though she was only in year seven, no one troubled her, no one jostled her. Being Ollie's friend awarded her a mark of protection.

But those days were gone. Now her association with Ollie Turnbald made her a target, someone to hate. With her head nervously bowed, she dropped into the first vacant seat she found and placed her tray upon the long table. She longed for the warmth of Dexter's company, wished he was still there to drop down next to her and flash her a wide smile. A girl with a bright red bob sitting opposite briefly looked up, but then returned to focusing on her food.

Grabbing her fork, Ruby stabbed half-heartedly at the mound of spiced minced beef atop a modest bed of limp pasta swirls. She reminded herself that she'd wanted this, that she'd pushed to exist beyond the four walls of her little room.

'You new?' the redhead was speaking, revealing chipped black nail polish on her fingertips as she dragged the back of her hand across her mouth now that she was done eating.

'I . . .' Ruby stared at her tray. She wasn't sure what weight her name held here. News of the outside world struggled to penetrate the high walls of the facility. Television time was monitored, same for listening to music. Everything the inhabitants did was regulated, ordered. But the truth still seeped in. A door to a staffroom would be left ajar, letting voices from the radio steal into the corridor, someone would change the channel in the common room when backs were turned. Within these walls was Ruby just Ruby or did the others know, had they heard the snippets of news, same as she had? And would they judge her? They too were prisoners after all.

'Because I've not seen you before.' The redhead leant back in her chair, openly scrutinising Ruby with her pale green eyes. She had several chickenpox scars on her fore-head, one wedged within an eyebrow at an unfortunate angle which made it seem like she was perpetually scowling. Her pale skin was peppered with freckles and, though she was sitting, Ruby could tell that the girl was tall, her long arms giving her away.

'I've been in isolation for a while,' Ruby admitted quietly, forcing herself to stare at her inquisitor. It's what Ollie would urge her to do if he were there.

'Show no fear,' he'd demand. 'Always look someone in the eye, even when you're in the wrong, it makes them nervous.'

Where was Ollie now? Was he also sitting beneath the glare of fluorescent lights, picking at almost inedible food and fielding questions from strangers? Would he be honest? Would he spread his arms and proudly proclaim that he was the King of the Stirchley Six, or had even Ollie's bravado been quashed?

'Ooh,' the girl's eyes lighted up at this. 'So you must have done something really good to be in here.'

'Or really bad.'

This made the redhead snort. 'I attacked my maths teacher, but the bastard deserved it, everyone knows that.'

Ruby said nothing.

'Once he wakes up, I should be able to at least get the hell out of here.' The redhead leant forward, resting her palms against the table. 'So what did you do? You look young, what are you, eleven?'

'Twelve.'

'So what did you do?'

Ruby wanted to return to the quiet of her room. Suddenly, being all alone didn't seem so bad. But if she hoped to survive her time in the canteen, she needed to at least answer this question.

'I followed the wrong person.' Because that was the truth. A very watered-down version of it, but still very much true.

'Ah,' the redhead leant back in satisfaction. 'Happens to the best of us. I'm Jayne.'

'Hey, Jayne, I'm . . .' She took a moment to swallow, to try and remember a time when saying her name felt natural and carefree. 'Ruby. I'm Ruby.'

'Hey, Ruby.' No shadow passed over Jayne's freckled features, her gaze didn't darken. She greeted the name Ruby like any other. 'You gonna eat that?' She pointed a chipped nail at the tray still laden with food.

'No,' Ruby was already sliding it across the table, 'I'm not all that hungry.'

Thirty

It was cold beyond the bed, as though summer had departed overnight. Beth hugged her knees against her chest and rocked back and forth as Josh dutifully ran his hands down the length of her spine.

'Shh, baby, it's okay, it was a dream, that's all.'

Beth couldn't speak, only whimper. How could she tell him that in the darkness she'd heard the screams of Caleb Walters, felt the warmth of his blood upon her hands? And in the terrible final moments before the nightmare released her, she'd seen his face staring up at hers, as pale and round as a full moon, only his mouth was hanging open in a howl, blood seeping out of it. And his eyes . . . they bulged maniacally in the sockets as he looked at her, gaze pleading. In her dream, Caleb only ceased screaming to rasp out his warning:

'You killed me. You fucking bitch, you killed me and now they'll kill you too. We'll never forget.'

'Okay now, deep breaths.' Josh's hand was still against her back, delivering some much-needed warmth to her frozen body. 'It's all right, sweetie, you're safe now. That damn break-in is just playing on your mind, that's all.'

She couldn't bear another second of his loving caress. Beth launched herself away from the bed and retreated to the corner of the room, to the shadows which swelled there.

'Hey, come on now.' In the dim light provided by the sole bedside lamp that had been switched on, she saw Josh's face sag with disappointment. 'I'm just trying to make things better, Beth.'

'No,' she held out a hand to him, noticing the way it trembled. 'Don't call me that.'

'Don't call you what?'

Beth closed her eyes and saw him still, Caleb Walters, alone and wailing in the woods, begging for someone – anyone – to save him. But in reality his screams had died away as the blood seeped out of him and he'd passed out, never to wake again. Had the dog walker screamed when she came upon his bloody corpse? If she did, she saved that detail from her account to the *Stirchley Star*. Perhaps shock had rendered her silent when she noticed the plump pale form within the grass that was slowly turning grey on top of a pool of darkening blood.

'You shouldn't be so nice to me.' Beth kept her hand raised as though Josh could advance towards her at any moment. And perhaps he would.

She could still remember the smell of drying rain as the sun peeked out from behind the clouds and she exited the taxi, looking towards her brothers on the cement porch. For a fleeting moment she'd felt safe, certain that they'd embrace her back into the fold and protect her. But their expressions – they'd looked at Beth as she deserved to be seen.

'Beth, what's got into you?' Josh was now perched on the edge of the bed, watching her with anxious curiosity. His bare chest was flushed from the warmth his body seemed to perpetually generate.

Hand still outstretched, still creating a barrier between them, she said, 'I deserve my nightmares.'

'*What?*'

'Trust me, I . . . I do.' Her chest was aching, her ribs especially. Beth was forced to drop her hand to caress them.

'Baby, you're being ridiculous. Dreams are just dreams. Now, come on and get back in bed, I've got an early start in the morning.'

It would be so nice to just climb back into bed, to snuggle beneath the sheets and resume the role she'd been playing so perfectly for years, of doting girlfriend. But the truth was no longer a well-concealed thing. Someone knew, someone had gone to great lengths to locate the six – now three – to attempt to pick apart the lives they had carefully crafted for themselves. How long until a different note was shoved through their door, one revealing Beth's real name?

Sturdy, stable Josh deserved the truth, even if he accepted it just as her brothers had. As she stood nervously cowering in a corner of her darkened bedroom with an owl softly hooting outside, Beth knew that she loved Josh as much as she could ever hope to love someone. Because now, finally, she was ready to be her truest self with him, something she'd vowed she would never, ever do with anyone. Circumstance might have pushed her to walk the plank, but she was the one deciding to jump. And perhaps he'd even understand, perhaps he loved her just as much as she did him. After all, love conquers all, right? Wasn't that what the fairy tales of youth preached?

'There's something I have to tell you.' The room grew colder as she spoke. Beth imagined icy tendrils reaching out of the shadows and wrapping around her wrists and ankles, trying to bring her to her knees.

'Beth, please, it's late.'

'Something about my past,' she continued, feeling oddly detached from her own words, as though she weren't the one speaking them.

'Sweetie—'

'Something about who I really am.'

This caught his attention. Josh dragged a hand over his scalp and ceased protesting. He raised his eyebrows in her direction and she saw the confusion in his eyes and realised it had been there for many years. Only now it was more pronounced, more vibrant. Had he always wondered who she truly was, merely pretending to accept her vague reasoning behind the estrangement from her family, behind the nightmares?

'Okay then,' he cleared his throat and lowered his hands to rest upon his knees. 'Who are you, Beth?'

Thirty-One

'My name . . .' Around her, the room grew still, as though they were standing in the eye of a storm. 'It hasn't always been Beth Belmont.'

'Right,' Josh remained perched on the end of the bed, shoulders relaxed, mouth held in a patient line. He had no idea what she was about to say. How could he? When they'd met in a nightclub a few years back, Beth had been wearing her mask of a pretty smile and too much mascara. There was no mark on her, no blemish or trailing shadow revealing her past. 'So what did your name used to be?'

Time. It both purified and degraded. Josh was old enough to remember the stories which had infected every news broadcast, would have seen the barbaric headlines strewn across newspapers.

Satanic Stirchley Six bleed out innocent boy
Sadistic Six kill boy in woods

The real story never surfaced: the one where fear had been the guiding hand for most of them. In the media, they were all demonic, all equally guilty. Once they'd each been plucked from their homes and taken into detention centres, their identities were fully released. Beth's young face would have peered out at strangers from the front page of the *Stirchley Sun* and old women with decay on their breath would exclaim to one another how they could see evil in her eyes. She had ceased being a little girl and become a monster.

'Beth?' Josh prompted, lifting a hand to rub idly at his eyes. He was tired. Perhaps she should save this for the morning.

'Everything looks better in the light of a new day,' was something one of her more naïve teachers had once told her. Clearly they'd never gone downstairs and found their mother face down at the kitchen table, the scent of stale liquor still thick in the air, and had to tiptoe around broken glass to reach the fridge, only to find that the milk was several days out of date.

'Ruby,' the voice didn't sound like her own. It was sore and strained.

'Ruby?'

'Ruby Renton. My name used to be Ruby Renton.'

She didn't have to wait long for recognition to darken Josh's gaze. He'd heard the name before, of course he had, the whole world knew the identities of the Stirchley Six. He would have read the newspapers, listened to reporters, got carried along with the tide of gossip in supermarkets, at the bank. And now all those sensationalist headlines might as well be painted upon the walls of her bedroom. In blood.

'Ruby?' From Josh's mouth, her name sounded dirty. Tainted. '*Ruby Renton?*'

Beth nodded. Once upon a time she'd thought her birth name so pretty, that of a precious stone. Now that stone was an albatross around her neck.

'Ruby Renton,' he was rising up, slowly getting to his feet. Now when he said her name, she could hear the accompanying disgust. 'As in . . .' Josh took a step forward and froze, looking at her as though for the first time. 'As in the Stirchley Six?'

'Yes.'

Staggering back against the bed, Josh shook his head. Back and forth it moved upon his thick neck as he absorbed the blow she had just delivered. Could he hear the walls of their perfect life crashing down around him?

'I wanted to tell you,' Beth extended a hand towards him. It was a lie. She'd never wanted to tell him, nor anyone else. She'd wanted to keep her secret until her dying breath. She'd hoped to die as Beth Belmont, with Ruby long since buried and forgotten. But the list. The list had changed everything. Beth needed to speak up before someone else did, needed to control the story this time around before she could be demonised by strangers.

'You . . . you . . .' Josh's eyes were wide as he stared at her. So full of . . . fear? Beth told herself it wasn't possible. There was no way he was afraid of her. They'd shared a life, a love, a bed. He *knew* her. 'You killed that boy.'

Caleb Walters was still haunting her, still demanding justice from beyond the grave.

'It was . . .' Beth pressed her palms to her chest, needing to control her breathing. Once again she was being forced to walk into the woods, forced to relive that terrible day. 'An accident. A truly terrible accident. Things got out of hand and—'

With a jolt, Josh stood up again, his eyes never straying from her face. 'Wait . . .' he pawed at his head as though trying to find long-stored memories. 'Didn't he . . . didn't he *bleed* to death,' he kept staring at her. 'That story, it was everywhere, it was all anyone talked about for months. He was cut up, shredded to ribbons. You fucking butchered him.'

'It . . . it wasn't *me*. I didn't, I mean—'

'You were there,' Josh's voice was low. Menacing.

'I was there but—'

'You could have called for help. Instead you ran away.'

'No, I . . . I never thought he'd die.' Beth's chest was burning, each breath she drew in filled her lungs with flames. She was telling Josh the truth, wasn't she? Perhaps just not all of it. Because her twelve-year-old self had known, had seen the strengthening flow of blood which pulsed out of Caleb's arm and sensed that the boy was in danger, that too much of him was being spilled upon the grass. But still she'd run away, let Ollie be the captain of her destiny even as he was driving them all towards the rocks.

'All this time,' Josh staggered forward as though his legs had forgotten how to work. He loomed just inches from her, shaking. 'All this time, you've been *lying* to me.'

'My old name, my old life, no one was ever supposed to know about it. For my protection.'

'*Your protection*?' he snarled.

Beth looked up into his eyes, searching their blue depths for some trace of the love that she desperately hoped he still felt. But there was only fire behind his gaze, hot and unstable. When he reached forward and grasped her shoulder, she flinched.

The ache in her chest sizzled anew, a reminder that even those who professed to love could be pushed over an edge, could be made to hate.

'You killed that boy. In cold blood. And you kept that from me. How are you even out and free?'

Beth whimpered as his grip tightened. Words were failing her. What did he want her to say? That she was twelve when convicted, seen in the eyes of the law as old enough to be culpable but too young to be condemned. Six years she'd spent in detention centres, six years talking to Glenda, who was probably searching for the evil that supposedly lingered in Beth's soul. But all of the six knew freedom again, at least a form of it. All except Annie. She'd had the foresight to know that even changing their names wouldn't release them from what they'd done. No matter what they were called, they were all killers, all had blood on their hands.

'I'm still *me*.' As Beth pleaded her case, she realised that 'me' was a very weak construct. At her core, she was still Ruby, but she'd tried to paper over her past, tried to outrun it every morning as she jogged, tried to avoid it in the shadows of the cinema.

'Fuck. Just . . . fuck!' Josh roughly pushed her back and then stormed out of the room. His footsteps landed heavily on the stairs as he hurried down them.

Alone, Beth dropped to the floor, chin against her chest. Her Green Day T-shirt was drenched with sweat. Hugging her arms around herself, she rocked back and forth. The truth was finally out, released like a caged bird. But the enormity of it was weighing down on her, crushing her, squeezing the air from her lungs.

The house shook as doors were slammed and cupboard doors banged with undue force. Josh had become a tornado of energy, bursting into each room and disrupting it. Beth remained kneeling on the floor, listening, as the fibres of the carpet dug into her bare kneecaps. She hoped he was just releasing his rage, venting at the objects around him before eventually returning to the bedroom, exhausted but finally accepting of what she'd told him.

Nothing needed to change between them. She was still Beth, just not in original name. He was still Josh. Things could remain the *same*.

Only they couldn't. How could they? Beth was kidding herself.

She heard the sounds beneath her begin to creep back up the stairs. Floorboards on the landing creaked and then

Josh came back, flicking on the main light as he did so. Beth squinted in the sudden brightness, shuffling back into the safety of the corner like the cowering creature she'd become.

'I don't even know you.' As he delivered his words, a pronounced vein throbbed in his neck and Beth noticed that his blue eyes were red-rimmed. 'I remember that story. I remember it being everywhere. The whole damn country was horrified over what had happened. My mum cried when she read the paper. Cried!'

'Please, Josh, just—' Beth forced herself to stand up, but didn't approach him, feeling better to keep some distance between them. 'I was twelve. I was stupid. I let bad people influence me and—'

'So you're saying that you're *not* a bad person? That you didn't stab that poor boy?'

'I . . . My hand was literally forced and I—'

Josh shook his head violently, raising a hand to silence her as he imagined the awful scene that had unfolded in the woods that day.

Lost little Caleb. He'd failed to comprehend what was happening to him, even when it was too late. His cognitive difficulties made the crime of the six even more heinous. They hadn't just targeted a peer, they'd targeted someone extremely vulnerable, someone who never would have been able to fight back.

But Ollie hadn't been alone in that. Cruelty was more prevalent in their school than the contraband cigarettes which everyone smoked during lunch and break times. Ollie had just succeeded in taking it further than anyone else would have dared, which had always been his style. If someone started a fire in a bin, he'd burn down a shed. Ollie would never be outdone.

201

'I was young and gullible.' Beth was repeating words she'd said to Glenda many times over in each incarnation of her office as the bespectacled woman moved around over the years. 'I followed my friends even though I knew better. But I've served my time, Josh. I've been punished. My life is now mine to live.'

'Why, why tell me now?'

The list.

Beth's knees knocked together as she thought of it. The list made the entire illusion that was her world a lie. It mocked her attempt at normality, picked apart the façade of a life which she'd worked so hard to piece together.

'The names.' Grabbing at her elbows, Beth knitted her arms tightly against her chest. 'On the list I found, there were five names.'

'But it's the Stirchley *Six*, right?' Some of the contempt had ebbed away from Josh's voice, which was a small mercy.

'It was. I recently found out that one of the . . . My friend . . . Annie . . . she hung herself. Years ago, when we were first taken away from our homes.'

Josh said nothing.

'The names, at first I thought they were nothing, just a silly prank, like you said. But they're . . .' Beth lifted her gaze to stare into the blinding sphere of the ceiling light above her. 'They're the names we were each given. Our new identities.'

Slowly, she lowered her head to meet her boyfriend's heated stare. His jaw was clenched, eyes wide and wild. But he was listening and not advancing towards her, not giving in to some archaic desire to dole out vigilante justice for Caleb Walters.

'Someone knows who I am. Who I *really* am. And the first two names on the list, they're dead. House fire and drowning. So, Josh, don't you see . . .' She shuffled closer to him, praying that he could see beyond Ruby Renton and find the Beth Belmont he'd fallen in love with. 'I'm in danger. Someone is out to get me, to hurt me. Maybe even to kill me. Please,' a single tear sliced its way down her burning cheek, 'I need your help.'

Thirty-Two

'I need you to breathe in for me . . . and out.'

Ruby breathed. She could feel the cold pressure of the stethoscope against her exposed ribcage; hear the rattle in her lungs.

'Okay and once more.'

Dr Swanson was young, with a thick head of dark hair and chestnut eyes which infused his face with warmth. Ruby visited him on a fortnightly basis. Whilst Glenda was concerned about Ruby's mind, Dr Swanson's focus was on the physical damage she'd sustained.

'That's great, Ruby. Relax.' He removed the stethoscope and reached for her wrist, pinching it between his thumb and forefinger as he began taking her pulse.

It was cold in the examination room. Goosebumps covered Ruby's flesh as she sat on top of a bed, clad in only a hospital gown. A female nurse hovered close by, taking notes each time Dr Swanson spoke. He uttered a set of numbers in her direction and straightened.

'I think we're making good progress.' Now his brown eyes were on Ruby. 'Do you feel like you're experiencing less difficulty when breathing?'

Ruby involuntarily inhaled. She felt the inner ripple of torn flesh scorch through her, followed by the lingering afterburn of pain. But she was doing it, she was breathing by herself, unaided. The hiss of the oxygen mask whispered in her memory. How long had it been since she'd first met Dr Swanson? His had been the face she'd seen as she stared, bleary-eyed, at the bright overhead lights and feared that she was in heaven. Despite the circumstances, despite the public hatred towards her, his voice had been kind, reassuring.

'You're going to be fine,' he kept saying. 'Everything is going to be all right, Ruby.' Her arms were locked in casts that she couldn't recall being constructed and her chest – it was the epicentre of a volcano: molten and spitting, burning everything around it. Pain, there was just so much pain. When the morphine touched her, it didn't bring respite, instead it allowed rats to enter the walls and scratch at her, causing her to scream into her plastic oxygen mask until she was coughing up blood from her damaged lungs.

'It still hurts,' Ruby admitted quietly. She could feel the nurse's eyes on her. Was she staring in judgement, thinking that the little girl on the bed deserved everything she got?

'You suffered extensive damage.' Dr Swanson relieved the nurse of her clipboard and scanned over its contents. 'Broken bones in both arms, broken ribs, a ruptured lung. That's a lot of trauma.' He returned the clipboard to the nurse and steepled his fingertips beneath his dimpled chin. 'I'm confident that your lungs have healed, but I'll need to do an X-ray to check the alignment of your ribs. I'm concerned that they may not have set correctly. Things were so hectic that day you came in, everything was done in haste, which means we might spend the next few months tidying things up for you.'

Ruby's first encounter with Dr Swanson was a blur of colour and shouting within her mind. It started back at her home, as she got out of the taxi and saw her brothers on her porch. She had run to them, arms outstretched, still so woefully naïve after all that had happened. Ruby had expected them to embrace her, to promise her that everything was going to be all right, the way that they always did. But the hands that greeted her were balled into fists.

She couldn't be sure who struck first, but they connected with her right shoulder, causing her to stagger back. The second punch, delivered squarely into her ribs, caused her to fold like a paper doll and then collapse against the ground. Ruby had stared up at the burning face of the sun as her brothers kicked and beat her. She wanted to scorch away her sight, to see nothing but blinding whiteness as she couldn't bear to watch them doing that to her. Blood left her mouth in a startled cough, tears soaked her cheeks and still they kicked, still they cursed her.

'You bitch, you fucking bitch. How could you do this to us? To Mum? You've shamed us, Ruby. How could you?'

Someone must have eventually called the police. Was it the taxi driver? Or a neighbour standing twitching their curtains, who didn't have the stomach to witness the death of a teenager? Had they endured the sight for a while, agreeing with Ruby's brothers and their laments? At what point did they turn away from their window and reach for their phone? Was it when the porch to the house became splashed with crimson, or when Ruby ceased sobbing, ceased begging her brothers to stop, almost ceased breathing altogether?

Help came in the form of an ambulance, but Ruby was no longer lucid. Her memory of being hauled onto the gurney felt more like she was floating through an endless blinding white sea. The sun was hot on her face, her blood and tears sticky on her cheeks. She closed her eyes and when she opened them again, she was looking up at Dr Swanson, some twenty miles away from the home she had grown up in, from the estate which had always protected her.

'People change.' That was the lingering sentiment offered by Glenda. 'Your brothers changed towards you, I'm sorry for that.'

After several weeks, Ruby summoned up the strength to ask what became of them.

'They're awaiting sentencing.' Glenda had adjusted her glasses as she spoke. Her lips sagged at the corners. 'I imagine the judge will be lenient, considering the circumstances.' When she wanted to, the lavender-scented woman could throw a punch just as well as Ruby's brothers. But she wasn't acting out of hatred or vitriol, just a stoic pragmatism, a desire to help her young charge see the world as it now was.

Ruby accepted these developing truths with stiff nods and furious blinking to suppress her desire to cry. So her brothers weren't going to be thrown into a detention centre like the one she was currently held in? They'd soon walk free, feel the sun on their backs as they traipsed around the estate, barely punished for almost beating their little sister to death.

The unfairness of it all was a shard which stuck in Ruby's side, made her laboured breathing even more agonising. Had she not been connected to Caleb's death, then her brothers would be the monsters, not her. She'd still be free.

'They were meant to protect me,' Ruby heard the shake in her voice as she addressed Dr Swanson and bowed her head shamefully. She sounded too much like the scared little girl she was and she didn't want him to see that, she wanted him to see her as strong.

'You're doing great.' He clasped a hand against her shoulder and squeezed. 'Let's schedule another X-ray and see how those ribs are looking, okay?' Though his back was to her, the nurse was scribbling away, noting down this latest addition to her workload. 'Try not to dwell too much on the past, Ruby.' His hand lingered on her shoulder. 'You're healing well, breathing on your own, it's all great progress. Let's focus on that.'

Back in her room, alone, Ruby tried to remember the brothers who had taught her how to ride a bike, who had given her their old Walkmans and cassette tapes. The brothers who would come and curl up next to her in the night when they heard her whimpers through the paper-thin walls of their little home.

'Don't worry,' they'd tell her, 'Mum will be herself again when she sobers up.' They were so like Ollie: equal parts cruel and kind. Ruby always felt privileged to see their softer side, just as she did with the leader of her friendship group. It was like being given VIP access at a concert – everyone else saw the star through their stage persona, but Ruby got to peek behind the curtain, see the real person who existed in the shadow of the myth.

It never once crossed Ruby's mind that she'd ever see the feral, ferocious side of her brothers. When they'd got into fights, stolen cars, smashed windows, their behaviour was always excused by their mother's insistence that they were good boys, decent boys. And they proved this in the way they looked out for their little sister. Ruby wanted to keep remembering them as these kind-hearted misfits who only she understood. But each time she thought of her brothers now, she remembered the power of their punches, the strength in their kicks. They had done more than broken her body that day out on the porch; they'd killed her spirit.

Thirty-Three

'I can't help you.' Josh thundered past Beth and swung open the white doors to their shared built-in wardrobe.

'But someone is trying to *kill* me.' What terrified her most was how certain she was of it. The first two names on the list were already dead, she was clearly next.

Josh bent down and rummaged around at the base of the wardrobe. He launched an empty holdall towards the bed, followed by a selection of jeans, jumpers and boxer shorts. Beth watched the clothes mount up in a messy pile as a lump of despair gathered in her throat. He was going to leave.

'Please.' Dropping to her knees, she joined him by the white doors, breathed in the lingering scent of fabric softener which clung to all their garments. 'Josh, please.' Her hands found his thick shoulders and clung to them. 'I need you. You can't just abandon me.'

He flung her off like she were a nuisance insect.

'I'm not staying here.' He was resolute as he turned to the bed and began shoving clothes into the holdall.

'Where . . . where will you go?'

A brief pause. 'I don't know.'

'Will you come back?'

This question required no deliberation upon answering. 'No.'

'Josh!' Beth was at the edge of the bed, thrusting her hands into his holdall and throwing out each item he packed. Joggers landed beside the radiator, socks were strewn across their pillows. Just an hour ago, they'd both been sleeping, the room had been peaceful. Only Beth was never privy to the calmness of night. When she closed her eyes, there was always screaming, shouting, panic. Now the lines between the waking world and her nightmares were blurred. The terror she found in the darkness had seeped into the bedroom, into the clenched muscles in Josh's jawline, the throb of the veins within his neck.

'Fuck, just stop!' He grabbed her wrists, thick fingers closing around delicate bone. Beth froze. So easily Josh could fill the room with the sickening sound of something snapping. He was breathing deeply, nostrils flared.

Beth closed her eyes in nauseated anticipation. She braced for the inevitable throw across the room, for the way it would feel when her back connected with the metal of the radiator. Then, as she slumped to the ground, felt the roughness of the carpet once again digging into her knees, Josh would reach her like a sudden storm. Fists would pound the flesh on her face into an unrecognisable pulp and her lungs would burn afresh after several well-placed kicks. And Josh would surely walk away from the brutality as easily as her brothers once had, because no one would condemn him for attacking a witch, a monster.

With a grunt, Josh dropped his hands, forcing Beth's to float down to her sides. 'Just get the hell out of here; I can't even stand to look at you.'

Her mouth flapped open, but there were no words. Instead, she just gasped repeatedly, almost panting.

'Beth,' Josh winced at his own mistake, 'Ruby. Whatever the fuck your name is, get out of here. Now.'

But she couldn't leave. Josh was her shield. When he kissed her, enveloped her in his arms, it was a reminder that Beth deserved to be loved, deserved to live. Once, she had been a little girl with desires and dreams and he made her inner child feel safe, sometimes even hopeful.

'I'm serious. *Leave.*' There was gravel in his voice. The tenderness which had previously existed there had been torn to shreds.

Beth left. She waited in the hallway, at the base of the stairs, as she heard Josh moving around the bedroom, yanking open drawers. Hugging her arms to her chest, she reassured herself that this was all just theatrics. Josh had already passed the test – he could have beaten her, hurt her, but he rose above those baser instincts. He was a better man than her brothers, than Ollie. And a better man would stay, would stand by the woman he loved.

When he appeared at the top of the stairs, Beth's heart seized and nearly missed a beat. He loomed so large, especially with the holdall slung over his shoulder, adding to his bulk like an oversized hump. Josh took a second to look at her and then hurried down, taking the stairs two at a time. His feet were already clad in the Skechers trainers Beth had bought him the previous Christmas, the pair which until now had sat in their box at the back of the wardrobe, temporarily forgotten. Seeing the shoes allowed the flicker of hope within her to grow into a fully formed flame. They were surely a message, an unspoken sign that she still mattered to him. That *they* still mattered. He wasn't really leaving, how could he when her life was truly in danger? Josh had seen the list, knew what she was up against.

'You were twelve.' There was a hollowness to his words, which set Beth on edge. The flame of hope that burned internally was suddenly buffeted by an icy blast. 'Ten is deemed the age of culpability, when a child is fully aware of morality and right and wrong.'

'Josh—'

'You could have told someone, anyone. It took time for that boy to bleed out. You could have saved him. You chose not to.'

'It wasn't that simple!'

'Yes, Beth . . . Ruby . . . whatever. It was. And now he's dead and you're getting this sick second chance at life. Where is the fairness in that?'

'I did . . .' Beth gasped as she defended herself, 'my time. I did my time.' She had been punished in accordance with the law and a judge had ultimately deemed her worthy of freedom, with the caveat that Ruby Renton ceased to exist. And Beth had initially been excited to sever those ties to her past. But she should have known that she was bound to her crime by more than just her name. All of the Stirchley Six were. 'Don't act like you're a saint! People make mistakes!'

He held her in an icy stare and released a stiff breath. 'I've been done for drunk driving. Yes. Don't go pulling skeletons out of my closet to try and feel better about the shit you've done. I've never *killed* anyone, Beth. I'm not a fucking murderer.'

'Neither am I!'

'I can't be here with you any more, try to understand that.' When Josh reached out for the handle of the front door, Beth didn't stand in his way. After twisting the lock, he pulled it open and allowed the cool night air to blast into the hallway. It wove between Beth's legs, making her feel numb.

'Don't go,' anguish was strangling her throat, her words. 'Please, stay. I love you.'

Telling him the truth had proved that, hadn't it? Josh was her world, her anchor to normality.

'Goodbye, Beth.' There was so much sadness in his eyes as he slid past her, enough to drown in.

'Please.' Gripping the door frame with both hands, Beth let the night air engulf her as she watched Josh stalk through the shadows towards his van, gravel crunching beneath his new trainers. 'Don't do this.'

The passenger door creaked open and Josh threw in his holdall, then he rounded the van towards the driver's side. It was still so early, the rest of their neighbours were sleeping soundly in their beds. Beth knew she couldn't risk making a scene, couldn't risk inviting questions which she could never dare to answer. Josh knew her truth, but she couldn't let it spill beyond him, taint the doors which were lined up next to hers in their little cul-de-sac of terraced houses.

In the distance, leaves rustled in the woods, as though already whispering about her. Beth watched Josh clamber up into his van and close the door. So many times she'd watched him depart like this, usually beneath the glorious glow of early-morning sunlight. She'd wave him off, grinning widely, already dressed for her morning jog. But this was different. This was finite. This was goodbye.

Josh gunned the engine and then released the steering wheel to crack open his window.

'Just . . . just stay safe.' His words were almost drowned out by the hum of the van and then he was reversing, sliding over gravel and turning away from the house. It took less than ten seconds for him to disappear from view entirely, the groan of the engine drifting away on the night air.

Beth stood, stunned, in the doorway, the cool breeze continuing to thread its way past her legs and into the house. She stared at the empty lit street, at the vacated space where Josh's van had been just moments ago. A tawny owl shrieked, the sound shrill and sharp. Beth kept peering at her driveway, at the pool of light cast upon it by the nearby lamp post.

When the piercing call of the owl came again, Beth stepped back inside and slammed the door closed, taking care to turn all of the locks. Finally, she laced the golden security chain in place and then rested her forehead against the plastic, breathing hard.

She was alone.

The truth of it swamped her like a damp cloak, making her skin prickly and clammy.

Not for the first time in her life, those who professed to love her had turned on her. Beth permitted herself to cry as her body sagged towards the floor.

Thirty-Four

I can see him. My brother. He's so close. And he's giving me that look, holding out his hand, and my fingertips are almost against his, just a little further and—

Something slams shut. Loud enough to wake me up, to cause the animals lurking in the darkness with me to scurry deeper into the shadows. My heart has leapt up into my throat. Coughing, I shove it back down, reach for the tree and try to stand up. I feel as stiff and wooden as my bed for the night. I've been falling asleep here too much lately, waking to find my clothes damp with dew, muscles stiff with discomfort.

The sound of gravel crunching underfoot carries over the fence to me. Was it coming from her house? I stagger forwards, willing the blood to hurry up and reach my feet, my fingertips. I'm almost at the fence when a car door opens. More gravel shifts. It's him. Even from this angle, I recognise her boyfriend, the beefing bulk of him. Is that really her type? He seems so . . . generic. I remember being a little disappointed when I first saw him. There's nothing brooding behind his eyes, nothing untamed fighting to be released. And I thought that's what she was drawn to. What she was always chasing.

Now I can see him behind the wheel of his van. With the interior light on, I can make out the red of his cheeks, the way his eyes are bulging. I know anger when I see it. My pulse quickens. Twice he slaps his thick hands against the steering wheel, lucky not to set off the horn. Then he's shoving it into gear and the *brakes are screeching as he hastily backs off the little driveway, kicking up gravel. He speeds down the quiet street, turning at the junction without his brake lights glowing.*

My mouth is dry as I keep watching the driveway, waiting for more fireworks. Did they have a fight? Has he just stormed out in a rage? Has she cheated? Has he? Or maybe, deliciously, has she confessed? Was the truth finally going to start bleeding out into the world? Her perfectly constructed life might be about to come crashing down and here I am with a front row seat to it all. I should be smiling. But instead I'm numb against the fence – hands hooked over the top, clenched against the rough pine, peering in from the darkness.

She wasn't sure how long she stayed curled in a ball beside her front door. When Beth finally lifted her head, she saw that the sky outside had lightened to grey. With some effort, she dragged herself onto her feet, bones creaking. Numbly, she stumbled into the kitchen. Everywhere was so quiet, as though the little house had been sucked into a vacuum.

'You need to keep being strong, can you do that for me?' That had been Glenda's parting question at their last meeting.

Keep being strong.

Is that what Beth had been doing all these years, showing strength in her ability to bury the past? Because she didn't feel strong, far from it. She felt weak. The life she had built for herself was not the life she had envisioned as a girl.

Like most children, she'd had naïve notions of greatness. All of the six did, in their own way. Ollie intended to become a notorious master criminal – something he had achieved much earlier than even he could have intended. Annie wanted to work in a library, help others fall in love with books, and Jacob often spoke of his desire to join a band and tour the world. Each of them wanted to move far beyond the shabby shelter of their claustrophobic estate. They wanted to see oceans that stretched out far enough to touch the sky, mountains capped with snow. They wanted *more*.

But so few got that. Beth understood that now. Her own mother must have once had dreams, ambitions, but somewhere along the way she lost hold of them and they fluttered away from her like a plastic bag caught on a breeze. Linda Renton proved to be resourceful, finding other ways to escape her life.

Beth clicked the kettle on. The sound of boiling water filled the space around her, but it couldn't quite reach the edges, still she felt the emptiness within the rest of the house coming down the stairs, searching for her.

'Keep being strong,' she gritted the command through clenched teeth as the kettle ceased shuddering and she made herself a strong cup of coffee. Exhaustion hadn't found her yet, but she knew that it would, once the despair and adrenaline within her system had been spent.

When she'd first been placed in her cold, stark bedroom at the detention centre, she had been certain that she wouldn't sleep, that she'd just spend each night staring up at the tiled ceiling and dwelling on all that she'd lost. But even the most troubled souls succumb to sleep eventually. It's a bittersweet kind of torture. For in dreams there is escape, and those moments when you first awaken, blinking at the light of a new day, you're disorientated, confused, and for a few precious seconds – truly free. Then reality slams into the serenity with the force of a freight train, memories bubble to the surface of the tar pit of the mind.

There had been a time when sleep meant freedom. But the nightmares soon found her, reached beneath her skin and hooked with talons to her soul, refusing to let go.

Her coffee tasted bitter. Threading both hands around her mug, Beth wandered into the living room, stealing a glimpse of herself in the glossy black surface of the flat-screen television Josh had bought in a sale the previous September. He'd been so proud when he brought it home, grinning like an excited schoolboy as he unloaded it from the back of his van.

'Sixty inches,' he boasted. 'Imagine how great *Game of Thrones* is going to look on this.'

On the screen, Beth could see how gaunt she had become, the way her cheeks appeared hollowed, the bones of her face too pronounced. Her legs were spindles beneath the short hem of the T-shirt she'd slept in; skin still mottled pink by the bristled caress of the carpet she'd been curled up on for hours.

Really she needed to shower, to attempt to wash away some of her pain, to watch it disappear down the drain with shampoo. But she couldn't even think about entering the bathroom and blasting herself with hot water while she felt so vulnerable, so alone.

Her purchases were still on the kitchen table; all the deadbolts and locks she'd hastily grabbed in Homebase. Beth darted out to the shed at the back of her small garden, moving as swiftly as the little sparrows which were now flitting amongst the trees in the early-morning sunlight. She returned, panting, feet damp with dew, clutching Josh's drill and hammer.

For the next hour, she worked. Beth fitted the locks, the deadbolts, not perfectly but adequately enough to make the house more secure. When she was all but spent, she collapsed on the sofa, grabbed her laptop and quickly fired off an order for security cameras and padlocks for the side gate.

Safe.

The word played on a loop in her mind. She needed to keep herself safe.

Your house always looks so inviting. I envy that. My home never felt like that. My mum was never on the doorstep to greet me from school. I used to spray myself with her perfume when she was out so that I could pretend that I smelt like her because she'd held me so close, hugged me so tightly. How pathetic is that?

I wonder if my mum has slipped into senility? It came for my grandma early. She was barely sixty when she was leaving saucepans boiling on the hob overnight. She'd tap her withered fingers to her temple and shrug. I like to think that when people told her what happened to my brother, and then to me, she was horrified for one awful moment, but then her mind pressed rewind and she just forgot. Maybe to her we're just still two kids creeping into her kitchen to pinch Malted Milks from her biscuit tin. I think that's better than knowing the truth, because the truth is so awful, so corrosive. I feel like it ruins everyone it touches.

I wonder what has become of my mum. Is she in a home somewhere? Not that I'd ever consider visiting her. Why would I? We're strangers now. My hair is long, ends split. My cheeks are too gaunt; my dead grandma would say you could slice cheese on my cheekbones. Is my mum even still alive? Or has the devil finally claimed her?

'You're a beauty,' my dead grandma would exclaim as she cupped my chin and my mum looked on scornfully. 'You're lucky, beautiful girls have it easy.'

Oh if she could see me now. My beauty has only worked against me. Like the first time Roger slid his hand onto my knee. I'd flinched, but he kept it there, parting his lips to reveal crooked teeth. 'Come on,' he said as his hand continued north beneath my skirt. 'Pretty girl like you, you must have been with lots of boys.'

The answer to that was no, but who would believe me? Who would care?

Showering seemed too swift. Beth knew that the ache in her joints needed to be massaged by warm water and so now that she felt safer, she was in the bath, surrounded by cherry-scented bubbles. She listened to the ripples as she kicked out her legs, dipped her arms fully beneath the waterline. It was up to her chin, her hair collected atop her head in a messy bun, but she could still feel that the tendrils at the back of her neck were damp.

Josh had not returned. Was he now at work, moving round the site at the foreman's behest without revealing any outward signs that something was wrong? Because Josh wouldn't open up to his colleagues, wouldn't cry to them, he wasn't that kind of guy. He'd store his sorrow in the pit of his stomach, where it risked turning ulcerous and deadly. Or *had* he talked? Had he arrived at work along with the dawn and started to tell his friends what had happened?

'Do you remember Ruby Renton? The Stirchley Six?' Anyone well into their twenties would nod that, yes, they remembered.

Beth couldn't breathe. She imagined Josh at the building site, surrounded by an enraptured audience hanging on his every word. Soon, a chorus of hatred would ring out from them. Whilst they might not grab pitchforks and torches, they'd equip themselves with whatever they could before they marched, en masse, a mob, towards her home, prepared to kick the door in and deliver the justice they felt had been so grossly neglected in her sentencing.

Her vision blurred. Beth had dipped her head below the waterline, letting her spine fold along the base of the bath. Blinking, she peered up at the bubbles which now floated above her like foam-filled clouds.

Five names on a list, the third one is yours.

And who had written it? The question continually plagued her, fanned the flames of her pre-existing fears. Was it someone connected to Caleb? It had to be. Who else would seek revenge after so long? He had family, people who loved him, mourned him. Where were they now?

The case . . . it had been so high profile. On every news channel, on the front of every paper. What if someone became fixated, what if someone obsessed over it all, channelling their interest into dark intent?

There was tightness in her lungs. With a spasm, Beth's back lifted off the floor of the bath and her body lurched upwards, desperate to find air. Releasing her hands from the water which was now tepid, Beth gripped the sides of the bath and held herself down, beneath the bubble-clotted surface. She could hear her feet kicking, thrashing, a part of her still desperate to live.

Is this what had happened to Vikki and Ollie? Did they receive a list and make the terrible connection to their past and fail to live under the mounting pressure of their true identity being revealed? Beneath the water, Beth understood their desperation, their pain.

Her body breached the surface, sending water off the edges of the bath, cascading down to the tiled floor. Beth gasped, staring fixedly at the shrivelled rouge hue of her hands. She had been unable to hold herself down in the depths. Her lungs were burning from deprivation and old wounds. Shaking, Beth dragged herself out of the bath and dropped against the floor, letting the coolness of the tiles press against her hot, soaked skin.

The worst part of it all, the part which clung like a rabid monkey to Beth's back, was the fact that if she were to do it all over again, given a chance to right so many wrongs, she couldn't be certain that she'd do anything differently. A terrible part of her would still follow Ollie, still want to believe that he could save her, that he knew best.

But Ollie was gone. Along with Josh. Along with her old name. Beth was alone and she needed to stay strong.

Thirty-Five

'Please, I just want to see them.' Ruby sat on her hands, chewing her lip and peering over at Glenda. It was raining. She could hear the soft patter against the window, had briefly glimpsed the ashen sky beyond the canteen when she ate her breakfast. The porridge in her bowl had been tasteless, her toast dry.

Ruby longed for the runny eggs her mum would make on the rare occasions she didn't wake up with a pounding headache. On those mornings, their little house would be filled with the alluring scent of cooked grease and frying bacon. Ruby would wake up to it, salivating, and her stomach would churn in delicious anticipation. She'd bounce out of bed as giddy as Pinocchio after he'd lost his strings. A house crammed with the smells of a fry-up always meant one thing: that it was going to be a good day.

The canteen always held the same odour, the crispness of burnt toast never quite gone.

'Ruby, we've been over this.' With a single finger, Glenda pushed her glasses up the length of her nose and readjusted her weight within her chair. Her long skirt was a deep red, matched with a beige blouse. The colours of autumn. Ruby wondered if the days had turned over enough times for a new season to commence whilst she remained within the centre, cut off from the rest of the world. Were her classmates starting school, returning to one another with the sheepish reservation of estranged relatives who'd suffered a great loss? Was Ruby's name now on their lips? As they walked to registration did they speak of the six, speculate on what might have become of them?

'I know but—'

'The answer is no, I'm afraid.'

With a sigh, Ruby sagged against the sofa, let the fabric absorb the weight of her disappointment. In truth, she'd known what Glenda's answer would be before she'd even asked the question. But she had to ask. She'd thought that the privileges which allowed her to roam beyond her room would help to reduce the size of the empty hole that swelled within her, but it hadn't worked out that way. The hollowness remained. At night, Ruby would lie in bed, wide-eyed, tracing the cracks in the ceiling and wondering how many similarly empty minutes the rest of her life held for her.

'My mum,' Ruby pressed. 'Can't I at least see her?'

Linda Renton was made for places such as these. With booze-hardened features, she'd scrutinise the staff, the nurses, send them cowering away from her with a steely stare. Linda could be fearless when she wasn't fixing for a drink. Suitably satiated, she could almost pass for normal. It was only when the monkey began scratching on her back anew that she became feral, desperate, almost childlike in her single-mindedness to have just one illicit sip from a bottle of liquor.

'You don't know what it's like,' she'd seethe at her children through cigarette-stained teeth. 'It's all I think about, all I want.'

'Those kinds of cravings, they'll kill her,' Jacob had once quietly told Ruby as they sat on the swings in the local park beneath a pale moon. He'd yet to be proved right on that point.

'My mum will want to see me.' It was a lie and Ruby could taste its bitterness in her mouth. She almost wanted Glenda to try to lure Linda, to offer her a bottle of vodka – not just the store-brand stuff, the good stuff – if she came to see her daughter. Her lips were puckering to make such a request when the woman opposite shook her head and clasped her hands in her lap.

'She won't come. I know that it's hard to accept, but—'

'Then my friends. Where are they? Annie, Jacob? Ollie, where's he? Kate? Vikki? They must be staying somewhere like this. Can't I just see one of them? They're . . .' she wanted to insist that they were still her friends, but was that even true any more? Towards Annie she still felt an affinity, a connection, but a canyon was opening up between her and the others. Each time she caught a glimpse of a contraband newspaper that had been smuggled in, or heard the clipped RP pronunciation of a broadcaster through the crack of a door denouncing the Stirchley Six, she thought of Ollie, of how he had instigated the game, ordered them to run. The rest of them were just the monkeys to his organ grinder, but did that matter in the eyes of a judge? In the eyes of the public?

'Ruby,' her name was accompanied by a stiff sigh. 'It's not safe for you to see people from your past. I thought you understood that.'

'I . . . I do.' She swallowed against the growing lump in her throat.

'And now you're able to go in the canteen, the common room, connect with people your own age.'

'I want to go back to school.' Tears threatened to slice down her cheeks. Releasing her hands, she gripped at her elbows through the thin fabric of her faded green jumper. Even her clothes didn't feel like her own any more, they carried the lingering odour of burnt toast, same as the canteen. 'I just want to go back to everything being normal and—' she stopped when she noticed the tilt of Glenda's head, the sad slant of her lips, the way the older woman's eyes were misting over with a pitying sheen.

'I know that this is all a lot to accept.'

'Am I going to be locked up forever?' Ruby could scarcely say the words. She shuddered fitfully as the question left her and the rain lashed louder against the window. Was this her fate, to forever be a hamster in a cage? Would she grow to forget how the sun felt when it was warm on her skin, the gentle tug of the wind in her hair?

'Ruby—'

'Because that's what I deserve, right? Since Caleb is . . . gone.' To say dead felt like a step too far, a condemnation too finite for her to be able to recover from.

'Don't think about things long term,' Glenda urged, her voice soft with kindness. Ruby often considered how the woman must have an ox's heart, much bigger than a human one, as it seemed to have such an irrepressible capacity for compassion, more than any other adult Ruby had encountered in her young life. 'Right now we are preparing for the trial. Once that is over, we can start to move on.'

'Move on to what?'

Glenda leant forward, eyes still fogged with their sad sheen, 'To whatever sentence the judge delivers for you. But don't stress over it, Ruby. Whatever happens, we'll cope.'

We.

Not you.

We.

Ruby clung to that as more rain whipped against the windows.

Thirty-Six

She was at the car park. Beth had made it this far. The door beside her was still open, one hand nervously clenched around its upper metal body. Less than a hundred feet away, the cinema loomed up against the tarmac, red signage shining brightly in the early-evening sunlight. Just a few more steps, then she'd be swallowed by the air-conditioning and shadows. First she needed to close the door, then lock the car. One foot in front of the other, she knew what needed to be done, could visualise her hurried saunter towards the main entrance. But Beth wasn't moving. She was frozen.

'Come . . . on,' she whispered to herself through gritted teeth. Her uniform, though crumpled, was in a passable state. Her dark hair was pulled back in a tight ponytail. All that remained was to physically enter the building.

'Oh my god, no, really?' A group of teenage girls were walking past, heads bent together in a rainbow of peroxide and ombre shades. 'She *didn't*?' They were giggling, gossiping. Beth watched them as though they were a flock of exotic birds. Arm in arm, they sidled across the length of the car park, making for the cinema. The tallest of them glanced over her shoulder, throwing a look in Beth's direction. She scowled, revealing eyes the colour of muddy water and a mottled complexion poorly concealed by copious layers of foundation.

Beth's throat tightened, strangling her. Did the girl know? The look lasted barely a second, then she was tossing her bleached hair over her shoulder and laughing heartily with her friends.

'Seriously, though, what a *bitch*,' the girl joined in the conversation, keen to throw her slanderous comment into the mix.

She couldn't know. Beth used the thought to help her muscles unclench, to allow air to reach her lungs once more. The girl was a teenager, possibly not even born when the scandal of the Stirchley Six broke.

But she could still know. A darkness unfurled in her mind like a slither of smoke. People passed down tales through generations, especially those of the more sordid, scandalous kind. Beth had grown up hearing about the Moors murders, although she hadn't lived through them. Hateful tales had a way of lingering around the dinner table.

'Do you remember when . . .?' people would begin, eyes bright with morbid interest.

'Awful, so awful,' others would remark whilst tutting and shaking their heads.

Had Beth become a myth shared down the generations? Her knuckles turned white as she kept holding on to her car door with a fierce might. She watched the gaggle of girls disappear inside the cinema. *Her* cinema. They were in her safe place, tainting it with their mean gossip and icy stares.

Did they know?

Were they standing inside, gathered close to the popcorn stand but peering back through the doors towards the car park?

'That woman,' the tallest could be pointing out, now unseen by Beth, 'by the car. Have you heard about her? What she did?'

'No,' Beth was already nervously easing back into her car as she choked on a sob. 'No. No, no, no.' Her keys jangled noisily in her quaking hands as she shoved them back into the ignition. Twice she stalled. On her third attempt, she managed to reverse out of her space, to storm across the tarmac, tyres screeching.

I need to stop sleeping in the woods. My legs are numb, along with my back. I can't tell if it's from the cold or from lack of movement. I've seen the boyfriend leave. He's still not returned. Is he gone for good or just working away? He seemed to leave in haste last time, late at night, slamming doors.

Have you finally talked? Did your ugly truth drive him away?

Maybe this is when I should strike, make my presence known more absolutely. It would be so easy to go over, to cross this final space existing between us. What would you smell like? Something floral, I imagine. Or vanilla. Maybe a mixture of the two.

I want you to see me. To look at me and remember him. My brother.

Conveniently, the police station was located just five minutes from the cinema, the buildings clustered around the main shopping centre like planets circling a sun. Different car park, same postcode. Beth swerved into an empty space and hauled herself out into the sunlight. She was surrounded by vehicles streaked with blue and neon yellow. Her heart rapped manically in her chest.

This was a mistake, she shouldn't be there. But she'd called Glenda's office twice that morning and gone through to answerphone. And Glenda had wanted her to go to the police, hadn't she? Beth was only doing what she had advised. So why did it feel like she was willingly walking into a snake pit? But she needed to feel safe. And the police would protect her, wouldn't they? Weren't they sworn to serve and protect? At least in America . . . Did the British police make a similar declaration, like when a doctor takes the Hippocratic oath? Despite all she had done, she was still a citizen, still worthy of their care. Right? They wouldn't instantly turn on her the moment they knew who she was? Who she *really* was?

Beth was taking short, sharp breaths, her pulse climbing. It was a bad idea. A terrible one.

But the only one.

There was nowhere left to turn. The list, it was a threat. Beth was certain of that. And with Josh gone, she was alone. Alone and vulnerable.

Her tongue had turned to cotton wool by the time she approached the reception desk in the main waiting room. Hands which refused to stop trembling were shoved down into the depths of her black trouser pockets. Beth looked at the uniformed man on the other side of the glass with a scared smile.

'Hi. I . . .'

He leant forward in his chair, buttons straining against a beer belly in its infancy. 'Can I help you?'

Beth's smile fell. He looked to be in his late twenties, maybe early thirties. But his freshly shaven thick chin might have been misleading her, making him appear more youthful than he was. Would he know? If she said her true name, would a shadow settle upon his features as it had with Josh? Would he judge her? Condemn her? String her up against a lamp post outside and leave her to wait for the author of the list to catch up with her?

'I'm in danger.' Her words ran together, making her sound as desperate and uneasy as she felt.

'Okay.' The man's chair squeaked as he shuffled atop it. He neither looked nor sounded concerned by her declaration. 'I'll need you to fill out an incident report; can you do that for me? You having trouble with a boyfriend, partner?' Pale blue eyes swept over her. 'Are you currently inebriated in any way?'

At this, she nearly laughed. She wasn't drunk, but she wished she was. Wished she shared her mother's proclivity for the sauce. What Beth wouldn't give to find some semblance of detachment at the bottom of a bottle. But all these years and she'd remained clean, and sober. Something Glenda regularly commended her for back when they were having more consistent sessions.

'I'm just in danger.' It was an effort to keep her voice level, her words audible without a jangle of nerves carrying through them. 'I need protection.'

You need more time. I get that. And I'll keep waiting. How long has it been since you found my note? One week? Two? Days flow together too easily for me, I lose track.

'Get a diary,' Roger told me. 'It'll help you stay organised.'

He didn't realise that it'd just remind me of how many days I'd lost. Absence, grief, it's like a hole in the pit of your stomach that your body keeps on excavating until you disappear down it completely.

I don't need a diary to tell me that I'm running out of days. My hollow cheeks, my concave stomach, these tell me how close I am, how I'm teetering. But she'll fix it all. I know she will. She'll have to face up to the past and stop hiding behind her new life, and then I can get mine back too. I just need her to act. Then we can both emerge from the darkness together.

Or do I maybe need to push her? I pushed before, with the others, and look what happened . . .

Pushing was wrong. It was too much, too sudden. But she's not fragile like the others, is she? She has her house, her job.

She had her boyfriend. She's great at pretending everything is fine. So do I risk nudging her, sending her closer to the edge?

With a shake of my head, I disregard the question, but the gesture makes me woozy. Leaning back against the tree trunk, I peer up at the sky, a vast expanse of clear blue spread above me. Here, in the shadows, I can hide and I can wait. But I'm running out of time, I can't wait forever.

An hour later and Beth was sitting in a stuffy interview room, a humming strip light taking up most of the tiled ceiling. Twice her phone had buzzed: first with an incoming call from her manager, Colin, and then a text message.

Beth, where are you? You're late for work.

Her reply had been blunt, factual:

Sorry, I'm at the police station. Not sure when I'll be done.

Colin was cut from the same cloth as Glenda, always keen to see the best in people. It took less than five minutes for him to respond and Beth could imagine him staring down at his phone, paling fearfully.

Right, okay, well, hope everything is all right. See you tomorrow, Beth. If you need anything, anything at all, let me know.

Kindness was a rare commodity. Beth felt particularly drawn to it. It was what had made her notice Josh, after she'd taken in his broad shoulders and confident smile. He was the kind of guy who slowed down for pigeons in the road,

232

who always bought a can of dog food when he was doing his grocery shop to place in the charity bin near the exit. Josh was *good*. But he was gone. Would Colin abandon her too if the truth got out? Would Beth be left with just Glenda, once again knowing that her counsellor was the only person in the entire world who would ever accept her for who she truly was? Should she try and call her again, ask her to come down and support her? Was there time?

'Right, Miss . . .' The officer who'd just opened the door to the interview room with a creak was looking down at the clipboard in her hand.

'Belmont,' Beth finished for her.

'Miss Belmont.' With a tight smile, the officer sat down across from her in a plastic chair – the same style as the one Beth was currently slumped down in, hands clasped against the cool metal of the table that acted as a divide across the room. 'What can I do for you?'

Not for the first time, Beth wished she had accepted the man at reception's offer of a cup of tea. Her tongue felt more like woodchips than cotton wool now, loose and bone dry. She swallowed and clasped her hands even tighter. A cup of tea would have given her something to hold, somewhere to channel the nerves which jostled inside like a hive of angry bees.

'I . . .' Beth nodded at the clipboard which surely contained the incident report she had filled out. 'I think I'm in danger. It's all there, what happened, with the note. The list.'

'Uh-huh,' the officer tilted her head and narrowed her eyes. She had blonde hair that stopped abruptly at her shoulders and a once-pretty face, creased by time. Worn red lipstick strained to add a touch of glamour to her tired demeanour. 'So you're saying that your real name is Ruby Renton?'

'Right.'

'Of the Stirchley Six?'

'Right.'

Fear gathered at the base of Beth's spine as though she were sitting on a bag of ice. She waited for the officer's eyes to harden with hatred, for her to shout out into the corridor for backup, for handcuffs. Is that why Beth had come there, to hand herself in?

I need protection.

If she couldn't even convince herself of the statement, how was she supposed to get a stranger to agree to help her?

'Okay, well, Miss Belmont . . . Renton, whichever you prefer to go by,' the officer tapped at her notes with the tip of a thick nail, 'this list that you describe is troubling, but not necessarily a threat. You claim that you've experienced no other harassing behaviour?'

'No, not yet, but—'

The officer held up her hand and Beth grew silent. 'I'm sure that it feels like you're in danger, but what you're presenting us with here is speculation. Without something more concrete in terms of a threat, there's nothing we can do at this point.'

'But . . .' The cold was racing up her spine, spreading across her shoulders, reaching down to the tips of her fingers.

Nothing.

The word echoed through her. No help. Nothing.

'Want my advice?' The officer leant back, stretching her palms out over the clipboard that was now resting upon the desk.

'Um, sure, yes. I mean, yes please.'

'You've been given a new identity for a reason, Miss Belmont. Stick to it. For my part, I can ensure that this report gets stored away safely, away from prying eyes.'

234

'Okay, but—'

'I left my prejudices at the door when I came in here. I chose to see you for what you are – a scared woman at her wits' end. Others won't be so kind. Or forgiving. Do you understand me?'

'I do. And the list, that's . . . that's what scares me.'

'It is not in this station's jurisdiction to investigate the origins of that list. At this point, I'm afraid, it is not a concrete threat, and until it is, our hands are tied, we can't do anything. I can only advise you and respond if something more menacing occurs. Go back to the people who gave you your identity, they might be able to provide you with some answers.'

'I have, I mean . . .' Beth dropped her head into her hands. 'And they said to contact the police if anything else happens—'

'Has anything else happened?'

Beth bit her lip and sighed. 'No.'

'Look, you're Beth Belmont. *Be* Beth Belmont. That's all the help I can give.'

The officer was getting up, chair scraping across the floor. Beth hastily shook out her arms and did the same, her legs uneasily supporting her weight.

'Th-thank you.' She hurried towards the officer, reaching out and touching her arm for support, needing a moment to steady herself. Beth could feel gravity trying to claim her.

'I'm just doing my job,' the officer told her pragmatically. 'Now go live your life. You've been given a second chance, don't waste it.'

Beth wanted to say more, but the officer was already withdrawing from her grasp and departing along the corridor.

It was dark when she left the station. Night had descended and brought with it shadows that swelled around the cars still lingering in the car park. Beth paused to let a stiff breeze sweep past her. The coppery tang of fear settled upon her tongue. Swallowing it down, she hugged her arms against herself, knowing that she'd go anywhere, give anything, to feel safe again, even just for a moment.

Thirty-Seven

Street lights glowed in the distance. Beth eased off the accelerator, letting her car slow to a crawl. Since leaving the police station, she'd followed the road as though it were a ribbon unwinding before her. She had no direction, no purpose, just a need to be moving somewhere. If it were daylight, she'd surely have gone jogging, but to do so under the cover of darkness in the woods near her home was both foolhardy and dangerous. Under the dense cover of trees, not even moonlight could reach the leaf-speckled path which spread through the woodlands like a network of tangled veins.

Pulling up against the curb, Beth killed the engine and sagged back in her seat. The world beyond the windscreen was instantly familiar, as though she'd walked into a dream. Crumbling fences bordered neglected front gardens, where the weeds claimed dominance over a few feeble blades of grass. A strip of houses stood clotted together like stained teeth, crooked and forlorn, shoulder to shoulder without even the slither of an alleyway to separate them.

Beth had parked up outside number eighteen. The numbers on the faded blue door were eroded by time and only just legible. A single light was on downstairs, bringing a glow to the lower left window. The kitchen. Beth released the steering wheel and began to massage her hands together.

Outside, so little had changed. The exterior of the house was still covered in blemished white paint, the window frames still splintered and cracking. Even the little patio at the threshold was the same: chipped cement pelted by years of wind and rain. It was not a welcoming sight. From where Beth sat, it looked more like part of a prison than a home. But this was where she'd grown up. She could still recall the wheezy creak of the gate when she pushed it open and began stalking up the narrow path leading to the front door, hoping that her mother wasn't passed out on the sofa or slumped across the kitchen table nursing the last dregs from a bottle of store-brand vodka.

Home.

She stepped out of the car and felt no pleasant sense of nostalgia envelop her like a welcoming hug. It was late, the night air damp and restless. A loose slat of wood slapped against a neighbouring gate and somewhere a dog was barking, rasping loudly over the stillness of the estate. If Beth lingered there long enough, she'd surely soon hear the squeal of sirens, the magpie cry of a disgruntled house-wife, followed by the resonant growl of an angry husband. The estate never slept. Like a vat of poison, it constantly simmered and boiled.

Her legs marched her up to the gate, hands finding the latch. She listened to the familiar wheeze as she passed through it. The sound followed her as she approached the front door, intensifying the ache in her chest.

Just turn back.

The thought was like a wasp, constantly humming. She could turn back now, climb in her car and drive down the motorway, speed along the empty lanes and be back in her own little terraced house before dawn. No one would ever need know that she'd returned.

But she *had* returned. Something had led her here; a salmon swimming back to where it was born. She'd been powerless against the impulse. And now she was back on her front porch, on the step that had once been stained with the crimson of her own blood. What was she hoping to find beyond the old blue door? Forgiveness? Closure? Comfort?

A bubble of laughter burst from her mouth. The one thing she'd never found in the dilapidated little house was comfort.

Thrice she knocked on the door, slamming her fist hard against the wood. From the light on downstairs, she knew that her mother must still be up. Still it took ten long minutes and a further bout of knocking before Beth heard the chain sliding on the other side of the door, accompanied by the rattling cough of a woman much older than her years.

'Yeah, who is it?' The voice inside tried to hold menace, but sounded feeble, afraid.

'Open the door and see,' Beth challenged.

A lock was turned. The door juddered open and Linda Renton was revealed, clad in a thinning blue towelling robe, short blonde hair matted atop her head. And lines. Her face had become a road map. Time seemed to have focused much of its decay on the homeowner rather than the home itself.

Linda had once been beautiful; she loved to boast as much to her children. And Beth had seen the pictures. It was indisputable that years ago the mother of the Rentons had once gleamed as bright and brilliant as a shiny new penny. But those days were long gone. Beth had watched her mother decline as she grew up, saw the woman's spine start to curve, her shoulders curl inwards and her teeth turn from white to yellow.

Now Linda was as dilapidated as the rest of the estate. When she coughed, Beth noticed that several teeth were missing, replaced by gaping black holes. The stench of stale cigarettes, liquor and urine powered out the house and Beth couldn't help but stagger back in disgust.

'Yeah, who the fuck are you?' Linda cocked her head at her impromptu guest like a curious bird, blinking bloodshot eyes in confusion.

Beth frowned. Could her own mother not see her there – the young girl now clad in a woman's body? Or was Linda simply too drunk to register what she was seeing?

'Don't you recognise me?' Beth tried to peer past the woman, tried to catch a glimpse inside her childhood home. In the light of the hallway, she could see that the wallpaper hadn't changed: still a dated design of red roses growing their way up towards tarnished coving. Framed pictures filled the wall towards the far door, leading to the lounge. Beth wondered if her face was still up there, smiling innocently for the camera in her school pictures.

It was the one expense Linda had indulged in. 'Saves me having to take any,' she'd mutter as she filled in an order for school photographs for each of her three children. Beth would wander through the hallway and look up at images of herself and her brothers, seeing each of them turn from cherub-faced toddlers to gap-toothed children and, for her siblings, eventually chiselled teens with acne and scowls. Her progress on the wall would be stilted, her pictures stopping just as her chest began to swell. In the hallway of her old home, she was forever a little girl on the cusp of womanhood. Provided she was even still there.

Beth kept looking over her mother's shoulder, keen to catch a glimpse of her own face. But she could imagine her brothers tearing down her pictures, smashing the frames and then shoving the remains down into the depths of the wheelie bin.

'Recognise you?' The gaps in her teeth brought a whistle to her words. Linda placed a bony hand against the door frame and leant forward, wavering slightly, as she scrutinised her guest. Beth could smell the neat vodka on her breath. She had not timed her visit well.

'Mum, it's me.' Beth reached forwards, palms upturned. 'Me,' she tapped at her chest. 'Ruby.'

The name felt rotten in her mouth. Beth almost retched saying it. She was Ruby Renton no longer, now she was Beth Belmont. But the roots of the past were clamping like vines around her legs, drawing her back to where it all began and pinning her there.

The list. This regression. It had all started with the damn list.

'Ruby?' Linda blinked and her mouth gaped. Skeletal fingers reached for her chest, for where her heart was languishing and beating in a concave chest still fighting to keep the fraying woman alive. '*My* Ruby?'

'Yes, Mum, it's me. Something . . . something happened. Someone knows about me, about my past and I . . .' Beth was faltering. Why was she on the doorstep of the woman who had abandoned her? The woman who had consistently failed to visit her whilst she was locked away from society? 'I came to see you. I wanted to see you.'

She was twelve again, climbing out of the taxi and buoyed with hope that her family would still love her, still support her, despite all that had transpired. Because that kind of loyalty was supposed to be unconditional, wasn't it?

'Oh, no,' Linda was shaking her head back and forth in an almost demonic way. One hand was shoved forward to create a feeble barrier. 'No, no, that can't be. My Ruby is dead. Long dead.'

Beth ground her back teeth together. She was most definitely not dead.

At least not yet.

Whoever had written the list had yet to catch up to her in person and she was trying to outrun them, trying to outrun the past that haunted her.

'Mum, you know it's me. I have a new identity now, a new life, but it's still *me*.'

If Linda chose to see it, she'd easily find Ruby there; in the straight line of Beth's nose, the smooth cheekbones, the dark eyes and strong jawline.

'You're too much like your father,' Linda would remark. Not that Beth had ever been able to draw such a conclusion herself; she'd never known her father. Her brothers were lean and muscular, all three children tall. The boys had inherited their mother's narrow shoulders and long fingers. Beth was broader. A PE teacher had once declared that she had the perfect athlete's physique – 'decent height, solid bone structure'. She was just about to graze five foot nine when she stopped growing.

'You need to leave.' As she spoke, Linda's lips curled over her decaying teeth like a dog about to commence growling. 'I don't know you. My daughter died years ago.'

'Please.' Beth took a step forwards. If she wanted to, she could easily knock the fragile woman aside and force her way into the home. But she sought an invite, was that too much to ask for? 'Mum, I'm not the monster you think I am. That day with Caleb, it wasn't my fault. You must understand that. I was just a kid and—'

'Don't make me call the police.'

The threat felt as sharp as a slap across the face. Beth leant back, smarting. Her mother loathed the police, felt that they were always interfering in her business whenever they scooped her up off the street or threatened to send social services round her house.

'Good-for-nothing pigs,' she'd seethe and then spit on the ground. It was a sentiment she'd passed down to her boys – one that was shared widely around the estate. No one respected the authorities, they were the enemy and only called in truly exceptional circumstances.

Beth couldn't speak. Was her mother really that desperate to send her away?

When she'd crashed against the porch beneath the force of her brother's fist, Beth remembered wondering where her mother was. She tried to call out for her, but her breath was being kicked out of her lungs, taking away her ability not just to speak, but even to scream. Hot tears had cut a path down her cheeks as she waited for the beating to be over, for the pain to end. Linda Renton failed to materialise that day. Had she watched her sons pummel her daughter from behind her curtains as the neighbours had? Did she even care about what had been happening?

'I'm your *daughter*,' Beth's voice was growing hoarse as her throat became clogged with emotion. 'But you never acted like a mother to me. Not once.'

'Don't you come here and say to me—'

'Someone wants to hurt me. Someone wants revenge for what happened that summer. I guess . . .' Beth shrugged and gripped the bridge of her nose, eyes squeezing shut in frustration. 'Fuck, I don't know. I suppose I wanted to see you one last time. Wanted to see my *mum*. But you were never there for me, never came to see me. Why should I expect you to give a shit now?'

She was walking. Back towards her car, back towards the glow of the street lights. Beth slammed the gate open, the slap of wood cracking filling the night. She strode with purpose, shoulders square, chin high. This time, she would leave her childhood home with dignity, with poise. This time, there would be no blood, no broken bones.

As she climbed into her car, she heard the screech of her mother's voice scratching across the night air like a wounded banshee.

'Ruby Renton is *dead*. You hear me – *dead!*'

Beth gunned the engine and sped off, tyres squealing. She didn't look back.

Thirty-Eight

'Beth . . . Belmont.' Ruby uneasily read the name typed on the slip of paper she had been given.

'Has a nice ring to it, doesn't it?' Glenda asked, her face lit up by a bright smile. 'I think keeping the alliteration will help you adapt to it.'

Ruby leant forward, offering the paper back to the woman in the chair. Once it had left her fingertips, she shrugged and looked down at her feet – at shoes kept pristine by a lifetime of wear inside, never being given the chance to get covered in mud and leaves, to get stained green by wet grass. Outside was a world Ruby no longer got to explore. The main yard was all concrete, housed within the centre of the complex like a cement heart. The only flashes of emerald in there came from the hardiest of weeds which had sprouted up between the gaps in the slabs. But there were fields, many of them, which bordered the building in which she was now sitting. They were filled with trees and farmers' fences and were ripe for exploring. Only Ruby was no longer free. She kicked against the base of the sofa in agitation.

'You don't like your new name?' Glenda smoothed out the piece of paper on which Ruby's new identity, new life, was written. 'I think it's really rather a lovely name.'

'But I'm Ruby.' She sounded so obstinate, so much younger than she felt. Her thirteenth birthday had come and gone the previous month, marked only by a cupcake from Glenda. The jubilant pink frosting and solitary candle had been more than Ruby could bear. She'd forsaken the gift and spent the night crying into her pillow. The trial soon followed her arrival into her teenage years, taking just three weeks for a verdict to be reached. Ruby was to remain in detention centres such as this one until she was eighteen, then she would be set free. With conditions.

'Like the judge said,' Glenda raised a hand to readjust her glasses, 'it is no longer safe for you to be known as Ruby Renton. The whole world knows that name.'

'I'll be eighteen when I get out. People will have forgotten by then.'

'That's too big a gamble. If you're to have any chance of getting past all this, of moving on, you need to change your name.'

'And the others?' Ruby rubbed her knuckles against the base of her nose. Annie, Ollie, Vikki, Jacob and Kate – how would she find them once they were all finally released if they too had been given new names?

'You have all been assigned new identities and given the same sentence.'

'The . . .' Ruby swallowed, 'the *same* sentence?'

Glenda released a strained sigh. 'Believe me, Ruby, I pushed for leniency for your case. But you've all been tried as minors and deemed to share,' her head tilted to the left, creases deepening in the corners of her eyes, 'the guilt. The judge passed the same sentence on you all.'

'So they have new names too?'

Glenda nodded.

'But I'm Ruby.' She was tugging at the sleeves of her sweatshirt, pulling them across her slim wrists. Her clothes were new, since she'd outgrown the ones she had brought with her. But these new garments weren't chosen for her, they were plucked out of the charitable donations collection. The green sweater she was wearing was several sizes too big; same went for the jeans hanging off her frame. She kept growing taller, just like the weeds in the yard.

'You just need time to adjust. And it is a big adjustment,' Glenda admitted softly. 'But soon enough you'll feel more like Beth than Ruby, I know it.'

'I don't even like the name Beth!'

Being Ruby Renton was all she'd ever known. It was the name written on all of her schoolbooks, noted in felt tip inside her school uniform. It was the name her mother had chosen for her.

'Because you were a little gem,' Linda had recalled in a rare moment of tenderness.

What would Beth be? That name didn't belong to a precious stone. And it had been selected by a stranger, someone who didn't know her at all.

Beth. Beth Belmont. Already she hated it.

'We couldn't have hoped for a better outcome at the trial,' Glenda was trying to placate her. Her voice remained level, like a gentle stream. 'Changing your name means you get to leave places like this one day, you get to go back out into the real world and have a second chance at life.'

'Five years.' Ruby's head dropped as her chin met her chest. 'I won't be eighteen for another five years.'

'Try not to think about the time. Think about things on a smaller scale, day to day.'

'Will I always be here?' Her room was so small, so barren of any sort of identity. She wasn't permitted to put up any posters or pictures, no one was. Ruby spent her days drifting between the canteen, the common room and the yard. The faces at the tables changed as people left, their sentences less severe than her own. Ruby became a loner, letting the isolation of her room follow her around the facility. She didn't need friends. She'd had friends once and it had ruined her life. Now she didn't even get to keep her name. It was as if her old life simply ceased to exist.

'At this facility?' Glenda tapped her clipboard and frowned thoughtfully. 'At this point, I can't be sure.'

Ruby felt her cheeks beginning to burn. 'Then when will you be sure?' The reality of being a prisoner was setting in, filling her body with a septic-like poison. Five years. Half a decade. Ruby wanted to howl at the epic scale of it. 'This is my life, Glenda, and I'm spending it trapped inside like I'm some sort of . . . of *rat*!'

The facility was her cage, the yard her running wheel.

'Like I said, you were tried as a minor.' Still Glenda's anger didn't flare. She rested her hands in a steeple on top of her clipboard as she addressed her young charge. 'You were deemed of sound enough mind to understand the implications of your crime. As such, rehabilitation was seen as the most appropriate outcome for you. I know it doesn't seem like it yet, but this is the best-case scenario you could have. In time, you'll come to see that. One day you are getting out of here, that I can promise you, and you'll get to live a life as Beth Belmont.'

'But I'm Ruby.'

'No,' Glenda gently corrected her. 'As of a week ago, you're officially Beth Belmont. Time to start getting used to your new name.'

Thirty-Nine

The trailers had concluded and the lights were dimming, taking the theatre from twilight to dead of night. Beth peered through the porthole in the projection room and noticed all the vacant seats. It was no surprise that the theatre was empty, given that it was an eighteen-rated movie being shown at three in the afternoon. She was on an early shift. Beth was thankful for her two o'clock start since she'd failed to sleep at all the previous night. After driving home, she'd sat at the kitchen table drinking coffee and staring dead-eyed at the space around her.

Everywhere felt so empty. With Josh gone, she realised how huge his presence in the house had been, how just hearing his footsteps creaking around upstairs brought great comfort to her. Now the only thing that creaked were the pipes in the walls.

Colin had briefly enquired if she was all right as she strode into work, still in the crumpled uniform she'd inhabited for almost eighteen hours straight.

'Yes,' she told him curtly, 'I'm fine. Just fine.'

Did he see the exhaustion etched on her face? The shadow of despair hanging beneath her eyes? If he did, he didn't mention it, stepping aside and assuring her that he was there if she needed anything.

'All right, as long as you're okay in yourself.'

Yourself.

She wanted to spin round and laugh at him. But he was just being kind, wasn't he? Her senses were so sluggish, her mind so raw, that her nightmares were starting to spill over into her waking moments. Already since walking into work, she'd spaced out several times. One moment she was in the foyer, then suddenly in the corridor, as though she were sleepwalking around the place.

The film can within the projection wheel fluttered as it began to be fed through the system. Beth was watching the screen, waiting on the opening credits since she had twenty minutes to kill before she was due to prepare the next theatre. Afternoon shifts were always slow. All the seats in the theatre were empty, but still the movie had to play, even with no audience.

Her eyelids drooped. Then closed. An explosion on the screen snapped her back into the moment. Beth blinked, briefly stunned.

Beneath her, in the darkness, something stirred. Beth looked down and saw a pale figure moving down the aisle. She watched them with vague interest until she noticed their gait, the slump in their step. They were limping, moving like someone in great pain.

'Dammit,' she scrambled away from her porthole. It was her duty to check, to alert management if she spotted someone in the theatre who needed medical assistance.

The corridor smelt of warm popcorn as she hurried towards the main theatre doors, pushing through them and entering just as the screen lit up with the scene of a brutal murder. Beth glanced down the aisle. In the shadows, a figure still hobbled, making their way up to the back row. Why were they even in there? She thought this screening was empty.

'Hey,' Beth advanced up the first step and froze. She heard the gentle smack of her foot connecting with something wet. At first, she thought it must have come from the screen. The theatre would have been thoroughly cleaned before this new screening, so any spillages of Coke would have been mopped up. 'What the . . .' By the light of the screen behind her, she could see inky footprints threading up the steeped aisle. Footprints made from something dark and wet, glistening in the dim light.

'Hey,' raising her voice to be heard over the ominous music of the movie, Beth kept advancing upwards. The figure now atop the steps had their back to her. 'Hey, are you okay, is your drink leaking or—'

When she was just several rows away from them, they stopped. Beth stared at their back, could hear the harsh gasps of her own nervous breaths. 'Look, are you—'

Screaming. It bounced off the walls, flew at Beth like poisoned darts. It wasn't coming from the screen, it was coming from the back of the theatre. Cupping her hands to her ears, she kept looking at the shadowy figure's back. The screaming grew louder and Beth felt tears gliding down her cheeks. She reached for the back of a nearby chair to steady herself and missed, hand slicing through open air.

Then she was falling, dropping through the air until her back connected with the edge of the steps and her head slammed hard against the ground.

Cold. I'm always so fucking cold. Like there isn't enough flesh on my bones any more. People are walking around in shorts and crop tops and I'm in heavy jeans and a thick hoody. And I'm still shivering.

'You should see a doctor for that chill,' Mrs Norris had once shouted as I passed her on the stairs. I'd kept walking, head down. Nosy old crow. I'd seen doctors. Many of them. And while my Crohn's gnawed on my organs, refused to be subdued

by all the pills shoved into my system, I was going to feel the fucking cold. But I wasn't about to stand around and inform her of my medical history.

'Physically there's nothing wrong with you,' Roger had told me. He'd hung on that first word . . . physically. I knew what he meant. I'd been telling him how cold I was, how my stomach felt like I'd swallowed a bag of nails that were now digging into my guts, piercing my soft internal flesh. There was something wrong with me. Stress. Guilt. Fear. They were a lethal cocktail in my system, a slow-burn poison. And Roger would just shrug as though I were complaining about a cold. Maybe if he'd listened, if help had arrived sooner, I wouldn't be wasting away.

Time. It's always working against me. I just need to stay stronger a little longer. Things are going to change, I know they are. I'm just so sick of the cold.

'Beth . . . Beth, are you okay?'

It was bright, so terribly bright. Beth's eyes grudgingly opened and she winced at the brilliance shining down on her, certain she was going to go blind from the dazzling white.

'Beth . . . can you hear me?'

'C-Colin?' she croaked the name the voice seemed to belong to.

'Yes, Beth, it's me.' He moved closer, blocking out some of the light, and Beth began to realise where she was. The smell of popcorn, the cool of air-conditioning. She was in the cinema, in a theatre. Only—

'Where?' She shot up, felt the blood rush to her head, making her dizzy. 'Where is he?'

'Whoa, now, take it easy,' Colin's hands were on her shoulders, keeping her sitting on the steps. 'You must have fainted in here. Amy found you when she came in to clean up. Paramedics are on the way to give you a once-over and—'

'I *fainted*? No.' Beth looked down at her hands with distrust, at her creased uniform. She was in the aisle, curled up like a child. There were no bloody footprints and the film had finished. Now the house lights were up and on full, leaving no darkened corner for someone to hide in. 'I was . . .' She tentatively touched the step she was on, 'There was . . .' Her back throbbed and she felt like someone had placed an ice pick behind each of her eyes.

'I know you've been under a lot of pressure lately.' Colin gently eased his hands off her shoulders. He looked scared but also concerned. 'I think you should take some time off, rest up, get well.'

'But I'm not—' Beth looked past him, up into the higher regions of the theatre. Caleb wasn't there. Of course he wasn't. He was buried in Stirchley Cemetery, not hanging around a movie theatre. Was she going mad? Is this what it felt like to go crazy – to start seeing things that weren't even there?

'The paramedics will be here soon and they'll check you out, okay?'

'Colin, I'm . . . I'm sorry,' she struggled to swallow, her throat felt like it was filled with tar.

'Don't apologise.' His hand found her shoulder again. 'You gave us a real scare there, Beth. Do you need me to call someone? Josh? Can he come and pick you up?'

'Um, no.' She was shaking her head and trying not to focus on the reality that there was no one she could call, no one who would come and pick her up. Even her own mother would rather think her dead than give her a second shot at life. 'I'll . . . I'll be fine.' Reaching out, she gripped a nearby seat and used it to haul herself up onto her feet.

'Whoa, Beth, take it easy,' Colin handled her carefully, as though she were a bomb which might explode at any moment. 'At least let's wait and see what the paramedics say, all right?'

'It was just a faint.' Now standing, Beth could brush a hand across her forehead and move it around to feel the sticky cluster of blood gathering at the base of her neck. Had she been passed out for the entire movie? Why was she struggling so much to keep track of time? 'I'm feeling much better now. Really.'

It was a lie, but a necessary one. As they waited for the arrival of the paramedics, Beth kept peering up into the top corner, fearing what she'd seen.

My brother. I'm not supposed to think about him. What was he labelled as? A trigger? Was that it?

'Don't think about him,' Roger would urge me. 'Focus on something else. Anything else.'

But how are you supposed to forget a person? Someone who was living, breathing? Someone who you raced down the stairs with on Christmas mornings to see if Santa had been. And my brother . . . he wasn't like other brothers. He was special. Unique. And now he's—

Rain. It patters loud and hard against my window, breaking through my thoughts. That's the last thing I need. Today, I was meant to be heading out, I was going to go and see her and—

Thrusting my legs out of bed, I let my bare feet connect with the cold floor, braced for the shiver that shoots up my shins and reaches to ice my spine. No excuses. I'm going. Today. I'm not going to lie in bed and stare up at the spreading stain whilst wallowing in the past. I'm going to shower, get dressed and get the hell out of my stuffy little flat. Roger would be proud. He was always telling me to go out and live my life, and, well, here I am doing just that.

Hair still damp, I shrink beneath the flimsy hood of my coat and wait for my bus. Rain bounces atop the shelter. Where the road is worn down, it puddles, as dark as the sky overhead. For a moment it feels as though the world has forgotten that it's summer and this pleases me. I've never cared for sunlight, for the pressure those long, heady summer days bring.

'Get out of the house,' my dad would order when the sun shone. 'Get out and get some fresh air.' To anyone listening, it would have sounded like a reasonable request, well-intentioned even. But I knew the truth. He wanted me and my brother out of sight, and the feeling was mutual.

Thankfully, I get to spend my bus ride alone. I lean my head against the window and watch the cars and streets stretch by, their image mottled by the rain gathered on the glass. As we reach my stop, the sun begins to shine, as though fate is urging me on with my quest, approving of today's task.

Backpack resting neatly on my shoulders, I depart, even managing to smile at the driver, but she doesn't notice. She looks right through me as though I'm not even there. The old me would be bothered by that, would dwell on it. But the new me, the me with purpose, can depart the bus with only a parting 'fuck you' thrown her way. I'm really growing.

The world bakes as I walk the final part of this journey. I weave between cars, chin to my chest, hair draped over my ears, covering most of my face. I'm beside a Nissan Juke, black and shiny like a beetle, when I lift my gaze, expecting to see the glass entrance doors, the darkened, cooled interior of the foyer beyond. Only my usual view is obscured. I stop, feet locking together, one hand slapping loudly against the boot of the Juke, its metal shell hot beneath my palm.

An ambulance. I can feel the blood rushing to my head, throbbing behind my temple. That neon strip. Those blue lights. There's pressure against my chest, an invisible hand pressing down, trying to turn my heart, my lungs, to pulp. I swallow, take a shaky breath. My hand, slick with sweat, slides free of the car, and I stumble forward but manage not to fall.

'Focus on something else.'

I do as Roger always willed and stare at the car parked opposite the Juke, a white Range Rover far too cumbersome for such a tight space. I read the letters and numbers on its glossy plate. Then I read them again. As my breath begins to even out, I look back at the ambulance. From here, I can't make out what's happening behind it, where the paramedics are. My mind goes straight to her, knowing that the ambulance could be for anyone. But a coldness creeps across my heart, telling me that of course it's for her, it has to be. She's hurt herself. She's hurt herself and it's all my fault.

I want to surge forwards, to crash against the small crowd forming around the entrance and fight my way to her, before it's too late. I'd tell her . . .

This gives me pause. What would I tell her? That I'm sorry. No, because that would be wrong. Because I'm not sorry. The names, the note. It's necessary, it's needed. My jaw clenches. I'd tell her to hold on because we're not done yet. She's not done yet.

'Oh my god, what do you think's going on?' Three teenage girls sidle past me, hair poker-straight, lips glossed varying shades of pink.

'An ambulance,' another chimes, 'shit, do you think we'll miss our showing?'

I'm frowning at them as they walk by, wondering if I was ever that self-absorbed? I catch a glimpse of my reflection in the Juke I'm still standing beside, a ghost beneath a flimsy coat. If I went to the ambulance, if I found her on a gurney, what then? Would she look at me and see a ghost too?

More people pass by, gravitating towards the ambulance like it's some macabre spectacle. I've lingered too long. I can't be within a crowd. But what if she has hurt herself? What if—

I read the licence plate on the Range Rover again. Focus. I need to focus. She's fine. She has to be fine. The ambulance is just an inconvenience, a way to test me.

'Life isn't going to be easy,' Roger had warned. I'd almost choked on my laughter.

'When has it ever been?' I asked him. He didn't have an answer to that.

I watch the ambulance leave, running my list of names over in my mind anew. Maybe I'll follow it to the hospital. Because if my fears are correct, it is her. Which means she'll be alone there at some point, on a bed, hooked up to an IV, unable to move. And anyone can walk into a hospital. Even me.

Forty

The sky was amber when the taxi pulled up outside her house. Beth had spent three hours at the hospital whilst her blood was taken, her BP monitored and her heart rate checked. Finally, she was deemed fit enough to go home but not permitted to drive. Her little car was still parked up by the cinema.

'Thanks.' She shoved a crisp ten-pound note into the driver's hand and walked up her driveway, listening to the shifting gravel underfoot. The windows of the house shone blood red as they reflected the setting sun. Beth didn't pause to admire the beauty of the evening. She pushed her key into the lock and twisted. Hinges winced as she opened her front door and stepped inside.

Silence.

It was the only thing that greeted her. Beth slammed the front door shut, letting its plastic rattle provide a brief respite from the quiet. Then the silence returned, as thick and clotting as mist. There was no creak of a floorboard upstairs, no gentle hum of voices coming from the television.

'Dammit.' Beth began shedding her uniform as she climbed the stairs, keen to rid herself of its itchy nylon touch. Leaving her shirt and trousers in her wake, she made for the bathroom. Turning on the shower, the hot water hissed, and it didn't take long for steam to fill the small space, misting up the mirror.

Beneath the shower, there was noise. And warmth. Beth gladly absorbed both as the hot water cascaded down upon her. Dragging her hands through her hair, she traced the line of her scalp, felt the bumps along her skull. The last few days had felt like an eternity. Now at least some of her pain was being washed away, flowing down her legs and then gathering in a whirlpool at the plughole. Beth looked down, blinking against the droplets in her eyelashes, and watched with interest as soapy water spun at her feet and then disappeared.

She stayed in the shower until her skin was pink, then she stretched to switch off the water and allowed the silence to return. It hung around her as she enveloped herself in a large towel.

Josh.

The towel held his smell like a signature. Beth grabbed a corner and pressed it against her face, her nose, breathing him in. He was Lynx and oil, sweat and cedar wood. And here, in this bundle of fabric, he somehow lingered. Beth kept inhaling, like an addict with glue. But already the scent was losing its potency, overridden by the smell of her own damp skin and strawberry shower gel.

'You left me,' she muttered to the towel before she let it fall to the floor. 'Why did you leave me?'

Because everybody leaves. Because you're a monster.

Beth hurried out of the bathroom towards the bedroom, the steam and her own savage thoughts following her. It was early evening and she was supposed to be resting. She plucked her Green Day T-shirt out from beneath her pillow and then, with a grunt, tossed it towards the far corner of the room.

Skin still flushed, she paced the room, kept glancing at the bed, at the crispness of the sheets, mocking her with how undisturbed they were.

'Argh,' she stormed over to the wardrobe and flung open the doors. The landscape of clothes had changed. Gone were Josh's Superdry T-shirts and dark pairs of jeans. Gone were his trio of shirts and plethora of polo tops. Dark gaps loomed where his garments had hung, like the shadowy gaps in her mother's sneer. It wasn't natural, wasn't right. The wardrobe should still have been packed to capacity. Beth reached in for some joggers and a T-shirt, quickly slipping them on over her underwear. Twice she bounced on the spot, feeling the restless energy gathering in her limbs. 'You said you loved me,' she told the gaps. 'You said you'd always be there for me.'

Lies.

So much of her life was built on lies, right down to the very name she went by.

'Ruby Renton isn't dead!' Beth was shouting the words as she surged towards her bed and ripped the duvet from it. And she didn't stop there. She tore off the sheets, the pillows, tossing them all onto the floor. 'I'm not dead, I'm not dead!'

The silence. She knew she had to fill it.

Beth turned back and threw her clothes out of the wardrobe, knocking over the vintage full-length mirror she'd found with Josh at a car boot sale the previous summer.

'It looks old,' he'd remarked as he ran a rough hand down its chipped white exterior.

'It's shabby chic, it's supposed to look old,' Beth explained as she eagerly handed the store attendant the fifteen pounds.

'I suppose you want me to carry this back to the car then?' Josh was trying to sound annoyed but failing. He loved to be helpful, useful. His large hands were happiest when being put to work.

'If you don't mind.' Beth had pushed herself onto her tiptoes to kiss his cheek, feeling the roughness of his stubble beneath her lips. The sun was shining, the sky was clear and blue and Beth felt free, felt like her life was finally starting to become her own.

The mirror didn't break as it met the floor. Beth wasn't sure whether to be annoyed or relieved.

She moved on from the bedroom, her footsteps bouncing off the walls as she raced down the stairs. The kitchen was next. As soon as she passed through the door, Beth reached for the little bistro set of table and chairs and sent them scattering across the tiled floor. How many times had she sat with Josh at that table and eaten a meal, shared a joke? It would surely be in the hundreds. Hands bunching into fists, she kicked at the cupboard doors until the wood began to indent with her imprint.

'You're supposed to love me,' she yelled at the space around her as she unclenched her hands to grab the micro-wave, not even bothering to disconnect it from the wall. Beth threw it at the floor and it connected with the tiles with a crunch of broken glass and plastic. 'Why would you hurt me?' she demanded as she flung the plastic drainer off the sink before chucking a carton of eggs at the far wall. She paused to hear the soft cracking of shells.

Beth was twelve again, looking eagerly up the path at her brothers, at the boys who had always provided the bookends of her safety. Between them and Ollie, Beth had never had to know fear, not truly. Each time her mother lashed out, drunk and unpredictable, either her brothers or her friends would be there to pick up the pieces, to remind her that she was loved, that she was special.

On the taxi ride from the police station over to her estate, she'd thought about what was going to happen, of the promises her brothers would make her.

'We'll keep you safe, Ruby. Everything is going to be okay.'

And maybe Ollie would be there waiting for her too. Because he was going to fix everything; he always did. He had probably already explained to the police that what had happened in the woods was just a terrible accident. Besides, how could they be prosecuted, they were just children, after all?

Beth had been giddy at the sight of her brothers waiting on the porch, certain they were there to protect her. But the darkness in their eyes had shone as black as coal.

'You failed me.' Beth had opened one of the upper cupboards in her kitchen, and mugs and plates were now raining down, shattering on the tiles in a waterfall of sound. 'You were supposed to be there.' A glass smashed. 'You were supposed to care.' A mug connected with the wall and broke into six pieces.

Silence. It followed every outburst.

'No.' Beth felt her knees beginning to tremble, the quake slowly extending throughout her body. She was clutching a Manchester United mug: Josh's favourite. Another reminder he'd neglected to take with him when he left. 'No,' she screamed out the last of her vitriol and watched the mug fly from her gasp and shatter upon the tiles in a medley of red and white ceramic. 'No.' There was nothing left in her. With her back to the cupboard, Beth slid down and settled on the floor amongst the debris.

I wanted to follow you to the hospital. Truly I did. I intended to. But exhaustion found me first. I woke up on a park bench, icy and alone. I'd been walking to see you, I swear. We were about to meet. Fuck my wasted body. And all my damn scars.

I was in his office when I opened up my wrists – Roger's. While he left to grab some tissues to clean himself up, I grabbed the letter opener on his desk. It had a heavy wooden handle and a sharp silver blade. But I'd still had to really dig deep, biting through my tongue as I tried to deal with the pain. When he'd returned, there was blood everywhere and I was feeling so very cold and so, so tired. He caught me as I dropped, gazed down at me as he pleaded for my silence, begged me not to say anything about our 'special relationship'.

In the hospital, they bandaged me up, watched me for twenty-four hours and then sent me back. Back to him. There was no freedom to be found. Not living this lie. I was his, held captive by my past. But the names – when I eventually forced them from him later, I knew the tide was turning. Again and again, I had searched the drawers in his desk, filing cabinet, even gained access to his computer. But I'd found nothing. Roger was smart; he kept important information under lock and key. A man with as many secrets as he has learns to be smart like that.

But I was smarter. I had to get the names, had to break free, and to do that I asked myself one simple question – how far was I willing to go? And just like that I had a plan.

She sat there as the light outside dimmed. She watched with dead eyes as the street lights came on, as cars curved their way round the bend at the far end of the cul-de-sac in which she lived. Still she didn't move. Her legs tingled and then became numb. Beth remained slumped amongst all the broken crockery, comforted by the scene of destruction. Now her house looked how it felt: dangerous and uninviting. Were the new locks she'd placed on the doors even enough to keep out the author of the list?

Feeling her head grow increasingly heavy, Beth realised that the locks' true purpose had been to keep something in. To stop Josh abandoning her. And they'd failed. Now she was alone with only shadows for company. The screams from the cinema rattled in her mind. Had she dreamt them? But the footprints on the floor . . .

Kneading her temple, she forced herself to think of something, anything, other than what had just happened at work.

'Do you love her?' Beth recalled asking Ollie long ago, keen to dig deeper into his feelings for Vikki. They kissed so often that they definitely *seemed* to be in love. Beth needed to know what love looked like. She was still invisible to Jacob, but that didn't mean he'd never love her, never see her that way, did it?

'Ah, Ruby,' he'd shaken his head in a wistful manner that made him seem so much older than she was, so much wiser. He took a long drag from the cigarette he was holding and let the smoke curl out into the night air. Leaning against a lamp post with his other hand shoved deep into his coat pocket, he was danger and delirium held together by a crooked smile and a cavalier attitude. 'Love is complicated, you know?'

But she didn't know. How could she? She was twelve. The only boy she'd ever kissed was Jim Rogers during a game of spin the bottle, and it had been a completely unsatisfying experience involving too much of his tongue and saliva. Yet when Ollie kissed Vikki, she saw a hunger there, something raw which made Beth feel an ache in the pit of her stomach. She wanted Jacob to kiss her like that, like he needed her.

'Would you do anything for her?'

At this, Ollie had released a dry laugh. They were alone on the street corner, waiting for the others to show up, but to Beth they could have been the last two people in the entire world. She prayed that no one else would arrive, that they could stay locked in this temporary bubble of solitude forever. Because this was her favourite Ollie, the one who lowered his walls, who treated her kindly, who made her feel seen, not stupid, for all her questions.

'Anything?' Ollie cocked his head in her direction and lifted the right side of his mouth, something he always did when he was amused. 'Most things, maybe. But *anything* . . . that's a hell of a commitment.'

'But you love her.'

'Ruby.' With a sigh, he flicked the last of his cigarette down at the pavement and stubbed out its smouldering tip with his trainer. Whenever he said her name, he took the time to pronounce it completely, carefully. He didn't run all the letters together in a hasty blur like some people did. In Ollie's mouth, her name sounded as it should: like a precious gem. 'Don't get so hung up on love, okay? You've got your whole life to experience it. Don't sweat it yet. Like I said, it's complicated.'

'But that doesn't mean it can't happen, right? Like, maybe Jacob will . . . you know.' The cider she'd drunk down at the park with Annie earlier that afternoon had made her uncharacteristically bold.

'You're too young for all that shit.' The right side of Ollie's mouth remained raised and he held her in a gaze so intense it made her shiver. 'Don't rush away being young, Rubes. You only get one first time, try to remember that.'

Beth hadn't heard the approaching footsteps of the others. She'd been so utterly lost in the spell of him, in the wisdom in his words. Her brothers never spoke to her like he did, never *actually* listened.

'Gone.' In the darkness of her kitchen, Beth rubbed the heels of her hands against her eyes and felt the blood start to return to her extremities. With a laboured stretch, she managed to stand up, legs now tingling with renewed sensation. Carefully, to avoid all the broken mugs and plates, she picked a route towards the hall, letting the light of the moon and the street lamp filtering in through the window guide her. 'He's gone.'

In the hallway, she flicked on the light, momentarily blinding in its intensity. She was thinking of Ollie, of the boldest boy she'd ever known. At twelve, she thought he could accomplish anything – hell, in her eyes he could have become the prime minister. Instead, he'd ended up at the side of a river, drowned and alone. Beth tried to imagine his face swollen and bulbous, his eyes wide and pale as the light left him. Had the man been so very different from the boy? Did he grow up to be coy, introverted, having realised the cost of his boldness, his charisma?

Trevor Hoskins

Beth was thinking of the list, of his assumed identity, neatly inscribed just above her own. Had he been presented with those names? Had he wondered who Beth Belmont was?

'Ruby Renton isn't dead.' Beth was reaching for her handbag which had been abandoned on the stairs, along with her uniform. Once unzipped, she delved into its depths, searching for a slip of something white. As her fingers closed around it, Beth's stomach plummeted to her feet.

The list.

Beth stared at it in the garish light, at the now curled corners and neat penmanship. Someone had written it, had left it in the woods for her to find. Someone who had intended to hurt her, the same someone who had probably hurt Vikki and then Ollie. Had Kate and Jacob

266

received such lists? Were their lives like hers, small and in the dark? Thinking of Jacob made her heart flutter, even after all these years. If he saw her now, what would he think? Because to him she wouldn't be Beth.

'I'm Ruby fucking Renton.' Beth shoved the list into the pocket in her joggers and stooped down to grab at her trainers which were beside the front door. She was no longer frightened, she was furious.

Forty-One

Beth. Belmont. Beth Belmont. No matter how many times Ruby rolled the name around her mouth, it refused to fit. She had a name; one which she'd had thirteen years to get used to.

'You're still you.' Glenda crossed her legs, letting the hem of her long brown skirt briefly rise. Behind the thick lenses of her glasses, her eyes were tinged with sadness as she sensed the uncertainty within the young girl across from her on the sofa. 'A name is just a name.'

Ruby squirmed. Her jeans were hanging too low on her hips, the sleeves of her jumper swaddling her wrists in a swathe of excess fabric. But now it wasn't just her clothes that were a poor fit.

'Can I ever go back?' She asked the question which had come to her shortly after lights out the previous night. It had crept up close in the darkness and whispered in her ear. With her back firmly pressed against the stiffness of her mattress, Ruby thought of home, of the cramped terrace she shared with her mother and brothers. Would she ever see the place again? Would she ever get to smile to old Mrs Simpson three doors down who loved to stand in her front garden pretending to prune roses that were actually weeds?

'Your name is just too infamous now,' Glenda said with a shake of her head. The mass of her bulbous chin shifted for a moment and then settled like a snood against her neck. 'Moving forwards, you have to be Beth Belmont. For your own safety.'

'I meant, can I ever go back home?'

What had become of her bedroom that was little more than a broom cupboard? Had her mother taken down all of her posters that she'd once so carefully stuck to the wall with Blu-Tack? Had her brothers trashed the small single bed as their restless anger travelled through the house? Ruby remembered the way a spring had broken loose just at the base of her back, how if she slept in the wrong position it would needle her all through the night. Back then, she hated the discomfort of it all, now she longed for the metallic pressure on her spine, the reassurance that whilst not perfect, it was still home.

Glenda's eyebrows dropped to form a level line and the sigh which rattled from her lips gave Ruby her answer. 'I'm afraid there is no going back. Not to your old name, nor to your old home.'

'But . . .' Ruby picked at the ends of her nails, wondering how her home could go on existing without her in it. Was her mum drinking more to compensate for the loss? Or was she relieved, glad even, to be rid of her only daughter?

'I know that it's an awful lot to process and it's only natural to want to go home. But, Ruby,' Glenda paused to clear her throat and adjust her glasses. 'But, *Beth*,' she leant heavily on the new moniker, 'it is vital to your future that you never go back. It just isn't safe. Better you leave here at eighteen ready to start a whole new life.'

Ruby used to wonder who she'd be at eighteen. Would she be even taller? Would her hips sway when she walked like they did with the older girls at school? Would she have a boyfriend, be in college, maybe even making plans to attend university? She'd be the first person in her family to do so. Eighteen used to feel like an adventure, a song she'd yet to learn the words to but instinctively knew she'd end up loving.

But now eighteen was no longer a mystery. Ruby would be Beth Belmont, clad in clothes that weren't her own, leaving an institution to enter a world in which she had no one – no friends, no family, nothing. The isolation felt both claustrophobic and overwhelmingly vast in its uncertainty.

'Like I've said, we just focus on the now,' Glenda ploughed on, offering Ruby a verbal life raft to cling to as she floundered in the depths of the unknown. 'We're hoping to set you up with a tutor over the coming months to help begin to prepare you for your GCSEs. You'll still get your education, Beth, a chance at a decent future.'

'I hadn't even decided.' Ruby kept picking away at her nails.

'On what?'

'On who I wanted to be. The others, they all kind of knew. Ollie was going to be a prince of thieves and Annie, well, she was all about going to university. Will she still go?' She levelled the question at Glenda, who pressed her back more firmly against the back of her chair, straightening in an almost regal way.

'Try not to think about your friends, about your past connections. It will only serve to hold you back over the coming years.'

'I know but—'

'Focus on your dreams. On what you want from life. Actually,' Glenda tapped her clipboard with a podgy finger, 'that was next on my agenda for us to discuss today.'

'What was?'

'Your next steps.' The older woman was smiling, her plump cheeks lifting and growing rosy.

'My next steps?' Ruby almost baulked at the suggestion. For her there were no 'next steps', just five long years locked up from the outside world.

Glenda tapped her clipboard more fervently, the sound travelling between them. 'Yes. Your next steps. This was only ever meant to be a temporary solution for you here, Beth. Now that you've been sentenced, you'll be able to move to a more long-term facility, somewhere slightly more . . . welcoming.'

'So I'm leaving?' Ruby shuddered at the prospect. Going somewhere new would either be a great thing or a terrible one. And she already knew that wherever she went she wasn't about to find her friends there, just more strange faces.

'Your transfer is scheduled for the end of this week. Think of it as a new adventure.'

'And you?' Ruby looked up through heavy lids at the one constant in her life. 'Will you be coming?'

'Yes, of course. I'm your counsellor, I'll always be here to support you.'

'Promise?' The plea was more befitting of someone who was three rather than thirteen, but Ruby needed to hear the answer, needed to know that she wasn't about to be abandoned by anyone else.

Glenda's smile remained, infused with kindness. 'I promise.'

Forty-Two

Darkness. It gathered around Beth as though she were running through a swarm of bats. She could almost imagine that the night air whipping against her cheeks was beating wings, drawing too close to her skin.

The safety of the lights on her street was behind her. She'd been running for just over five minutes and was about to enter the woods. Already she could hear the nightly serenade of the owls and foxes calling out from the shadows.

When Beth passed through the treeline, she slowed her pace, lifted her feet with care, for fear of connecting with a raised root and crashing down to the leafy ground. But still she ran. Hands pumping at her sides, she swerved along the path, navigating by memory alone.

It was so dark. Though the moon was shining, its silver glow couldn't find the floor of the woods, couldn't light up the leaves crackling underfoot.

Woodsmoke lingered on the breeze. Beth imagined teen-agers huddling around campfires and telling ghost stories until their bravado cracked and they hurried home to warm beds. She twisted her body against the curve in the path she knew was coming.

Wind whispered through the trees and Beth could almost hear the sound of long, jubilant laughter. She remembered riding the tyre swing, head thrown back in delight as the sun burned on her cheeks. Ollie would push her, always too hard, always keen to test the strength of the rope which marked the difference between this world and oblivion. Kicking out her legs, she'd beg him to push harder, higher. Around Ollie, she could be fearless, his own bravery infectious.

Something screamed. A fox? An owl? Beth could feel the adrenaline pumping around her system, sharpening her senses. The woodsmoke mixed with the scent of damp earth, of wet leaves and freshly turned soil, cut grass and sap – Beth could smell it all. Blinking, she realised her eyes had finally adjusted to the night and she staggered to a halt. She had reached her destination.

Around her, dark shadows swelled. Long tree branches stretched across the starlit sky like sinister fingers. Beth took several steps forwards, hands on hips, drinking in the night air, which cooled her burning lungs. It was here that she'd first seen it – the list. A slip of pure white against a world of mottled browns and greens. Spinning, she tried to cast her gaze in all directions. Beth strained to see if she'd been followed, but her vision was poor, the darkness too dense. Behind her lay a maze of shadows, each with the power to hide something . . . or someone.

'Well?' She raised her hands and her voice. 'I'm here. I'm fucking here! This is what you wanted, right? To scare me? To call me out? Well, here I am!' She was shouting into the void, spinning around to let her voice travel in all directions. 'I'm *here*. What the hell do you want with me? You wrote the damn list – at least face me! Who are you? Why do this?'

Her temple throbbed. When had she last slept? The world in her peripheral vision blurred, as though she were still spinning. 'Fuck,' she needled the bridge of her nose with the tips of her fingers, 'come on.'

She dropped her hands and waited for screams to swell around her, for ethereal shadows to gather at her feet, for limping spectres to scuttle just out of view. But she was alone. Only the surrounding leaves whispered back at her in response.

The wind whistled past her, brushing away some of her fatigue, allowing her anger to refuel.

'Ollie, Vikki – did you hurt them? Did you leave little notes for them too? What about the others?' Tears splashed against her cheeks, which Beth didn't bother to wipe away. She let them linger upon her face, cooling in the night air. 'Jacob, Kate, we all did our time. We paid for what we did in more ways than you'll ever know! You need to leave us the fuck alone!' Her anger was a force. It clenched her hands into fists and made her heartbeat quicken. 'You know who I am!' she was almost screaming, felt her vocal cords flame. 'You know that I'm Ruby Renton. So what? Who the fuck are *you*?'

Beth wanted someone to rise to her challenge, to emerge from the shadows holding their own hands up. Who did she expect to find? Caleb's parents? His sister? Her own mother? Who would want to push the remaining members of the Stirchley Six to the point of hysteria?

'Face me!' Beth demanded of the night. '*Face me!*' She needed to meet their judgement head-on, needed to feel their hateful stare on her skin. Ruby, the girl cocooned in a woman's body, just wanted a chance to defend herself.

It was an accident.

A stupid game.

I'm sorry.

All this she'd said before – in court and to Glenda. But they were just words and they held so much less weight than actions. Nothing she could do or say could bring Caleb Walters back, could turn her from a monster back into a girl.

'Please.' Beth's resolve weakened with each passing minute. Slowly, her body sagged towards the ground until her knees connected with the dirt of the path. She crouched in the middle of it as though praying at some darkened altar. She listened to the fluttering leaves, to the shrill cry of a tawny owl . . . and she waited.

Hours passed as she held on for the crunch of leaves underfoot. No one came. Above her, the sky turned from black to navy to grey. Soon the sun would be up. Beth wiped her hand across her eyes, blinking away any lingering tears, and then staggered to her feet, bending to brush the dirt from her joggers.

'You should have come,' she told the emptiness around her, 'you should have faced me.'

'Rebecca Terry.'

He was so matter-of-fact in his delivery, leaning back in his chair to zip up his fly. 'It has a nice ring to it, don't you think?'

Rebecca Terry.

The name was a fucking insult. I was Kate. Kate Turnbald. Where was Ollie? Surely he wouldn't stand for this shit. Apparently we'd all received the same bullshit sentence, but there was no way my brother would accept it, no way he'd pretend to be anyone other than who he was. Or so I once thought.

What did Roger expect me to say? That I loved it, that it was nice, that I was thankful? I told him over and over that changing my name wouldn't change anything.

'I'm going to find them — my brother, the others,' I warned. Because this wasn't me. This wasn't us. We didn't hide from who we were. Ollie, he wouldn't stand for this new-name bullshit.

Once we were all eighteen and free, we'd be together again. I'd been so certain. And Roger had been so smug.

'This is the way it has to be, Kate. Moving forwards, you're Rebecca now.'

'No, no.' I remember shaking my head, being defiant. Feeling defiant. God, I had been so full of fire back then. And inch by inch Roger had taken it from me, had worn me down. When there was nothing left, I tried to find Ollie.

Ollie, my big, bold, older brother.

But he was gone. I found meek Trevor Hoskins, who was living this . . . this lie. Working a shit job in a shit town, driving a shit car. That wasn't my brother. I needed to shake him out of it, remind him of who he really was. So I left a list under the windscreen wipers of his car, just like I left one for Vik in her letter box. I wanted them to read it and break free of this fucking spell we're all under. I wanted them to wake up.

I was hiding behind it, my list. I see that now. But I couldn't face Ollie, Trevor, whoever the hell he considered himself to be, and be rejected, to look into the eyes of my brother and see a stranger staring back. He had to become Ollie before we could meet. And I thought he could do that. I thought that Vikki would find him, break the shell of his lie and slowly, one by one, reunite us. Repair what was broken. I was wrong.

I needed them. Vikki, Ollie. I needed my big brother to tell the world that this was all bullshit, that we weren't ashamed of who we were, that we weren't going to live these half lives any more. But they broke, both of them. Perhaps I should have approached them, let them know who I was, what the list was. I was being patient, waiting for them to realise the truth. Waiting for them to want me, the real me. To flames and water, I lost them. I waited too long.

But the people I found . . . they weren't Vikki – the tart with a heart who sucked my brother off outside the garage in town and almost *got caught* by the police. They weren't Ollie, *the hero* from my childhood. They were ghosts. Broken relics.

Ruby. She's different. I see that now. I should have gone to her first. Instead, like always, I defaulted to Vik and Ollie, as though the world still revolved around them, as though it never stopped.

Ollie's life . . . it killed me to see it. To see him. He wasn't the boy from my memories. Driving a piece-of-shit car, working nights, always alone. So, so alone. That wasn't my brother. I didn't follow him to the river. I hoped he was just running away, finally breaking free of the house of cards he was living in. I wanted him to be free.

But I saw Vik burn. I sat in a nearby park and breathed in the smoke on the air. I felt numb, knowing she'd gone. And, for a moment, lost. She was supposed to figure out the riddle of the list, come find us. Instead, she sent all my hopes up in flames. Maybe I should have seen it; the way she walked with her head bowed low. The way she moved with quick, nervous steps, flinching if someone so much as passed her by. She was ready to implode, I just provided the spark.

Ollie . . . he surprised me. When he didn't come back. That's when I knew it had to be you next. You were like me, shadowed by big brothers. You knew what it was to be pushed down. If anyone was going to want to break the chains of our new lives, it was you.

Rebecca Terry. That's who they want me to be.

I hate the name. Never use it. And Roger still called me Kate. Made me beg him for the privilege. He's as much a liar as the rest of us, as much of a monster. Some fucking counsellor he turned out to be. I hope he rots in hell.

But I believe in you. My third name on my list. You were so sweet, and so in awe of Ollie. So hopelessly in love with Jacob. I remember how close you were with Annie, the two of you in

277

some kind of club. But it didn't matter. Not around Ollie. With him, we were all part of something. We were whole.

Kate. Kate Turnbald. That's who I am. It's who I will always be. And together, Ruby, together we're going to reclaim our past, our lost lives. Together we'll move forwards. But first you need to wake up. Because I can't make the first step. I'm too sick, too weak. I'll even admit; too afraid. I can't do it alone. You need to come into the light and drag me with you, then we can suffer the slings and arrows together.

I need you to tell the press, the world. To give our lost lives a voice. We'll admit who we truly are. We can apologise anew. But we can be ourselves, don't you see the beauty in that? No more hiding. No more lying. Just us. Us against everyone else. The way it always used to be.

We were always stronger together. You need me just as much as I need you. Tell the truth. Let us be free. Don't let Vik and Ollie have died in vain. Don't make me find the final person on the list . . . don't make me look for Jacob.

Forty-Three

Dirt and sweat clung to Beth like soiled morning dew. She jogged the short distance home, lungs still burning, as birds began to chirp in the trees. When she rounded the corner of her street, the sun was up, but the world remained calm and still. It would be another hour before car engines roared to life and voices filled the air as her neighbours bid one another goodbye before leaving for work and school.

Her hands trembled as she forced her key into the front door and turned it, listening for the unclasping of the internal lock. Walking into the hallway, she sighed, letting the sound fall away from her. She was desperately tired. Every muscle was fraying and her T-shirt was damp, plastered to her back.

'Shit.' The shrill melody of china and glass scraping on tile greeted her as she nudged open the kitchen door, the room still in a state of wild disarray. 'Shit,' Beth repeated as she pressed the heel of her hand against her eyes and winced. So much had been destroyed – mugs and plates shattered beyond the point of repair. If Josh could see her now, what would he say?

Beth had to lean all her weight against the sink when she thought of him. Devoid of his laughter, the strength of his presence, the end terrace house was beginning to feel like the prison she'd once been held in as a teenager.

Four walls and a bed did not a home make. There needed to be warmth, love. Safety.

Her head snapped back in the direction of the hallway. The newly placed deadbolts, locked as she'd come inside. The chill of the night had followed her home, cooling the perspiration on her skin. She'd called out for them: the author of the list. Challenged them. But no one had come. She'd been alone.

Plucking her phone from the pocket of her joggers, Beth stared at the screen, her heart settling into an uneasy rhythm. She remained scalded by her visit to her mother, the memory so prickly it threatened to burst any last dregs of confidence or security she held inside. Someone had to still love her. She was worthy of forgiveness . . . wasn't she?

It was just after six a.m. Wherever Josh was, she knew he'd be getting up, settling into his regular routine of rising at dawn and showering, climbing into his van and setting off for work. Beth scrolled down the screen of her phone and found his number. How many times had she called it over the years? Hundreds? Thousands? And he always answered. Josh was more reliable than the tide. Pressing down on the green button, she pushed call. With each drawn-out ring, she anticipated what he might say when he picked up.

'Beth, what do you want?' He'd be hostile, but present. And that was the bridge she needed. If he answered and was willing to speak to her, she could start to cross over, to journey back to where they had once been.

'Josh, I need you,' she'd tell him softly.

I don't want to be alone.

Several long rings dragged out as Beth blinked sleepily at the screen. 'Come on,' she urged. Why wasn't he picking up? Was he still in the shower? 'Just *answer*,' she willed both Josh and the device. 'Just answer me.'

After the seventh ring, his answerphone kicked in.

'Hey, you've reached Josh. Clearly I'm busy right now, so just leave your name and I'll get back to you when I can.'

An automated female voice instructed Beth to begin recording her message. She pressed the red cancel button and slammed her phone down onto the kitchen counter.

'I'm busy right now.'

What was Josh doing? Was he still showering, lingering longer beneath the heated water since he'd left her, needing those extra minutes of contemplation each morning? Or was he with someone else, had Beth already been replaced in his life?

'Dammit.' Beth kicked at a nearby shard of plate and sent it bouncing across the cluttered floor. She wanted to phone Josh again. And again. She wanted to keep phoning him until his resolve cracked and he finally answered. But she was already in enough pain. Beth knew that each time he didn't answer, each time his answerphone clicked in, she'd die a little more. And there was already hardly anything of her left. She needed to preserve what remained of her strength.

As though in a dream, she drifted out of the kitchen and up the stairs, collapsing onto her unmade bed, too tired to care about the lack of pillows and sheets as she connected with the mattress. The compulsion which had drawn her to the woods – had powered her legs to run – still pulsed through her, but it was weakening now, her breaths slowing, becoming less laboured.

Sleep. She needed sleep.

But when she closed her eyes, she heard the screams, smelt the coppery tang of Caleb's blood in the air. She'd fainted in the cinema, hallucinated. Right? Because he couldn't be coming back for her, could he? He was dead. Cold and rotting in the ground.

And yet the screams, they'd raised the hairs on her arms. Now they didn't come only in her nightmares, they were invading her world. Destroying it.

He doesn't come back. Not that night, nor the next. Two whole days pass. I know because I stay. I sit within the fringes of the wood, one ear tilted in the direction of her home. Listening. Waiting. I've drained the last of the water in the bottle in my backpack and pissed in a nearby pile of leaves more times than I care to count. Home. I need to go home. I am waiting for you. You're going to break soon, come forwards, end this lie. I know you are. I can feel it. I'm tired, aren't you? I should go home.

But my home is a shitty little flat beneath a deaf old bat who hoovers at night like it's a fucking sport. My home doesn't have a nice front door and two floors. They all had better homes than me. Better lives. Like they each just set out into the world as though nothing had happened, as though they had a right to act normal, to act like everyone else. Maybe if we weren't strangers, I could ask how they did it, how they lived a lie when just living is so damn exhausting. Will she tell me? Would she tell me?

I wonder if she's waiting on his return, imagine her sitting at her kitchen table, gazing sadly at her half-empty driveway, willing his van to come and disturb all the gravel.

My brother didn't even miss me. Carried on his small life as though I – as though we – hadn't existed. He bandied his new name about, wore it on his uniform with pride. That fucking stung. He'd once told me we'd be Turnbalds together until the end. I suppose he was half right. We were almost together until the end. I watched him slink away from his flat at a time I knew he didn't have a shift to get to. I wanted so badly to believe that he was leaving his shitshow of a life, that he'd finally woken up. I wanted my Ollie back. I wanted to watch him smack anyone who stood against us in the mouth, to break down Roger's door and snap his neck. Instead, this new Ollie existed in a solitary orbit. He forgot about me.

I had to admire Vik for being so rattled by the list. But, like a coward, she just reacted, didn't spend enough time trying to figure it out, didn't follow the breadcrumbs I'd left to find the others. That was the plan: one name would lead to the next and then finally they'd find me. Once they had Jacob, living his life as Harry Jensen, I'd be all that remained, the last piece to our puzzle. Sometimes I can't help but wonder if I went about it all wrong. The list was cryptic, but it had to be, in case it fell into the wrong hands. I thought that it'd be the jolt everyone needed to snap out of the stasis they were in. And if Roger had released all our identities to me, maybe the others had also pressed the people tasked with caring for them?

My mind . . . it betrays me. My thoughts wrap around one another and when the pain in my stomach takes me, everything I've been thinking about goes up in flames. Roger, more than once he called me crazy. He was wrong. I'm just unravelling. We all are. That's why I was so desperate to find us all, to reunite us.

If my plan worked, we'd be a group again. We'd be whole. Remember how it felt, the six of us? We were infinite. The universe stretched before us, wide and limitless. We believed in a better world. We let that be stolen from us. And I tried to give it back.

The old Ollie would have understood. The old Ollie would have applauded my efforts. But the old Ollie is gone, long before fucking Trevor washed up in some grimy river. They broke him. But I won't let them break me. Us. It's you and me now. Together. We can fix this. We can reclaim who we are.

I'm cold and it's late, I can tell by how bright the moon is. Mrs Norris is probably dragging her barely functioning hoover back and forth across her threadbare carpet. And my flat is empty and bare.

Forty-Four

Ruby lingered at the edge of her room. Even with what few belongings she could claim as her own gone, it looked the same: stark and cold. A stony sky filled the little window wedged high up the far wall.

'Are you ready?' Glenda gently pulled at her elbow, drawing her into the corridor. It felt strange to see the woman in a different setting, to see her standing, long skirt sweeping down to the floor and hiding her shoes from sight.

'I'm . . .' Ruby stole one last glimpse of the space that had been hers for the last few months. 'Yeah, I'm ready.'

'I promise that you'll like this new facility.' Glenda fell in step with her as they walked down long corridors, passed through security doors which buzzed as they granted them access. Ruby saw herself in the few teenagers that they passed: all hunched shoulders and downward glances. No one was vibrant. No one was laughing. The entire building carried the air of a vast tomb, only instead of holding corpses, it housed lost souls. 'I'll give you a week to settle in and then we'll resume our sessions, that sound good to you?' Glenda's words were the only source of brightness in the bleak tunnel they traipsed down.

Peering out of the corner of her eye, Ruby realised she was now in a part of the facility she'd never been in before. There were fewer security doors, larger windows.

To her left, she could see a field stretching like a green carpet towards a heavy sky.

'Here we are.' Glenda's hand clamped down on her shoulder and Ruby knew to cease walking, stopping in front of a closed door. They'd reached the exit. The corridor they were in opened out into a glass-walled foyer. Security cameras perched like angry birds in every upper corner, red eyes blinking down on them. There was a loud buzzing and then the door before them eased open and let them into the wide space.

Ruby stepped forward, leaving behind the dense stench of desperation and sweat clinging to the interior walls. Now there was only a set of heavy-duty double doors separating her from the rest of the world, from freedom. She could see the sparsely filled car park, the wall that bordered it, and, beyond that, green, so much green. Trees stretched up high, their leaves already turning golden. It was all so achingly beautiful.

'We'll just wait on the transport to get here.' Glenda's hand had remained on Ruby's shoulder as they edged forwards. Two guards were close by, clad in black uniforms and expensive-looking earpieces. Ruby wondered what they'd do if she tried to run. Would they chase her? Wrestle her to the ground? Break her bones?

She breathed in and felt the rattle of her poorly healed ribs tickle against her lungs. She wanted so much to run, to sprint away from this oppressive place until her legs were on fire and sweat was pouring down her back. But instead she remained at Glenda's side, held in place by a hand and the bond of trust that had been forged between them.

'How far away is this new place?' Ruby asked as her gaze settled on the fluttering leaves on a distant tree. It looked like it was going to rain. The sky was darkening, closing in.

'About forty minutes. Not far.'

Ruby nodded as though Glenda's words made perfect sense, when she didn't actually even know where she currently was, couldn't anchor herself to a location, a point on the map. Was she still in Shropshire?

'You'll have your own room there,' Glenda chattered on, 'and similar facilities to here, but there will be opportunities to learn, to finish your GCSEs. There's a library, a gym . . .'

It became difficult to pay attention. Glenda spoke like she was describing a prestigious school, but Ruby knew better. She was being sent to yet another prison, another institute, another place with guards at the doors and bars on the windows.

The guards at the front doors never once looked over at her, their postures remaining rigid and alert, eyes focused ahead with indifference.

'Here's the transport.' Releasing her shoulder, Glenda pointed to a silver transit van just turning into the car park. Ruby saw the lettering on its side as it pulled up outside the main entrance:

The Priory Home for Wayward Youths

Was that what she was? Wayward? Her fear and sorrow began to ball together in her throat in a tight cluster.

'Okay, Beth, well, take care and I'll come and check in on you in your new home soon.' Glenda embraced her. It wasn't forced either, like the times when Linda bothered to hug her. Glenda held her tight, squeezing her close, and for a second it seemed like she didn't want to let go. But then her hands were returning to her sides and Ruby felt alone and untethered, like one of the leaves recently shed by the bordering trees – forced to exist on the whims of the wind.

More buzzing, shrill and close. The uniformed men were opening the final set of doors and fresh air rushed in to press against Ruby, to bluster against her cheeks and tangle in her hair. She could smell the manure in distant fields, the dampness of impending rain, the lingering odour of petrol released by the parked cars. In that second when nature engulfed her, she felt more alive than she had in months.

Something dripped against Ruby's forehead. Rain. It was timid at first but quickly made its presence known. As she was ushered into the back of the van, it was already hammering on the roof like dozens of little feet dancing a chaotic jig.

'Good luck, Beth.' Glenda waved as she retreated out of the rain, back through the main doors. 'This is the start of your future, don't be scared! Embrace it!'

A guard slammed the door to the van closed with jarring force and Ruby was once again cut off from the world, from its intoxicating autumnal aroma.

'You belted in?' the heavy-set female driver turned and asked from the front seat. Ruby nodded.

'All right, Janice, let's go.' A bald guard sat beside the driver, his flint eyes regarding their passenger in the rear-view mirror with open disdain.

Ruby sank low in her seat and watched the rain splatter haphazardly against her window. She was headed to another facility, another room that wasn't her own.

Eighteen.

She pressed her fingers into her palms as she focused on the number. Once she was eighteen, they were going to let her out, going to let her start living her life again. But not as Ruby, as Beth.

As the van shuddered along an A road, Ruby made a promise to herself – that this second chance wouldn't be wasted. Once she was free, once she was truly Beth Belmont, she'd do great things, would live an amazing life. One day she'd be released, one day she'd be able to run across the fields, feel the sun on her back. She just needed to wait for that day to come. Then she'd be happy again.

Forty-Five

It was the screams that woke her. They tore through the air like sharpened arrows, passing through her skin and piercing her lungs, making her gasp for air as she opened her eyes, looking around in panic.

There was sunlight everywhere. It swarmed the single window in the room and bathed the bed in a warming golden glow. Beth shrivelled against its potency, scurrying off the mattress like a vampire afflicted by the light. Standing near the doorway, she panted and spun round.

More screams. They wailed through the little house, rushed up the stairs and bounced off the walls.

'What the . . .' Beth slapped her cheek and then pinched her forearm. The pain did not stop the screaming. As the last grip of sleep released her, a sickening realisation gripped her entire body: someone was in her house. Someone was in her house, downstairs, screaming. 'No,' the word almost got stuck in her mouth, her tongue as dry as parched leaves.

Who was it? Was it Josh? Had he snuck in while she slept and decided to punish her for calling him?

No . . . the screams were too high-pitched to belong to him. Too young. Too feral. Beth had to force herself to leave the bedroom, gripping the door frame for support as she slid herself out onto the landing. The screaming was relentless. Again and again, it came in waves, a sound more pitiful and terrifying than anything Beth had heard before.

You're dreaming.

This was the thought she wrapped her shaking body in as she approached the top of the stairs and began to descend, tightly gripping the handrail which ran along the wall at a steep angle.

You're dreaming, that's all.

The screams filled the air, blasted her eardrums so violently she feared they might bleed and burst. It would be so easy to just hide in her wardrobe or the bathroom, to close herself in darkness and clamp her hands around her ears and rock back and forth until the screaming subsided. But if that didn't make it go away, what then? Beth knew she had to face the intruder. Was she finally about to lock eyes with the author of the list? What would she even say? What would they want?

I'm sorry.

Two words she'd once said with such regularity that they'd surely lost their meaning. Beth *was* sorry, *was* repentant. She'd spent her adult life paying for what she'd done.

She was in the hallway, the door to the living room ajar in front of her. The screams were swelling inside, a continuing howl. Beth flexed her hands over the silver handle.

You can do this.

The image of Caleb in the darkened theatre flashed in her mind. He'd been so bloodied, so swollen, toiled by time and decay. And his mouth had become a bottomless black pit through which he wailed incessantly.

Beth snatched her hand back and held her breath. Was Caleb now in her living room, standing on her cream carpet, soiling it with his rotting body?

He's dead. He's gone.

But in the cinema, he'd seemed so real. Too real. The sight of him had been enough to cause her to lose consciousness.

What if he wrote the list?

What if he's real?

If Josh were there, he'd have laughed at the suggestion – a hearty, deep laugh. He'd tell her she was going crazy. And perhaps he would be right. Was Beth losing her mind? At the cinema, she'd been so certain of what she'd seen, but when she came to, there were no bloody footprints upon the stairs, no withered spectral boy screaming at her. How could there have been? She was going crazy, losing her mind inch by terrifying inch. Is that what happened to Vikki and Ollie? Did their madness drive them to utter despair, lead them to a final goodbye?

Beth covered her mouth, muffled her own anguished breaths.

Someone was screaming. Someone other than Beth.

The sound. The cries. They were real, buffeting through her home. Beth forced her hand to clasp the handle and push the door open just enough to allow her to slip into the living room.

Silence.

It slammed into her so suddenly it felt stranger than the screaming had. Beth peered at her empty, sunlit sofa and blinked rapidly, waiting for her gaze to finally find the little boy who'd been making such a commotion. Only there was no one there. Her skin didn't prickle with the sensation of being watched. Everything within the lounge was still, calm. Only the ringing in her ears told her that the screaming had been very real.

'Where are you?' she demanded of the sofa, the plush carpet, the magnolia walls. 'Caleb, where are you? I'm here, what do you want?'

Not even a fluttering of the warm air in response. Beth was alone. Head spinning, she backed out of the room and made for the kitchen, reaching desperately for her phone, which was still face down on the countertop. She peered at the screen, breathing heavily.

There were no new calls. No new messages. Josh hadn't got back to her. Had he just deleted her earlier attempt to contact him without a second thought?

It was two in the afternoon, Beth had managed to sleep away most of the day. Her stomach churned with the desire to eat, but she couldn't concentrate on such basic needs, not now.

Boldly, with phone in hand, she marched back into the living room. 'I know someone was here,' she raised her voice, filled it with as much iron as she could muster. 'I heard you screaming, why hide from me now?'

Was that what Caleb was doing – hiding? Had he followed her into the woods the previous night and lingered in the shadows as she screamed out for a confrontation?

'Fuck no.' Pressing her fingertips to her temple, Beth collapsed onto her sofa. She was dwelling on the impossible.

Caleb Walters was dead. There was just no way that he'd been in her home screaming. It was ludicrous, it was—

Beth flung her phone across the room. It connected with the ground just shy of the wall, remaining intact. She longed for a drink, longed to lose herself at the base of a bottle the way her mother did. Her mind felt like it was being shredded to ribbons with each damaging thought that invaded it.

I'm going crazy.

Should she call Glenda, confess to her what was going on? What then? Another institution? Another new name?

The list. Beth kept coming back to it like an 'x' on a map. Everything had started with the list and that at least was very real. Josh had seen it. The officer at the station had seen it. A little slip of paper had unsettled Beth's entire house of cards. She needed to find the author, needed to ask them what they wanted from her. And whatever it was, she was willing to give it.

'I won't live in fear.' Beth slowly climbed off the sofa and crawled towards her phone. 'I won't.' But she realised with a plummeting sensation that she knew no other way to live. For over half her life, she'd scurried around in the shadow of oppression, had been living in the brace position, waiting for someone to uncover her terrible secret, for someone to demand that Ruby Renton finally atone for what she had done.

I wonder how you sleep. Are your dreams hollow like mine? Great black holes of nothingness which threaten to swallow me whole if I don't open my eyes fast enough.

Or do you see them – Caleb, Ollie, Vikki, Jacob, Annie, even me. Are we all frozen in time on that patch of grass, forever atoning for what we did?

Has time been kind to any of us? Or does it just make us older, not wiser or richer? You switch your lights off at night. All of them, I've checked. I guess the dark doesn't bother you too much.

I long to dream, to feel the release of somewhere new. Anything that punctures the emptiness is nightmarish. I see Ollie most. I see him crying until his tears become a river in which he drowns. Do you think he ever thought of me? Of you?

I'm so desperately tired. Here, in my spot in the woods, I like to pretend I'm inside your nice house, warm in your cosy bed, curled up beside you, both of us exhausted from laughing about happier times. Next to you, I'm safe.

*

The light was fading. Beth stretched, uncurling her spine from where she'd been pressed into a ball against the back of her sofa, sleeping fitfully. There had been nightmares. Caleb's pale face had illuminated the darkness of her dreams like a full moon. He had howled at her, stared at her with empty, coal-like eyes. Beth had been back in the woods with him, had felt the cool of the dew upon her feet, the heat of his blood on her hands.

Just a nightmare.

She repeated the mantra over and over until her heart rate settled.

She was awake, back in the familiarity of her living room. With a groan, she raised her arms up above her head and pulled her hands together until she felt a satisfying pop between her shoulder blades. She at least felt rested, despite the torment of her nightmares.

Standing up, she gazed through the large window overlooking her driveway. Absent of any cars, the strip of gravel felt unusually empty. Beth strayed closer to the glass, tipping her head upwards to see the sky bronzing and the street lights beginning to glow. She had no idea what time it was, but sensed it was late evening, perhaps eight, even nine. Had Josh called her back while she slept? Turning away from the window, she approached her discarded phone with eagerness, but then abruptly froze in the centre of the room.

A creak. Upstairs. She was certain she'd heard it. The bristling of her spine was all the confirmation she needed. Beth held a breath and strained to hear more. A second passed and then another creak, this one unmistakeable.

Josh.

The naïve thought that her boyfriend had returned flooded through her, drowning any logic as she hurried into the hallway, slapping on light switches as she passed them, and began ascending the stairs.

She was like a child on Christmas Eve, chasing rogue sounds through the house. But none of them were going to lead to a man in a Santa suit.

Beth had made it to the landing when the screaming started. It cut through the warm air of the house like razors, scoring her skin and turning the blood to ice in her veins.

'No,' leaning towards the wall to steady herself, Beth began to shake her head. 'No.' With her free hand, she swatted at her ear. 'This can't be real, I can't be hearing this.'

But she was. The screams from her dreams, her nightmares, they were once again inside her home, bouncing off the walls in an endless echo chamber. It was so loud, so piercing. Her knees contracted, bringing her closer to the floor.

'It's not real,' Beth felt the tremor in her voice as she leant heavily against the wall, pawing at it with both hands for support. 'You're not real,' she shouted at her bedroom door.

Still in her crumpled joggers and T-shirt, hair bunched in a loose ponytail, she crept forwards, eyes fixed on the white door just a few inches in front of her. If she pushed it open, surely she'd just find the chaos from earlier – the unmade bed, the strewn clothes. That would be it. There would be no source of the screams. How could there be when this was all just her own mind punishing her?

'This isn't . . . real.' With a grunt, she forced herself to stand straight, to square her shoulders. She was Beth Belmont and Ruby Renton rolled into one. She could do this. She could open the door and face her demons. 'There's no one there,' her voice dropped to a whisper as her hand found the door and applied just enough pressure for it to slowly creak open.

Between the sunset and the street lights outside, the room was bathed in a hazy glow. Beth stepped inside and saw him. She felt gravity desperately trying to claim her, trying to drag her down to the carpet. But she remained rigid, her bones shaking with the effort of staying upright.

Caleb Walters was in her bedroom. His bloody footprints had soiled the clothes around him, the beige carpet. He stood at the side of her bed, dark eyes glazed and unseeing, mouth hanging open. A worm wriggled from behind his teeth and lingered on his lip but went unnoticed by Caleb, who just screamed. He wailed as his paper-thin skin seeped out blood that churned with the dirt on his ragged clothes, pooling at his feet in a dark puddle.

'You're not . . .' Beth struggled to find her voice. 'You're not real!' she shrieked at him. He was a phantom, a figment of her imagination, nothing more.

The boy stopped screaming. He was frozen, forever thirteen, still clad in the tatters of his school uniform. Parts of his scalp had fallen away to reveal the white of his skull and his aura of decay reached across the room and curled around Beth, making her gag.

Now it was her turn to scream. Desperately, Beth backed out of the room as Caleb began to advance towards her. She all but tumbled down the stairs, her movements frantic and erratic. When she reached the front door, she kept screaming, her hands flailing against the locks, fingers loose and useless. But somehow she twisted them in time, flung the door open as she heard the footsteps advancing behind her, felt the acrid stench of Caleb's proximity. She staggered out into the late evening and started running.

★

The door opening. It pulls me back from the void where I'm trapped between dreams and reality. Like a mother attuned to the cries of her baby, I'm instantly awake, alert. If only my body were as competent as my mind. I'm dragging myself to the fence, legs stiff and reluctant. My fingers find the rough ridge and I extend onto my toes just in time to see someone running away from Beth's home. Twisting, I see her front door hanging open, light spilling out. Has she been attacked? Is someone fleeing the scene?

'Shit.' I cough against the tightness that has taken up residence in my chest, feel the weight of liquid in my lungs. 'Come . . . on.' I'm back on the soles of my feet and kicking at the fence. One of these boards is loose. I know because I'm the one who worked it free of its restraints, easing the wood away from its companions with just the right amount of pressure. Only now I can't find it. In the moonlight, the panels all look the same. Dammit. Damn! I keep kicking and nothing budges until . . .

A shift. Even my toes, numbed by the cold, can feel it. Bending down, I shove my fingers behind the panel and pull. It takes some effort, but it eventually moves to the side, revealing a gap I can just about squeeze through. With a strain, I push myself through and dust off my jeans, panting. It's a pointless exercise since I'm already caked in dirt.

The door. I run to it, a clammy sweat breaking out across my body. It's open, and inside there is a hallway and stairs leading to a golden landing. The walls are white, so very crisp, so very clean. I lean over the threshold, a stain on the interior. 'Hello?' I can barely rasp out the word and my chest, it's burning. Reaching for the door frame, I notice that my hand is shaking. Nerves? It must be. But I'm also so very hot. And normally I'm cold, so so cold. Now there is fire burning beneath my skin, making me pant, sweat. But there isn't time to question my symptoms. 'Hello?' I dare to speak louder, the word delivered as a bark, more animal than human. Is she there? Is she lying in a pool of her own blood, feeling the life pulsing out of her?

Focus.

Squinting, I press my fingers to my temple. The figure. The person running. They were slim. Tall. Female. It was her. It had to be. I'm in the wrong place. I take off as fast as I can, and at the end of her street, I don't hesitate. I turn left. The woods, she's surely going to the woods. Because for us it's always been about the woods.

Forty-Six

Beth ran. Her legs pumped furiously as they carried her over to the woods. She didn't lessen her pace once she passed by grand oaks and lean birches, instead she ran faster. Her hair bounced between her shoulders as twigs snapped beneath her feet. Beth couldn't – *wouldn't* – stop. She feared that the second she paused to double over and catch a breath she'd feel Caleb's clammy hand on her back, inhale his toxic odour.

But he can't be real.

The thought churned in her mind until it began to thicken. It was impossible and yet she had seen him, smelt him. If she'd reached out a hand would she have been able to touch him? Either Caleb Walters was haunting her or she'd lost her mind. Both were equally terrifying prospects.

She ran straight through the woods, flying as a crow would, direct from one side to the other. Ignoring the deviations in the little path, Beth sprinted up towards the core, where the darkness was most dense. There wasn't time to mind her footing. She just needed to keep running until she was out on the other side of the woods, until she was—

Her left foot caught on a spindly root. Beth tumbled forwards, quickly extending her hands before her as she connected with the ground with a loud thud. Dirt crept into her nostrils, her mouth. Her lungs had been flattened by the impact, screaming for air.

'F-fuck.' Beth kicked out her feet, letting them scramble amongst the leaves and patchy blades of grass as she tried to get up. Her hands were pressed against something hard and sharp – a rock. Choking on shock and adrenaline, Beth managed to get onto her knees. Her chest had caught fire. Each time she drank in the cool night air, she felt the flames overwhelming her lungs. 'Fuck.' Barking out the expletive, she tried to stand. A pulse had gathered in her left ankle, uneasy and throbbing. 'Dammit.' She shook her foot, tried to fling out the sensation, but it wasn't leaving. Pain started to shoot up her leg. 'No, no . . .' She bent down to massage her calf muscle with hands that were warm and wet. She was bleeding, but it was too dark to assess her wounds.

Doubled over, she chanced a glance behind her at the narrow slip of a path bordered by grand trees and swathed in shadow. She appeared to be alone. Caleb wasn't stalking after her, luminous and glorious in the night. But that didn't mean she really was alone, that she was safe. Beth tensed and waited for screams that never came.

Just go home.

This was the point where she should be staggering back to her little house, limping on her bad leg. But the end terrace with the gravel driveway was no longer her home. In so many ways, it never was. Beth couldn't face the destruction, the echo of Caleb's haunting screams.

She needed distance.

Moving with markedly less speed, she hobbled further along the path, edging herself ever closer to the far side of the woods. When she paused to wipe a hand across her brow, she felt the oily presence of more blood. The ache behind her eyes told her that a bruise would soon swell around them. Her fall had been a bad one. But she had to keep going.

I didn't follow Ollie. I watched him leave his house that night and didn't consider what he might be about to do. How could I have known that he was about to disappear for good? If I had, I would have followed. Stopped him. And with Vikki . . . again I hadn't seen it coming, not until it was all burning down. I won't turn my back on you. I won't let you leave me.

Faster. I need to go faster. There's no spectre ahead of me, darting through the trees. I'm surrounded only by darkness. Sputtering, I'm forced to stop, head lolling to my knees as I steady myself against an elm. And then I listen. There's the whisper of the leaves. The scurry of small feet against the ground, the hoot of an owl. Beneath that, further away . . . crying. Someone is crying. And not the gentle kind of crying. This is the real shit, the kind of crying that shakes your entire body, where your eyes weep along with everything else on your face capable of producing fluids. It's her. It has to be. But why is she running? Where is she going?

With my questions keeping me company, I carry on through the woods, letting the haunting call of her sorrow guide me. Perhaps something has happened. Perhaps the boyfriend sent her a cruel message, some taunt. But then why leave her perfect little home?

Does he know? The thought pierces me, cold and sudden. I want to drop to the ground, but I manage to keep pumping my legs, to keep moving, my elation giving strength to my weary muscles. Perhaps she has finally done what the others could not, perhaps she's finally broken free of the lie, embraced who she truly is.

But if she hasn't—

I need to get to her. Every second is crucial, I learnt that the hard way. But everything burns. My legs, my lungs. Gasping, I stagger to a halt, doubling over. Fuck my weak body. Fuck my failing muscles. Wheezing, I drink in the cool night air.

Focus.

I count to ten. With each number, I rise up, slow and certain. By fifteen, I'm staggering forwards. I'm coming, legs aching but complying. She's not alone any more. None of us are.

Owls seemed to hoot at her in observation as she picked her way through the woods. Beth tuned them out, along with the relentless whisper of leaves, as a frail wind whipped along the same path as her. Ahead, she could just make out the treeline thinning. Forcing her damaged ankle to connect with the ground, she managed to sprint out into the moonlight. She felt as though her bones had been replaced with glass and might shatter at any second, but Beth didn't care, she just needed to feel free.

Beyond the trees, the world opened up into a grand field, which lay beneath a sapphire sky, peppered with the scattered diamonds of stars. It was beautiful. The openness was a relief to her senses. Extending her arms, Beth slowly spun around, revelling in the sheer space of it all. Long grass brushed against her legs and she tipped her chin up to the silvery face of the moon.

Then she heard it – the crack of a twig. Her head snapped so quickly in the direction of the woods that her neck burned and stiffened. He was there. He had to be following her.

Caleb Walters was at the treeline and screams seemed to startle the birds feverishly from their perches. Beth stared. Twice she blinked. Then she did it again, felt dried blood gathering in her eyelashes. The phantom boy didn't disappear. He was advancing beyond the woods, coming for her.

Beth instinctively stepped back. Her body sang a painful tune as it protested each movement, each ragged breath.

'No . . .' the word whistled out of her. 'You're . . . you're not real. You're not.'

I've reached the edge of the woods and now I see her. She's running across a field, still crying. Her heaving sobs carry across the grass to me. And she keeps looking back, keeps twisting to shoot desperate looks over her shoulder. At the treeline, I freeze. Can she see me?

I open my mouth and call to her, as loudly as I can, 'Don't run,' tripping over the first word clumsily in my eagerness. The distance between us is still too great and it's extending with every step she takes. We need to be face to face. I need to see her, look her in the eye. It's what I should have done with the others, should have let them know that I was there, that my name was on the list too. I was too afraid that they'd turn me away, too committed to their new lives. Too ashamed of their past. I couldn't face that rejection, especially not from Ollie.

My fear cost them their lives. I failed them and I'm failing you. I just need to reach you, explain that the list was meant to remind you who you are, who we are – that we are a group, connected, that the world doesn't make sense without one another. But you're running away and I can barely breathe, barely stand. But I have to keep going . . . I have to see you. I have to make things right.

'Run.' There was a new voice on the wind. One Beth hadn't heard in a very long time. She didn't dwell on the how, just focused on heeding the command. Turning, she forced herself to run. Her ankle was so brittle, so useless, it slowed her progress, but she kept running, fleeing from the voice carried on the crisp night air.

The long grass began to give way to a steep incline. It dipped suddenly away from her and as Beth tumbled forward, she recalled that there was a railway track which ran along the back of the field. On clear summer nights if the bedroom window was open, she could sometimes hear the freight trains that moved through the night thundering along their route. It comforted her to lie in bed beside Josh and listen to the chug of the engine and imagine this other world which existed while she slept.

She rolled down the embankment, damp grass whipping past her. Over and over, she turned until finally she came to rest on her back, looking up at a distant array of stars.

The adrenaline in her system was keeping her fatigue at bay, but she began to feel it on the fringes of her consciousness, as though the lines between dreams and reality were beginning to blur. On her third attempt, she managed to sit up. Then, with some effort, she hauled herself onto her feet. She ground her teeth against the fresh pain engulfing her back and, looking down, saw that she had landed on the railway tracks. They stretched away from her in stiff, uniform lines.

'He's coming.'

A voice so close it could have been her own. Beth strained in the moonlight to find the figure beside her on the tracks. At first, they were blurry, like a shadow, but slowly they slipped into focus.

Ollie. Only as he had once been. Hair cropped close to his scalp, jawline chiselled and angular, a smouldering cigarette held in his hand, which he casually lifted to his pale lips as he nodded back up the embankment. 'He won't stop coming, you know.'

'C-Caleb?' Beth struggled to speak through teeth nervously gnashing together. She knew not to trust what she was seeing. Ollie the boy no longer existed. He had died as a man, as Trevor Hoskins. But here he was in all his youthful glory, standing beside her. She could smell the sweetness of cheap cider on his breath, the heady cloud of cigarette smoke that always clung to him, mixing with the Brut aftershave he loved to splash on his cheeks. 'H-he . . . I . . .'

'Just stay here, with me, and he'll go away for good.'

He exhaled and his breath was warm on her cheek. So warm and so real. Beth closed her eyes and felt her body sway, her head become light. Was she about to faint?

'Any second now and this will all be over,' Ollie assured her with that trademark grin of his, the one which was always ripe with mischief and confidence.

She could still hear Caleb's screaming coming closer. His dark eyes, his unearthly gaze . . . She never wanted him to look upon her, never wanted to have to face his decomposing corpse again.

'Why won't he leave?' she asked as the pain from her ankle started to shoot up her leg afresh.

'You know why,' Ollie breathed out a plume of smoke, which curled above their heads.

The field is wide, the grass cropped low. I'm running, but the air feels like treacle in my lungs, thick and cloying. I have to keep going, I have to find the strength to reach her. The ground. It's shaking. The sensation is gentle but constant. Still running, I look around, my eyes fully adjusted to the darkness.

I hear it before I see it. The rumbling. I almost topple down the canyon I suddenly find myself at the top of. The field steeply falls away, the incline peppered with weeds and rubbish. And at the bottom, in the shadows, I can make out train tracks. The light of an approaching train glows to my right. It's headed this way.

Something stirred beneath Beth's feet. The ground was vibrating as though there was a giant heart buried underneath, which had begun to beat.

'W-what's that?' She moved to leave the railway tracks, but Ollie's free hand shot out and grabbed her upper arm, anchoring her in place.

'That's salvation,' he told her, cigarette clenched between his teeth.

'Wait, what?' Up ahead, she saw the light at the end of the tunnel. For a second her senses couldn't line up with what she was seeing, but then she realised – it was the beam from an oncoming train. The tracks began to shake with fervour, rattling like old bones.

Still Caleb screamed. Beth heard the soft fall of rocks sliding down the embankment and she looked up to glimpse the boy, as pale as pure alabaster, standing above her, looking down with a torn face distorted by contempt and fear.

'Don't look at him, look at me,' Ollie had to shout to be heard over the screams of the boy and the roar of the oncoming train. 'Just a few more seconds and this will all be over, Ruby.' His hand was still on her arm, his grip surprisingly strong.

'Ollie, let me go.' She wanted to scramble up the far side of the embankment, to run away from Caleb, from Ollie, to keep running until she was truly alone, truly free.

'I can't do that.'

'Please,' Beth begged as the light up ahead grew brighter. 'Let me go, let me be free.'

'I'm not the one holding you here.'

With a start, she realised that his hand was in his pocket, not gripping her upper arm like a vice after all. Had he ever held on to her or had she imagined it?

'I . . .'

'Ruby, it's okay, don't be scared.' He laced his fingers through hers and, standing shoulder to shoulder, they faced the oncoming train. 'I'm right here. Soon you'll truly be free.'

His hand was so warm, fingers so long, so nimble.

Beth opened her mouth, intending to tell him that she was no longer Ruby Renton. She was Beth. Beth Belmont. Her desire to reveal this final truth grew within her like a sapling searching for the sun. Only no words came out. The train powered against the tracks, the guttural roar of its engine drowning out Caleb's wails. Beth stared at the incoming light, as bright as the sun as it bore down on her.

She thought of Josh. Of her mother. Of the innocent little boy she'd failed to save that day out in the woods. The sound of the train faded away and Beth could hear birdsong, sweet and soft. Her skin was warm as golden sunlight traced along her bare arms.

Free. I'm finally free.

There was laughter in the air, childlike and light.

And she's there, standing in the centre of the tracks, looking towards the oncoming train, left hand hanging in mid-air.

No! No, not again! This can't be happening. It's not supposed to end like this. She's not supposed to leave, she's the strong one. She's supposed to come forward, to declare to the world who she really is and bring me out of the shadows with her. She's meant to be making things better for us.

My entire body is trembling. I can't fail again, I can't. Vikki, Ollie, I made mistakes, grave ones.

I won't let this happen! I just need to get to her, to let her see me. Then everything will be all right; she'll look at me and know she isn't alone, that it's okay for us to be who we are.

Ollie . . . if he were here now, the Ollie I knew, the Ollie I loved, he'd be dragging her off the tracks. Instead, he's rotting in some grave. In taking his name, they'd taken my brother's entire identity. The six of us should never have been ripped apart. Together we could have overcome all the hate, the vitriol. Together we could have sought forgiveness. Redemption. And if we were to rot in jail for the rest of our lives, let us at least rot there together.

My tears mix with the blood on my cheek. I blink to stop my image of her becoming blurry. She was always so good. So kind.

The train, it's getting closer, the tracks creating a deafening death rattle. But she's not moving. She's staring at the light, helpless as a moth. I can't let it claim her.

With the animalistic cry of a powerful engine, the illusion was broken and Beth smelt sulphur and oil, felt burning heat against her face. Fire and brimstone. Was this it? The front of the train was almost upon her.

'Ruby! No!' My scream sears my throat, but I don't care. I rush towards her, hands extended. Using my momentum from the incline, I shove her hard.

A force. It came from the right, sudden and sharp, and knocked her off the tracks, back against the grass and shrubbery. Beth gasped, stunned, as her spine connected with the ground, then her hands. She wasn't alone. Beth stared at the figure bathed in the glow of the train's light, their skin so white it was almost translucent. Were they a ghost?

Beth blinked. It wasn't Caleb. There was no gaping mouth, no rotting flesh. This person . . . they were real. And they were looking at her. Right at her. Beth felt her mouth falling open. The packaging had changed, their hair now long and lank, skin stretched too tight over bones. But those eyes. Emerald fire. Beth had looked into them before, had seen the same sharpness in Ollie's gaze.

'Kate?' It was hard to speak through her tears. 'K-Kate?'

As she falls back, she looks at me, eyes watery and wild. I wonder if she knows it's me, if she realises that—

Raising a hand, Beth lurched forward to snatch the wiry figure from the tracks, but the train claimed her first. Kate Turnbald's blood washed over her like warm rain. Shaking, Beth's body turned rigid. She drew in shallow, desperate breaths. The train thundered by.

Forty-Seven

Five Months Later

Beth's day began the same way it always did. She woke up in her small flat, alone, in a ball with her damp sheets clustered around her. Following a feline stretch, she stalked into her bathroom and tried to wash off any lingering remnants of her nightmares. The mornings were dark now. Christmas was close.

Bundled in a thick dressing gown, Beth would head down to her kitchen, turning on every possible light so that not even a scrap of darkness could gather in distant corners. She'd flick on the kettle and as she waited for it to boil, she'd pluck her phone from her pocket and listen to the voicemail that had arrived almost four months earlier.

'Hey, Beth, it's me . . . Josh.' An intake of breath which told her he'd taken up smoking again. 'Look, I just . . .' Deep sigh. 'I'm just calling to say that, what I know, who you are . . . to me, you're still Beth. Okay? I'm not going to go telling anyone. Your secret . . .' Long pause. 'I'll keep it. Don't get me wrong, I know you're a m—' Beth always hung up at the very same point, unable to listen to whether she's a monster or a murderer. Each time she put down her phone, she swore she could smell him, feel the weight of his presence beside her as though that message had been able to erase time and bring them back together. But she was still very much alone.

She went to work. She came home. She read online about the death of Rebecca Terry. It was considered a suicide.

Terry, a recluse.

That was how the media had painted her. A loner. Someone without anyone. But Beth knew the truth. It had been Kate Turnbald who'd died out on the tracks that day. And she'd died saving Beth. The why of it all failed to present itself. But Beth picked at it, like a jigsaw she was compelled to complete even though she only had some of the pieces, not even the box with the final image on the front.

Kate must have written the list, she was sure. That was how she found Beth, followed her into the woods that night. But why not just approach her? Why hide behind a slip of paper? Was it shame? Fear? If she'd just reached out to her, knocked on her door, even phoned her, things might have turned out very differently. Beth would never know.

The alarm on her fitness tracker buzzed against her wrist. This morning was different. She wasn't going to work. She had an appointment to keep.

'So, how are you feeling?'

Beth was studying the small cactus on the desk, admiring its tidy little blue pot. Something like that would look nice in her new flat, over the little fireplace maybe, add some colour to—

'Are you sleeping better?' Dr Peters persisted.

'Yes,' Beth nodded, lifted her gaze and leant back on the sofa, hands neatly clasped in a basket in her lap. 'A lot better, thank you.'

'And the nightmares?' Dr Peters' fountain pen scratched against his notebook.

'He's the best,' Glenda had assured her. 'Seeing him will help, I promise.'

'They're . . .' Beth looked past him, over his shoulder at the array of framed certificates on the wall. 'I still have them,' she admitted. 'But the . . . the daytime visions have stopped.'

'Okay, well,' more scratching of the pen, 'I'm hopeful that in time the nightmares will also decrease. But you're sleeping well?'

'Yes.'

It wasn't a lie. She'd fall asleep looking up at the cracks on her ceiling and even though she still woke up sweating, heart racing, she'd learnt to drink in deep breaths, anchor herself with something familiar around her, a pillow, or a lamp, and then drift back to sleep.

'You've made a lot of progress these past few months,' Dr Peters ceased writing to smile at her. He was handsome, in an obvious way, with a square jaw and an impressively thick head of brown hair for a man his age. Given the dates on the certificates, Beth placed him as late forties. At every session, he wore a tweed waistcoat with a white shirt and his office always smelt of coffee and lemons. 'Do you feel that our sessions are helping?'

'Yes,' Beth dipped her head, remembering how Dr Peters didn't like one-word answers. 'They're helping. I'm sleeping better, I'm back at work. I'm in my own flat now and . . .'

She was still Facebook-stalking Josh. But that was normal, right? And Jacob. Beth's cheeks burned just thinking about it.

'You have to forget about it,' Glenda had told her as she comforted her in the police station that dreadful night.

'The list, the names, forget them. Live your life, Beth. Stop holding on to something you can't change.'

'Sometimes I think, what if she hadn't pushed me out of the way?'

'On the train tracks?' Dr Peters' eyebrows inched higher on his large forehead. Beth looked at his broad shoulders, imagined him playing rugby in his younger days.

'I . . .' she shook her head, trying to dismiss her own words.

'Do you wish she hadn't pushed you out of the way?'

'I mean,' she unclasped her hands to drum her fingertips against her knees. 'In the moment, when I was in front of the train, I kind of . . . I felt relief.'

'That you were going to die?' Dr Peters asked in a non-committal way. From anyone else, Beth would be a little shaken by his indifference, but five months in she knew this was just his manner.

'Yeah. I mean, living . . . living with being *me*. It can be exhausting.'

'I can imagine.' His pen returned to work. Scratch. Scratch. Scratch.

'I don't want to waste it. My life. This . . . this chance,' she was struggling to explain how she felt. Nervously, she tucked a strand of hair back behind her ear. It was slightly shorter now, with layers and highlights.

'I don't think you are wasting it, do you?'

'I wish she'd spoken to me.' Beth blinked away tears and drummed on her knees some more. 'It's like how can you miss someone who hasn't been in your life for over half of it? And yet . . .'

'The bonds forged in childhood are often the strongest we'll ever experience.'

'Um . . . yeah. That must be it.'

'Beth,' he said her name and held her in a deep stare, brown eyes burning into hers. 'You are doing well, trust me. Every week, I see improvements in you. Own that. In time, the nightmares will ease. Things are only going to get easier. Time heals even the harshest wounds. You must learn to move on and also to forgive yourself.'

'But I don't want to forget her,' Beth blurted. '*Them*,' she corrected, thinking of Ollie. Vikki. Even Annie.

'Forgetting and moving on aren't the same thing,' Dr Peters told her. 'We'll keep talking and you'll keep moving forwards. Growing stronger.'

'Thanks, I hope so.'

'You're stronger than you think, Beth.'

She raised her shoulders nonchalantly. 'Same time next week?'

'Same time next week.'

It was cold. The wind gnawed against Beth's cheeks as she stepped out of her car, even though half of her face was tucked behind her cream woollen scarf. Clutching an ivy wreath in a gloved hand, Beth walked with brisk, confident steps towards the far corner of Stirchley Cemetery. She could walk the route in her sleep since it had become her weekly ritual some months ago. She strode right up to a granite stone, etched with a neat inscription, and stooped down to rest the wreath on the short grass.

Straightening, she tucked a strand of hair behind her ear and then retrieved her hood which had blown down, tugging it back over her head. The wind swept across the headstones, rattled the branches of a barren oak tree. The sky was heavy with the threat of snow.

She looked at the name hammered in stone and finished in gold, bowed her head gently.

Here lies Caleb Walters. Beloved son and brother.

'See you next Wednesday,' she whispered before turning and walking back the way she had come.

Epilogue

Beth rubbed her eyes and straightened in the front seat of her car. It had been forty minutes since she'd pulled into her space and despite her thick parka and wool hat, she was starting to get cold.

The world around her sparkled. Snow had fallen over-night, making everywhere seem pristine and perfect. Even in the car park, the snow still lay unblemished, a few days away from turning to coffee-coloured slush.

Lights glowed in the front window of the store across from her. Red and green. Wishing her Season's Greetings. Christmas was just three days away. There was a small tree in her flat, almost crushed by the weight of the large star she'd placed atop it. But Beth wasn't watching the window of the furniture store with its welcoming arrangement of a plush sofa and festive tree. She was looking beyond it, to the glass doors leading towards an exclusive gym. And she was waiting.

There was only so much information she'd been able to gather online. She knew a location. And, thanks to social media, a vague time frame for Tuesday mornings. So she'd booked the day off work and made the decision to drive two hours to sit in a freezing car park in late December.

Regret was gnawing at her along with the cold.

What if she was wrong?

What if this was a mistake?

She could still back out. There was time. No one knew she was there. Not even Glenda or Dr Peters. Especially not them. This was her own little secret.

'Come on . . .' she twisted her wrist and pulled up her sleeve to check her watch.

Eleven a.m.

They were running late. If they were even there at all.

'Come . . . on . . .' she gripped her steering wheel and peered forward, through her windscreen, which was beginning to glisten with ice. If she was forced to sit there any longer, she'd need to turn the engine on, let the heating blare at her for a bit of respite.

The doors to the gym grazed open and a pair of young women strode out, buried beneath Puffa jackets and bobble hats.

'Dammit,' Beth released the wheel and sagged back against her seat.

It was a mistake. All of it. Her being there. The fact that she hadn't seen them was surely a sign. Reaching for the key in the ignition, she prepared to turn it, longing for warmth as much as escape.

The doors to the gym opened once again. A man came out. Broad-shouldered in a grey woollen coat hanging down to his knees. Wearing a backpack and trainers, he paused by the doors to turn up his collar, blew on his bare hands and then stepped towards the furniture store, taking care to bypass piles of snow which had been pushed to the far side of the walkway. His thick black hair shone, as though wet, and his jawline was shadowed by the faint trace of stubble.

Beth stared at him, chest clenched as she drew in a breath and then failed to release it, as though she'd forgotten how to breathe. He was past the furniture store, striding by a fashion retailer and a row of sweater-dress-clad mannequins when Beth exhaled and sprang into motion. Whipping her keys from the ignition, she pushed open the door, let her booted feet sink into the snow. The man was moving fast, weaving his way between snow and shops. Beth needed to be quick. Forsaking locking her car – there wasn't the time to shove the key into the old lock and turn it while applying pressure – she scurried through the snow, a cold wind scratching at exposed cheeks.

This is wrong.

This is a mistake.

She blew out her negative thoughts in a foggy breath.

The man had turned away from the shops, towards a section of the car park that was sparsely occupied, approaching an olive green vintage Range Rover. Beth froze beside the mannequins in their warm dresses. He moved with ease, unshouldered his backpack and reached inside for what she presumed must be his keys. He didn't glance around, didn't shy into the creases of his collar.

Turn. Back.

She remembered how it felt to watch Kate die. The warmth of her blood on Beth's cheeks.

Too long she had been alone. Too long had she carried the burden of her past in secret.

She started walking again, towards the Range Rover, hands clenched in fists at her sides. The man had opened the driver's side door, was tossing his backpack across to the passenger side when Beth reached him, stretched out and tapped him on the upper arm. Snow crunched beneath his trainers as he spun round, surprise deepening into shock. Beth cracked a half-smile at him, hope tentatively blooming in her chest.

'Jacob?'

Acknowledgements

I've been fortunate to work with some amazing people on this book. Firstly, my agent David Headley. Both he and Emily Glenister over at DHH were so passionate and kind about *The List* right from the start and I'm so grateful for their continued support.

My editor, Francesca Pathak. From the moment we met, I knew I was in safe hands. Her insight and enthusiasm has taken the book to a place I never could have reached on my own. Also many thanks to Lucy Frederick for her help during the editing process. Both of you were so patient with me and didn't judge my zealous fondness for a good head tilt and the fact that my northern roots will forever make me want to be sat down rather than sitting.

Huge thanks to my friends for unknowingly distracting me when I was in the query trenches or editing hell. Our shared, sometimes sordid history, our love of Disney, I'm eternally grateful to have each and every one of you in my life.

My mum and dad. Not only did you tolerate my dream of being an author, you even helped me chase it down, from reading early manuscripts I wrote to patiently listening to the myriad of ideas I've had over the years.

Sam. You believed in me even when I didn't. And you always listened. No matter how long the day had been, how tired we were. You listened.

The most handsome person on this list: my beautiful boy, Rollo. You have been my writing companion for a good seven years now. You nap nearby, sometimes twitching, often snoring, while I tap away at my laptop and occasionally utter something unrepeatable when I'm frustrated. You are the definition of loyal and give the best cuddles.

Finally, Rose. Because of you I wrote this book under duress. Making notes during night feeds, frantically writing while you napped. Pushing through exhaustion, ignoring my bed when all I wanted to do was sleep. And I loved every minute of it.

Credits

Carys Jones and Orion Fiction would like to thank everyone at Orion who worked on the publication of *The List* in the UK.

Editorial
Lucy Frederick
Francesca Pathak

Copy editor
Francine Brody

Proof reader
Jade Craddock

Audio
Paul Stark
Amber Bates

Contracts
Anne Goddard
Paul Bulos
Jake Alderson

Design
Rabab Adams
Joanna Ridley
Nick May

Production
Ruth Sharvell

Editorial Management
Charlie Panayiotou
Jane Hughes
Alice Davis

Finance
Jasdip Nandra
Afeera Ahmed
Elizabeth Beaumont
Sue Baker

Marketing
Helena Fouracre

Publicity
Alainna Hadjigeorgiou

Sales
Laura Fletcher
Esther Waters
Victoria Laws
Rachael Hum
Ellie Kyrke-Smith
Frances Doyle
Georgina Cutler

Rights
Susan Howe
Krystyna Kujawinska
Jessica Purdue
Richard King
Louise Henderson

Operations
Jo Jacobs
Sharon Willis
Lisa Pryde
Lucy Brem